Rebels Rein

Part Three of The Chronicles of Xannia

M.J. Moores

Rebels Rein: The Chronicles of Xannia

Copyright © M.J. Moores, 2017

Published by Infinite Pathways Press 2017
P.O. Box 4, Caledon Village, ON Canada L7K 3L3
Produced in Canada

ISBN 978-1-988044-07-1 Paperback Edition

The Chronicles of Xannia

Time's Tempest

Cadence of Consequences

Rebels Rein

Dedication

To my son, for understanding that "writing is work" and that even though I'm at home, I'm technically still at the office sometimes.

Acknowledgments

A book is so much more than just an author's ideas put into words to share with others. My inspiration for quirky, little things comes directly from personal experience, and the stories my friends and colleagues whisper in my ear (or on Facebook). As a writer I then add my creative flair so that even those sources of inspiration are no longer identifiable—but that doesn't mean they're not still there!

And now, for my "Academy Award" thank yous to those friends and colleagues who supported me behind the scenes. I raise a toast to Nanci Pattenden, my partner in crime, who kept kicking me in the butt to get writing and graciously acted as a first reader on the manuscript. To Linda Francis for pouring over the third book in a series for which she hadn't yet read, and gave me invaluable feedback (although there's still no glossary and only a tease more about Xannia's religion than before). To Erin Woodley, a fellow reader who looked at The Chronicles with fresh eyes and an honest heart, and to my overseas writing buddy, Melissa Barker-Simpson who always makes time for me and my crazy ideas.

Finally, I'd like to thank Wilma Reynolds, my copy editor, without whom this book would be riddled with misplaced modifiers, melodramatic phrases (I did keep a few), and unclear clauses. Without fail, she asks the hard questions and makes me consider angles to the story no one else does.

To book three!

The Races of Xannia

TALIAN:
Silvery-white skin, with black tracings for coliths*
The ruling race segregated from the commoners by a large Compound wall.

NIRIAN:
Dark grey skin, with jade green coliths

SHIMUG:
Light grey skin, with dark blue coliths

DANIETH:
Deep orange skin, with black coliths

GLAAON:
Pale pink skin, with silver coliths

MATIN:
Bronze-tanned skin, with red coliths

JERIDAN:
Black skin, with yellow coliths

METEK:
Deep-green skin, with gold coliths

BALANIS:
Pale-blue skin, with purple coliths

*Coliths are naturally occurring tattoo-like markings that cover most of the body. They are S-shaped and can coil around various parts of the body as a snake might. They manifest in varying lengths and thicknesses. Few to none don the face, palms, or soles of the feet.

The Followers of Xannia Flow Chart (turn to back)
Xannian Governmental Structure (turn to back)

Rebels Rein

Gerrund

Empty Promises

Daria grabbed the crying baby from my arms, gave him a bounce on her hip, and then whirled around to talk shop with her husband, Brid, and our parents. A few overhead lights glowed in the pre-dawn. The Underground Generators grumbled, working intermittently, at best. My best friend, Randek, snuck in from the shadows of a side-alley and tugged my elbow. I shook him off.

"Not now," I whispered. He shrugged, then leaned against the rocky front of my house. The overhead lighting flickered, lengthening shadows and intensifying the unspoken fear hovering around us in the main cavern.

"No, Brid, don't wait. I'll catch up. Your regiment needs you." Daria kissed his cheek, sandwiching their son between them. Baby Gelden cooed as Brid mussed his hair before locking gazes with Daria, a signal they'd used forever—see you soon ... *Gah, sentimental mush.*

As Brid dashed off down the cavernous tunnel, Daria turned to Mom, Dad, and my older brother Hez—each gave the baby a kiss on the forehead, before setting off after their *Leader*. Kaynee burst out the front door aiming to by-pass Daria.

"Mama!"

I grabbed her around the waist. Randek and I kept her still as Yadel, our neighbour, hurried out too. Daria dropped to one knee in place of Mom, her black pants and long-sleeved t-shirt nearly making her invisible.

Her arms circled our sister's shoulders, so Ran and I let go. "Kay, sweetie, Mom and Dad talked to you about this. Remember, we've got an important job to do."

"Gerry." Daria looked up at me. "*Gerrund*."

I glared back at her. "I wanna come."

"No. We've been over this. You're only eleven."

"I have just as much ri—"

"Stay. Here. Not another word. Help Yadel with Kay and the baby. *Don't* breach the surface. It'll be chaos until we take the Compound and get everything sorted out."

"*Daria* ..." Kay sobbed. "Don't go."

Daria pulled our kid sister into her arms, baby and all, and whispered something I couldn't make out. Kaynee whimpered, then gave Daria a squeeze before turning and hiding in Yadel's skirts. Daria stood and ruffled my hair with her free hand—I shook her off.

"It's time the people stood up for what's right. The government can't force us to live in hiding forever. Complacency is *not* an option."

Yadel tapped the face of her watch. Daria nodded, hugged my little nephew tight, kissed his cheeks, and whispered *I love you* before passing him over to Yadel.

Then, she mussed my hair again before jogging down the tunnel. I pushed it straight just as she looked over her shoulder and yelled, "We'll be back before you know it!"

Even after she disappeared into the yawning darkness, her rapid footfalls echoed back to us between Gelden's wails as we stood there, waiting for a miracle to happen.

PART I

Daria

The Massacre

" "W" atch out, Daria!"
Laser blasts smashed the wall above my head. I ducked, but sharp fragments of brick embedded into my skin like shrapnel. I choked on lingering teargas as Resistance Fighters fell back, clogging the narrow alleys, trying to escape the city of Darzeth after three hours of struggling to gain control of the Compound. Retreat hadn't been in our vocabulary until twenty minutes ago. The late-afternoon rays gave brick dust a tangible weight in the air.

The multi-race fighters, commoners turned rebels, now poorly protected, took heavy fire from the Justices and Contractors. Curtains jammed shut in the windows above as average citizens chose to ignore the fight for survival in the streets below. I changed the clip on the old-stock semi-automatic rifle, one of hundreds meant for the arms recycling plant. I pushed a loose strand of black hair behind my ear, and took aim.

"They're funnelling us back to the Compound!" Bridden shouted over his shoulder. *Blocking our escape from the city.*

Another volley of laser blasts struck the building, spraying more brick and dust. The Resistance Fighters behind us surged forward. Stumbling blind from the protection of the old complex, I tripped over a black boot attached to the leg of a Contractor—the government's *elite* guard. The standard issue black fatigues and matching helmet defied gender. The blood-traitor yanked the rifle from my hands and tossed it to one of a dozen or more Justices flanked nearby. I staggered forward. Brid's gun, and everyone else's for that matter, was chucked into one of the many piles now lining the deserted street.

Everywhere I looked, rebels and arms clattered into one long line moving *back*. Back the way we came. Back to the gates of the Government Compound run solely *by* the Talian race *for* the Talian race. I spat grit from the brick dust and wiped sweat from my forehead with an equally filthy arm—my dark grey Nirian skin now coated in a chalky residue.

The butt of a laser rifle cracked into my shoulder. Searing webs of pain made me stumble. Bridden caught my elbow and pulled me to his chest. His mouth moved, but his words were lost in the frantic shouts and general panic.

They rounded us up, a herd of captured rebels, stumbling over fallen comrades every other step—fighters whose bodies were tossed onto open wagons lining the streets. Sweat and fear hung in the air like wet laundry, as each breath was cut short by the stabbing pain of loss. Regardless of the long hours we'd fought, and the blood we'd lost, Xannia's three suns and their silent Gods, Zola, Zita, and Zerameteth, held vigilant in the mid-day sky—*a warning it had all been for nothing?* If only more of the commoners had helped, had even acknowledged what we were trying to do here today. No one was exempt from the suffering, except for the Talians.

Bridden squeezed my arm and nodded forward. I scanned the moving forest of heads, mostly hung low. Pride ignited in my heart. *I am not ashamed!* I held my chin high, refusing defeat.

Up ahead, a group of rebels spread out causing a blister on the side of our perfectly aligned column. Three Justices—average law-keepers—converged, leaving their positions. Flailing arms broke the stillness of the air, harsh voices raised in conflict. The black-clad Contractor overseeing this section of the Collection rushed to assist.

A gap!

"Run, Daria!" Bridden's hot breath shot from my ear to my heart.

I ran.

Others did too.

The bones in my fingers ached in Brid's grip. My heart hammered against my chest, as each foot slammed against the asphalt. Then a large black van swerved in front of us—six gunned and helmeted Contractors leapt from the back. *No!*

Six shots echoed down the street, the sound ricocheting off buildings, deafening us. Wet drops hit my face as Bridden's arms flung wide. I crashed into him, his legs collapsing as he landed hard against me. I just managed to wrap my arms around his chest to slow the fall. Rebels scattered—not forward toward escape, but back.

"Come *on*, Brid!"

I tried to pull him off my legs. His head lolled back against my breast. *NO!* But the shriek never made it past my lips. The barrel of a gun hovered between my eyes. Time froze until a comrade pulled me to my feet, dragging me back ... back to the tight column of bodies marching toward the capital, towards our fate. I struggled against the helping hands.

"Brid! No! I can't leave him!" Those hands held me tighter. Soothing words buffeted my head, but my ears refused to hear them as I fought to get back to him while the hands restrained me.

Cocooned in the middle of the mass of bodies, I strained to look back over my shoulder as we rounded the corner to Capitol Street. Black smoke billowed above. The closer we got to the Compound Gates, the more it spread.

I coughed and tried to wipe the soot from my eyes. The dark grey of my hands came back slick and red. I couldn't stop staring at them ... at the *blood* smeared on my arms, my chest. My body quaked. The arm around my shoulder tightened, but it and the squeeze by my elbow felt wrong. Nothing would feel right again.

I shut my eyes but only saw the image of my parents dropping their weapons less than half an hour ago, falling lifeless against the Gates, black holes searing the flesh of their backs. Then my older brother, leading the charge against the first wave of assassin-Contractors, a kind of madness consuming him, took out three of their guard before being torn apart by laser blasts. I opened my eyes, not really seeing, just lost in all the blood. If only the average citizen hadn't been so complacent—had realised we were fighting *for* them and for all our futures ...

At first, the marching slowed to a walk and then a shuffle. Fragments of exclamations broke the silence in my head.

"Zola, save us—"

"Sister Zita!"

"Suns Above—"

But if the gods had been with us today, we would have won—our sacrifices wouldn't have been in vain. My feet stopped moving as the mass of rebels halted. I looked up. Dense black clouds blocked our solar sentinels. The red blaze before me was not our largest sun, Zola, giving false promises of warmth. No, the blazing, two-storey tongues of flame engulfed the largest funeral pyre I'd ever seen; twice as wide as the damaged Compound Gates and as deep as Capitol Street. More wagons filled with our dead, backed toward the blaze as the bodies of our lost Resistance Fighters burned as one.

"NO!" The scream tore from my throat. Seconds after a gust of wind parted the black shroud above, I fell to my knees raising my face and my arms to the Gods Above. *Why? Why didn't you help us? We were supposed to win.* On the rooftop of the office complex, two dark forms leaned over the edge— one taller than the other, both thin and lanky. They weren't snipers—an outline I knew well. No, they were just kids. My younger brother Gerry and his best friend. Agony tore at my heart. My little brother now had to raise our younger sister and—I bit down on my lip to keep from crying, from giving the Kronik and his government the satisfaction.

Once again, the smoke cut off the late-afternoon sky. Everything from the noise of the rebels to the roar of the fire and our supposed *leader's* amplified voice shattered my thoughts—

"We feel your pain and are distressed by the violence ... follow in the path of Darius in search of Neto-Darzeth ..." *Lies. All Lies.* The Kronik only sought to placate and assure the meek.

Gravel bit into my knees, blood stung my cheeks. Two sets of kind hands lifted me to my feet—we were moving again. A score of black-shrouded Contractors stood before the decimated Gate, blocking sightlines and stopping common Xannians from entering the Compound, a place where only the privileged Talian race lived and worked and ruled from.

The Kronik stood next to Magistrate Delenon, the voice of the people, *of the Resistance.* From the front of the makeshift stage, it would look as though they stood in solidarity over the mass Ceremony of Release to Zola—but I caught the metallic glint of cuffs binding the Magistrate's wrists behind him, and the Talian Guard's gun digging into his back. The man who had rallied a nation to believe it mattered, stood as no more than a puppet in the Kronik's eternal game.

As we passed the blaze of bodies, brothers, mothers, neighbours, and friends of the Underground Resistance, I saw two things: row upon row of top-side citizens standing still as headstones on the opposite side of the pyre; and a massive sailing ship floating in the sea at the bottom of the hill.

I broke into a cold sweat as I stepped toward the new dock leading straight out into the sea. *The sea—guaranteed death.* My chest ached in protest—no, it was my breasts. I held my arms against my body, but two wet spots formed anyway. I refused to let myself cry. Not here. Not now.

A light touch came at my elbow. I turned. A pink-skinned Sun Guardian slightly younger than me tried to smile, to encourage me forward, but all I saw was my fear mirrored in her eyes. Two other Guardians trailed behind her. *How did they get caught up in this mess? Maybe the gods abandoned them today too.*

Forcing down gagging panic, I focused instead on not falling off the swaying wooden platform above the sea. I gave myself over to the single line of curved spines and bent heads disappearing over the upper edge of the enormous ship.

I looked up, instead of down. The centre post easily towered three storeys, surrounded by a strange basket, and rope-webbing. The post at the front stood nearly two storeys, but the one at the back seemed smaller. Giant bolts of loose fabric hung from horizontal poles that looked like arms, giving each post the appearance of a stick-drawn figure. The ship towered several storeys above, the only thing of substance out here besides the cliff-side of the Compound, which was now too far away to inflict its imposing heights on frail sensibilities.

The creaking, snapping, and moaning that filled the air wasn't from the rebels, but from the ship. The eerie sounds foretold our coming end. A Contractor wearing full, standard-issue combat gear, stood half-way down the length of the ship near the end of the floating dock. The tinted visor on her helmet remained down, and her firm, straight mouth matched the steel of the gun she gripped. I could only guess it was a woman by her slight form. Regardless of size, she was deadly with or without the weapon—a Kronik-trained mercenary disguised in plain sight by the normality of her day job.

Stepping before her, I turned and opened my arms to grasp the wooden ladder built into the side of the ship. My stomach heaved, not from the sway of the platform or the vessel, but from catching sight of Bridden's and my Binding tattoo on my left index finger—our marriage vows splattered in his dried blood.

The black-clad assassin standing beside me shifted. Swallowing everything down, I pushed myself to climb hand-over-hand up the curved side of the ship as the salty scent of seawater bit at the insides of my nose. I hadn't seen this coming. No one had. I thought we'd win; we had Magistrate Delenon's support. But that, and our army of misfits, hadn't been enough.

Now, the Kronik wanted us dead for our rebellion against *his* policies which claimed good farmland for expanded housing, silenced freedom of speech, punished unsanctioned technological advances, and policed with an iron glove.

The governing Council likely convinced him not to openly order our deaths. I knew too well how those elitist Talians crafted appearances. The pyre earned them the sympathy vote from the praying masses—a guised effort to show mercy to our dead by not completely disgracing the bodies. Dumping them into the

Deserts wasteland for its unholy creatures to consume was a tried-and-true spectacle other traitors had been condemned with. The commoners instead saw *us* as the problem and not the government, because of their subjection to relentless propaganda. A government so steeped in lies and half-truths they threatened to destroy our homes with ignorance and greed. The ship I climbed feigned a chance at redemption for us policy-haters. *Liberators.* But ultimately, it would bring us to our deaths.

Hitching one leg over the ledge, I dropped the short distance to the floor. Just before I turned, I caught sight of a soft, white, knitted Luma—the round-brimmed contoured hat Sun Guardians wore during Observances. The delicate pale-pink hand of the girl who'd supported me on the dock slipped back from the ledge. I leaned over, grabbed her arm, and helped her up.

The dark grey of my skin wound around her pale flesh, making me think of twisted rock-candy. Stupid, I know. She nodded her thanks and stayed to help her fellow Guardians aboard. I stutter-walked to the opposite side of the ship, trying not to fall as it lolled from one side to the other. A mass of bodies, the last of the living Resistance Fighters, crowded the upper decks of the ship.

By the time the last boot dropped over the ledge, well over one-hundred commoners stood glaring at three Talian men in pristine, tan-coloured uniforms, and one Contractor. The contrast of their silvery-white skin, exposed outside cuffs and collars, made them look all the paler beside the black, masked and gloved killer standing next to them — once a commoner of the lesser races, no longer one of our own.

"It was the Kronik's intent to open this reconstruction of Captain Darius' magnificent ship as a museum dedicated to his harrowing Nine Seas expedition over one-hundred years ago.

Instead, you *despots* have turned a work of art into what will likely be your death barge," the tallest Talian said.

The stocky one stepped forward and said, "We were intended as the curators of this vessel, and now we have but half-an-hour to impart a career's worth of knowledge to you rabble-rousers. This ship sets sail with the setting of the first sun whether you're ready or not."

The tall man walked to the centre post and placed his hands on its surface; the base of it now clearly broader than his arm-span.

"This is the *main* mast. That one's the *fore* and the other the *aft*. The fabric on the yardarms above are your sails ..."

He's telling us how to sail this thing?

"—you'll find the sail-hold. This is where extra fabric and the smaller sails are stored during ..."

Oh, meeka! What did I miss?

Each man spent ten minutes talking, just as they might have had we been average, law-abiding citizens taking a tour. The monotonous, feigned normality made my skin crawl. Every time I stopped to try and remember some fact or warning, I missed a new piece of information.

A low sound escaped my mouth.

I couldn't stand still. I had to move, get off this ship—*get home to my son.*

Then a Matin man, broader than Brid, with the cloying scent of fresh hay and manure—a testament to the working class who made up the bulk of the Resistance—said seven simple words in my ear.

"Pay attention to the next three points."

And I did.

I learned about the mizzen mast: why the sail was a triangle, how to manipulate the rigging, and when to use it. That's it. I focused all my attention on those three things and kept repeating them over and over again. Some small part of my brain also followed the farmer's progress, his bronze skin with its sinuous red s-shaped coliths acting like a beacon as he wove through the people on deck. A wave of intent, purpose supplanted blank stares and numb minds as he moved across the crowded ship.

When the third Talian concluded with a warning about food supplies, another person climbed over the rail and dropped to the main deck. The three men parted—everyone gasped.

Magistrate Delenon.

My heart rate doubled, as it did whenever he gave one of his rallying speeches, then stopped. The aura surrounding his tall, tailored frame, rich black skin, and gold coliths resonated power. Without him, we wouldn't have had the ability to fight back. Without us, he'd probably still be working to improve conditions for *all* commoners. But the Kronik had sliced off this ear to the people, just as fast as he'd burned our dead. This hero shared our fate. *What corruption will reign now? Who's left to stand against the madness?* The thought of my little brother defiant and wanting to fight destroyed what was left of my heart. My blood ran cold.

The small Talian presented two leather-bound books to Magistrate Delenon and said, "Guard these with your life. One will guide you to safety, and the other will keep you alive until you get there."

With that, the three Talian's loosened several ties, placed Delenon behind the Capitan's wheel, and descended to release the moorings.

Satie

Expectations

S ister Megrhen crushed the fingers of my left hand as Sister
Ellanir squeezed my right arm. *Oh, Satie, what are you going to
do?* I looked around the ship trying to get a handle on an
impossible situation. Both whispered The Solemn Prayer to help
ease their fears and those around us, their voices eerily in unison,
as people pressed in from all sides.

"—love those forsaken. May the warmth of your rays
brighten the dark—"

My voice stammered over the words, falling behind their
rapid pace, "—strength to the weak … those forsaken. May the
… rays brighten—" I couldn't keep up with my sisters or
understand their ability to concentrate. An older man directly
behind us, repeated something under *his* breath too—not a
prayer, but said just as desperately as he clenched and un-
clenched his heather-grey hands.

"The mizzen mast has a triangular lateen-rigged sail meant
to catch the wind blowing from side to side …"

Yes, that's right. A farmer told me to remember that. My gaze latched onto and followed the older man's navy-blue coliths as they wove over solid forearms. I tried to review the rest of the information I was tasked with by the farmer, but between Meg and Ella praying in my ears, and my own fumbled attempts to keep up the new Observances, my mind spun.

I shut my eyes tight, but the loll of the ship on the open water made me stagger, bringing my Sisters with me. The heavy scent of oily ropes and the reek of body odour brought bile to my mouth. I forced it back. We managed to crowd ourselves into a corner as voices, once silent during the Curators' lecture, now rose like dagger points.

"What now?"

"That's it?"

"Hey, watch it. You nearly got me in the head."

"Where are we going?"

"Don't stand so close."

"Is there any food?"

"There's nowhere else to go!"

"I'll give you somewhere to go—"

I couldn't concentrate on my prayers. The mass of races, crammed into such a confined space, no longer attuned with one another and a common cause, now sought to assert themselves in desperate need of grounding. I held my hands over my ears. Part of me ached with guilt, searching for the right words to calm and soothe the flock, as my logical side strained to figure things out. My thoughts whirled with a ceremony cut short, dead lining the streets, being cast away on a ship, discordant voices. I watched as heads turned rapidly, looking over shoulders and around the ship, and voices rose louder simply to be heard. My hands fell away from my ears, ineffective against the crash of sound. Staring at the back of the ship, the stern I think, I caught sight of the bronze-toned, Matin farmer climbing a set of stairs up to where Magistrate Delenon stood leaning against the wheel.

"Are you threatening me?" The nearby harsh words compelled me to turn.

"It's not a threat, it's a promise!"

Two Resistance Fighters heaved their chests against one another, arms spread wide, faces nearly nose to nose. A few people looked on, but no one intervened. Normally, I'd just walk over and say hello—however, today was not a normal day. Bound for a month to my new Observances, I could utter nothing but my prayers, although the Order preferred silence during this sacred time.

I have to do something ... but what?

The Resistance had chosen my day of Rebirth and transcendence to the Third Rite of Passage, *The Devout*, to stage the rebellion. The rebels' Underground tunnels led right to the basement of our Temple. Of course, the Order was glad to act as a Junction Point between the hunted and the hunters. But the end of the ceremony had collapsed in panic as frantic rebels sought refuge after nearly a day of focused fighting. Those still present were collected. *Thank Zerameteth, may his light guide the lost,* the Contractors never found the entrance to the caves. We were taught to believe everything happened for a reason. I had to trust that my being here, on this ship, was simply another test of my faith in the Suns above.

Delenon and the farmer spoke, neither actually looking out at the mass of people before them, aware of the growing unrest. Sails snapped and whipped about overhead, half-caught by the wind. Volatile, hurt, and frightened Xannians quickly lost the sense of purpose given to them earlier by the farmer when he'd directed us to listen to key stages of the curators' lessons.

The two arguing rebels pushed back from each other, falling into the already chaotic masses. They struck a fighting stance, shifting from foot to foot, gazes locked.

Huddling in the corner made no sense to me. I tried to pull my arm away from Sister Ella, but she held tight, reciting her prayers ever faster as her wide eyes darted from side to side. I moved to speak in her ear, then stopped. *I have to remain vigilant, speak only the words of the Holy.* So, I yanked my arm free instead, and pried Sister Meg's rigid fingers from my hand. The two mature Sisters stared at me as they clung to one another. I walked into the fray—someone had to.

"May the Trinity's Light illuminate your soul and its worth," I spoke the prayer aloud, touching the cheek of a woman hyperventilating. She locked her gaze to mine. I smiled. Her breathing slowed.

"Bring guidance to the lost"—gripped a young man's shoulder—"strength to the weak, love to those forsaken"—walked between the fighters and raised my palms to cover each man's fist. The ship listed to one side. Someone fell against the hostile man on my right. Instinctively, his other fist shot out and smashed into my face!

I bit my tongue and crumbled to the deck. Blood coated the inside of my mouth and spikes of pain lashed up and through my jaw. Gasps buffeted my ears as a wide circle of bodies formed around me. The two combatants disappeared into the crowd. My vision blurred as I lay writhing beneath a perfect blue sky, face wet with tears.

"Dear Suns! The Sister—"

"Where did they go? Where did *he* go?"

"Blasphemy! That's a double curse. You don't—"

Voices wavered around me as two sets of hands took hold of my arms; the circle collapsed as Sisters Megrhen and Ellanir dragged me back to the corner, whispering prayers of Observance. The sails above cracked. The crowd fell silent as Magistrate Delenon's voice finally called out, commanding order with its deep resonance.

"Fellow Xannians! Citizens—all hear me!" He paused just as a Danieth woman's deep-orange face popped down in front of my own.

"Saw that, I did. Both foolish and brave, I dare say. Name's Coreen but everyone calls me Eena. Here"—she reached out her hand; I glanced at the thin, black colith coiling from her wrist to her elbow—"let me look at you." A deft but gentle grip followed the line of my jaw while a critical and exacting gaze searched for things others couldn't see. Her cloud-grey hair sat piled in a loose bun high on the back of her head. Stray locks wisped about her smooth, rust-hued face tickling my forehead during her examination.

Delenon's words consoled the crowd, "The Resistance fought bravely today, and while this banishment may seem like a loss to our Cause, rest assured our voices were heard. Though I did not fight beside you in the streets, I took the political battle to the Kronik himself. Our sacrifices for the betterment of society will *not* be ignored any longer. Now, a new generation awaits to hold our government accountable."

Many raised their voices to cheer his sentiments, but not everyone.

Eena touched my nose; I winced. It hadn't been hit directly, but it hurt. I whimpered.

"Sorry, sweetie—I mean Sister. Nothin' seems broken but you'll have a hell— ah, I mean, a real bad bruise. Tender for a good few days. Doubt we have any red meat on this ship to cover it, and if we did, doubt anyone would let us treat you with it. Still, I'll see what I can rustle up for ya once things settle some." Eena stood, eyed Meg and Ella critically, shook her head and then disappeared into the crush of bodies. My stomach lurched with the bobbing of the vessel. I looked up, past the standing bodies of the rebels around me to the large beams of wood and lengths of cloth meant to keep us afloat, *alive*.

I refocused on the Magistrate's speech. "—two great books and your knowledge of this ship"—he nodded to the farmer beside him—"mean that we are *not* doomed. We *have* the resources to follow in the wake of the Great Captain Darius." The sails flapped above us as the crowd inhaled a collective breath. *But Darius set out with a fully trained crew and still returned alone on a wreckage.* The wire's programming would show the same old special about Darius, a hundred years earlier, looking for new land. Even then, people had seen the over-crowded cities growing ever larger between the sea and the Deserts. At least his sacrifice held merit—not like the slow death to which the Kronik doomed us. *Stop it, Satie, focus on the positive.* But nothing came to mind.

"First things first. No one person knows everything about this ship, and we need to control the sails. If you remember anything about this aspect of the lecture, join Marxx here on the poop deck. If you were a Company Leader, meet me at the bottom of the stairs by the quarterdeck—there's much to discuss regarding our supplies. Everyone else, take a moment to go over what you learned from the Talian Curators. Remain calm. I *will* update you on our findings."

Those who'd been summoned moved toward the back of the ship. Everyone else muttered among themselves and did their best to get out of the way. Pairs and then small groups formed as if at random. In the closest group to the Sisters stood the older, stocky, Shimug man with heather-grey skin and navy coliths, who'd mumbled about the mizzenmast. Beside him, the Nirian woman who'd helped me over the upper-edge of the ship stood with her arms crossed over a damp, dusty, blood splattered shirt—clearly she'd been in the thick of things before the Massacre. They shared what they could remember of their similar three points from the Curators' lecture—the groupings apparently not as random as I first thought.

A woman raised her voice, "I remember that part. The long pole-things, ah, jibs? Don't move." Her rough pale-blue arms showed signs of skin damage even as her deep-purple coliths followed the graceful sweep of her arms, belying her hard life with a natural beauty.

Wait. That doesn't sound right. I shifted to get up and tell them, but the Sisters held me down. My nose throbbed with the jolt, and my jaw burned as I ground my teeth. What could I do? The woman had it wrong. But even if I could say more than my prayers, I certainly couldn't speak properly with a swollen face.

"Well, now, hold on a minute there," the old Shimug drawled. "That may be true of the yardarm on the mainmast and the foremast, which need many hands to shift using them ropes, but not the jib on the mizzen. That one, as I recall, swings easily to catch the side winds and helps turn the ship."

Yes! Listen to him …

"You should get over to the wheel and tell the others," a tall, rail-thin Danieth man said.

"Perhaps I should." The old guy nodded and navigated the sea of bodies to the back where the farmer stood holding the wheel steady as a group formed around him.

A boy, with moss-coloured skin and gold coliths, pushed through the crowd. He stumbled toward the Sisters and me, looking decidedly off. We shifted deeper into our corner as he flung his chest over the edge of the ship and threw up. The rancid stench wafted up over the deck, and five more people ran for it. I tried to breathe through my sore mouth but wound up tasting the stink at the back of my throat anyway. His feet slipped out from under him as he cantered forward on his stomach. My heart leapt. I swallowed what little saliva I had and gripped the kid's leg to keep him from toppling over the edge to his death.

Daria

The Hold

I watched as the old Shimug wove through the shifting crowd making his way to the helm. The crack of the sail high above made the woman beside me jump. Crossing my arms, milk from my aching breasts soaked my shirt—how many feedings had I missed?

My body pulled at me to sit, but I couldn't. Not yet. I glanced with longing at the three Sisters huddled in the corner, wishing I could join them or maybe follow the kid the young Glaaon Sister now held onto, all the way over the side. But that idiotic woman beside me kept nattering on, relaying mixed up information about the three points Marxx had assigned us. Opening my eyes, I focused instead on the old man's head as it bobbed and wove through the masses on deck. His lithe frame and broad shoulders helped set him apart from the crowd. This time I was able to ignore the woman as someone else in the group corrected her. The old Shimug climbed one of the steep staircases up to the poop deck, passing Delenon's small group looking out for more Leaders. I narrowed my eyes.

What the hell is Camdin doing there? He assisted the munitions expert. He's no Leader. I frowned and pursed my lips. In fact, of the three soldiers who stood with Delenon, only one could legitimately claim the title. A voice at the back of my brain said "leave it alone" but I couldn't. I stalked off, manoeuvring through the crowd wondering what these so-called leaders were playing at.

"Hey! Where are you going?" the forgetful woman called. I didn't owe her anything, let alone an explanation. So I ignored her and spread my arms wide in order to slip between the backs of two large men. As I crossed the expansive deck, the Magistrate's gaze found mine. He nodded to me then pointed my way. The others looked too.

I glared at Camdin as I joined the group. His blue skin purpled high on his cheeks in a blush. The kid dropped his focus to the deck and scuffed a toe at the blond wood. Behind him, a dark outcropping of rocky cliffs framed his shame. My gaze lingered on all that remained of the city of Darzeth. A raw ache clenched my heart. I drew a shaky, salt-laced breath then focused on the boy of twenty before me.

"What do you think you're doing, Cam?"

He refused to look at me.

Delenon cleared his throat. I scanned the other faces watching their gazes jump from my tangled hair to my bloody, dirt-blasted clothes. I re-crossed my arms over my damp chest.

"I invited him."

I glanced at the man's shoulder patch—three suns in a half-circle above a seedling. "And you are?"

"Jippen Rakk, Leader of the Fifth. Cam out-ranks everyone else out there." He glanced at my patchless shoulder. "And you are?"

"Bridden Myyup's wife and Second Commander of the Third."

"Is he here?" Jip asked, looking around.

"Brid's dead."

"So that makes you Lead now," the woman with the pale, strawberry hair said, her shoulder touching Jip's in acknowledgment.

Something wavered behind Jippen's eyes. He'd lost someone too. But *I* hadn't lost just one ...

"I'm sorry, Mrs. Myyup," Delenon said.

"Daria." I looked at him, still frowning.

"Daria. Unfortunately, most of the Leaders appear to have joined Bridden in Zola's Blessed Embrace. We need to work with who we have." *And now we have you*, hung unspoken in the air between us. My lips pressed into a tight line, but I nodded. He was still the Magistrate after all. The voice in my head that had warned me not to get involved, sighed.

"There's much to do. Marxx has volunteered to look after the sails, but we need answers for everything else—verrin, food, water, medicine, tools, sleeping arrangements. My speech isn't going to keep these people calm for long. Tempers are getting short." His eyes flickered to the corner of the ship where the bow met the lower deck. I knew he couldn't see her, but the image of that Sun Guardian's swollen jaw flashed through my mind, too. Had anyone else gotten hit, a riot would've started. Talk about a blessing in disguise.

"The blueprints at the back of Darius' Journal"—he opened the thicker of two leather-bound volumes—"show three sub-levels. Camdin and I will take the first, Jippen and Reena the second, and I'd like you to search the hold, Daria. Report to the quarterdeck when you're done. Take stock of what's below as fast as you can, but be careful."

With that, the five of us threaded through the crush of bodies, past the towering mainmast, to the back of the ship. I paused at the opening and glanced to the side. The Sisters likely still cowered off in the corner by the hull, but too many nameless people stood between us for me to be sure. The wide eyes on the youngest Sister's face kept flashing in my mind. The terror that simmered beneath her shock struck too close to home.

I followed the leaders down a steep set of stairs. Going from the bright sunshine into the dark made it difficult to see. I ran my hand over the relatively new, sweet-smelling planks.

"Lanterns. Beside the door," Cam said at the bottom.

"Can you tell what fuels them?" Jip asked, as the shadow of his body moved to the opposite side.

"Most are solar—seem fully charged." His lean silhouette shifted over to the corner where the hall turned behind the staircase. "These ones have a large cavity on the bottom to put something in. Can't use them right now. We'll have to check into it later. Here." He activated and then passed out the solar-energy lanterns as we rounded the corner.

I held the thin metal handle before me; lamp's weight equal to that of the semi-automatic I'd carried only two hours before— before everything we'd worked so hard for was shot to hell. The low ceiling made the narrow hall feel cave-like. Jip and I staggered to one side. I caught my balance against the wall. Delenon clattered through a small doorway on the right. Cam grunted as the door at the bottom of the stairs grated open. Something hard cracked into my head.

"Ouch! What the—" I hit back, held the side of my head, and then raised the light. "Dammit." Unlit lanterns hung every few feet, suspended from hooks near the ceiling. I moved back to the opposite wall as Reena and Jip disappeared down the next flight of steps. The ship pitched, groaning in response to its unease.

I braced my arm against the wall—no railings here either—as I followed the others down ... the ship swallowing us whole. At the bottom of the next level, Reena shuffled her feet in a wide stance as the boat lolled again. My stomach sloshed in the opposite direction. *They bloody well better straighten this thing out.*

Jip and Reena separated by the time I reached the lower deck. Their lanterns cast small circles of light in the larger area. Angular shadows moved around me, cast by netting and fishing gear hung overhead. Groaning echoes from the surrounding wood played with my sense of depth perception. I staggered toward the last staircase, little more than a hole in the floor with a single rail surrounding it. *Why did I have to stick my nose where it didn't belong?* The quiet voice of warning answered, *you couldn't help yourself.* With no walls to guide me, and no railing to grasp, I stepped down into the bowels of the ship.

The reek of manure hit hard and fast. I coughed several times. The noise of baying animals floated in the thick air. *Food.* I raised my lantern, keeping the bottom stair-tread pushed into the back of my calf for support as I looked around. The ceiling here was higher again. Not quite two-storeys, but the lack of interior walls made it feel cavernous.

I cracked my shoulder against a pillar, jarring my entire body. My breasts ached with a raw need. I inhaled a shaky breath and rubbed them with the flat of my hand to relieve the pressure. Milk trickled over my swollen flesh. Shallow breath hitched in my throat. I blinked rapidly and bit the inside of my cheek to draw focus to a different pain. *You have a job to do. So do it.* I walked behind the open steps, following the sound of the animals, toward the back of the ship.

A soft, hazy glow blanketed the space. I moved toward the closest pen and slipped on some loose straw, landing hard on one knee, "Oh, for the love of Zola."

I grabbed onto a tall post near where a larger lamp hung. The light swayed; one of many. Something moist flicked over my knuckles. I jerked back. *What the hell?* A small, fuzzy face looked up at me with dark eyes. I scowled and scanned the area. Simple fences and gates held goats, goats, and more goats—no, wait. There were ganoo too, cocks and hens, in open crates stacked as a false wall toward the back. The large bird sported short blue and green tail feathers that looked more like my brother's hair in the morning, than any kind of masculine display. *Gerry.* The non-stop ache in my chest was too much. *I can't do this. I can't think about him or—No. Stop it, Daria. Focus on the task at hand.*

I gripped the fencing as I walked down an aisle easily wide enough for three people. Each pen I passed drew forth curious noses scenting the air. Behind the fencing, bales upon bales of straw lined one side of the hull as what I could only assume was hay, and straw lined the other.

A hot bubbling and frothing rose inside me with every animal or barn-like element I saw. My frown deepened as I pursed my lips and tried to swallow the bile that rose. I should have been happy to see how well-stocked this floating tub was, but my brain processed everything differently.

At the wall of ganoo, I slipped around the towering crates to a cramped maintenance space. I tried to take a deep breath to clear my head but the stench of barn coated my mouth. I looked up. A long beam rose to a spot just beyond the stacked crates of poultry—an arm of the tiller. I checked out several boxes marked "parts" or "supplies" littering the floor, bending down to inspect one in particular just as a loud creak and moan echoed through the hold. I looked at the hull. Several dark seams glistened. I straightened and kicked the crate.

"What is any of this doing here!" I staggered back and bumped the ganoo coup. Several squawks and the sound of flapping filled the hollow space, but the wall held.

Shuffling back around to the barn-side, I hurried past the animals and around the stairs. *Let's finish this.* No ambient light here to rein in the shadows, only the ink-black weight of ignorance stacked in tidy rows from floor to ceiling. Raising the lantern, I peered closely at a black brand and knew some part of me should shout for joy that someone had stocked the ship before casting us out to sea. But I couldn't have cared less.

Walls of sealed crates and barrels, branded with more black labels, screamed of our failed Resistance, overpowering rational thought. This ship may have started out as a floating museum, but spoke more to the preparedness of the Kronik and his government's presumption of winning—routing us out and making us disappear forever. Delenon got it wrong. The next generation would *not* continue the Cause … for fear of eternal persecution.

"Damn those Talian bastards!" I smashed my fist into the slats of a crate. The crunch of my knuckles made me whimper. *I've seen enough.* I turned back to locate the open-riser steps when a metallic clink and heavy shifting registered somewhere at the back of my consciousness—a sound so muffled I questioned whether I'd actually heard it. Pausing, I listened a moment longer. *Just my imagination.* But as I reached the bottom step, it came again.

I turned the glow of my lantern back toward the towers of supplies and forced myself to venture farther into the absolute dark. I had a job to do, and that meant taking stock of everything. *Meeka. Why me?* The black ate my weak pool of light, nibbling its edges more and more with every step. My shadow silently kept guard to either side. The weight of the dark clung to me as my breathing quickened. Not even in battle had I felt this creeping suffocation.

"What the Suns?" I growled, trying to throw off my unease. *Stop imagining things!* A heavy scraping ground against the wood flooring. I stopped. *Sweet Zerameteth. What was that?* The lantern's light quivered in response to my shaking hand. Grinding my teeth, I looked up at the looming barrels and boxes anchored to the ceiling by ropes and pullies. Seared labels contradicted the normalcy of their words, taunting me … taunting all of us. We'd been lied to. Not by Delenon but by ourselves!

The deep scraping of metal on wood came again. I looked at the dark opening leading to what I could only assume was another closet-like maintenance space. A hot flush rose in my cheeks as hate sizzled through my veins. I'd watched my husband die in my arms, my parents fall at the gate, my brother obliterated by tech weaponry, and our dreams of a better life drown in the sea. There was nothing left they could take away from me—even my son belonged to another woman now.

I stomped around the far side of the wall. Holding the lantern high, I saw a pen of crates spilling straw around a mound of old cloth. A foul, acrid stench infected the air. I gagged and held my hand over my nose. The mound shifted, rising higher and higher and higher.

I shrieked and ran.

The Green Sea.

Costal, Home.

The smack of a salt-laden wind bolsters the sails
and the crew's spirits. To the naked eye the
coastline disappeared hours ago leaving nothing but
the blue sky and the green waters frothed by the
wind. Some birds still glide overhead but as we put
more distance between the hull and the memory of a
crowded shore-line, I'm certain even those signs of
life will soon disappear.
The Second String are sleeping below deck as the
First String monitor the sails and check the rigging
and supplies. No one knows how long it will take to
find land, or if we will at all. Still, hope is high
that this will be the first of many voyages in the
years to come.
As I watch the water through the spy-glass, I can
make out schools of fish in the darker patches of
water. There's little room in the hold to stockpile
the fresh fish. Perhaps in a few more days we'll have
space below to accommodate the meat—if I can
convince a crew to man the rowboat.
All is calm and progressing according to plan.

Captain Darius

Satie

Children of the Suns

"Nothing's gone right," a large, stocky Glaaon man complained to three other men in his circle. His pink skin, darker than mine, looked tanned, and yet the bridge of his nose glistened brightly, already burning under the midday suns.

"After the gates came down, I thought for sure we'd won." The other man's bald, orange head glistened with a sheen of sweat.

"How many Contractors swarmed us up there?"

"I heard fifty."

"*Meeka.*"

"Yeah. Who knew there were so many?"

"What in Xannia are we going to do now?"

The Metek boy's mossy-hued skin paled as he slumped against the side of the ship, resting his head on the rail. The acidic scent of his, and others', stomach contents wafted on the breeze—likely not making it past the bulge in the ship's hull on the way down. I released his leg and curled back into the corner with Meg and Ella.

A Devout now, my Observances to Zerameteth were of paramount importance, especially as we sailed into the unknown. Keeping in the Sun Gods' favour might mean the difference between life and death. I joined my Sisters saying the Rising Prayer under my breath, though barely moving my lips for the swelling in my jaw. The prayer was traditionally sung on days of communal celebration; at its core it spoke of hope and guidance, both of which we desperately needed.

Broad shadows fell across us shifting ever closer, as if the men didn't see us huddled there. But they jostled aside when a whirlwind of commotion made its way across the deck. Even though I couldn't see from my vantage point, I could *hear* her coming.

"Look out now. Move out of the way. Slide to the side. Coming through."

The men scattered as Eena settled to rest in front of me. She held a dripping kerchief I was certain I'd seen one of the women wearing as we boarded earlier. She held the cloth out to me.

"Here, Sister. On your jaw with it now."

I recoiled at the stench of fishy salt-water, blinking rapidly. Holding my palms up, I shook my head, still whispering, "Of Zerameteth we rise as his steadfast glow …"

"It won't kill you."

I narrowed my eyes at her. As children we were taught to beware of the Liquid Death.

"You'd have t' bathe in the salt-water for ten minutes before you'd risk critical absorption and go inta sodium shock. This lil' bit won't harm ya. It's cold and we need t' get the swellin' down." She pushed it past my hands, onto my swollen cheek.

I shivered, my eyes widening. My heart ignored her words and pounded relentlessly. Still, she said it wouldn't kill me.

"I'll come back in a few t' refresh it for ya." She patted my good cheek, gave a curt nod, and whirled her way back through the crowd.

The ice-cold cloth soothed my flushed and puffy skin. I leaned back into the corner, rested my head against the sharp-cut evergreen scent, and closed my eyes. The ship lolled and swayed beneath me as the waves slapped the lower hull and the rigging creaked overhead. Another sail cracked, whip-like. My eyes opened just as fast, heart racing once more.

A change in the murmur of the crowd brought several men and women hurrying toward the front of the ship. As they climbed the pair of ladder-stairs to the forecastle, several other multi-hued bodies scaled the web of ropes up the mainmast. Soon everyone on board caught sight of the action; voices lowered as a hum washed over the ship. They looked confident—like they knew exactly what needed to be done. But a woman missed her footing and slipped! Gasps and cries rose up from below. She regained her footing and carried on, slower. Two others shimmied back down to the deck and collapsed to their knees, shaking. The height or the sway of the ship or both must have been too much for them.

Slowly, those remaining aloft took up the slack in the sails. I held my breath as they leaned over the jib to fight with the ropes tied in place. No safety net waited to catch these daring Resistance Fighters, not like at the circus. And yet they balanced on their stomach and straddled the beam with the same determination I saw on the faces of those fighters who came through the tunnels below our temple.

After a fair amount of trial and error, the pitching of the vessel lessened. I couldn't hear what they said to each other over the constant creaking of taut ropes; I don't even think they could hear themselves. Hand signals helped confusion morph into understanding. I could hear my heart pounding in my eardrums as I watched them swarm the rigging, cautious but confident. The ship steadied as the wind was finally harnessed. My lungs burned. I exhaled, not realizing I'd been holding my breath. Those people looked tiny, so high up—lost in the azure sky.

I glanced at my Sisters; Meg and Ella stared at their knees oblivious to the miracle our prayers had brought about. *How can they shut themselves off so completely? No, that's not right. They've given themselves over to the prayer—infused their very essence into each word. The Gods heard us because of them. This is what I have to do; stay focused on our teachings, our proven rituals. Only then will I be able to contribute as they do.*

A shriek yanked my attention from the Sisters up to the mainmast.

"Watch out!" several voices cried.

"Ohh!" a wail carried. Multiple riggers who'd returned to the deck scrambled back to the latch-points on the rail and swung into the lower netting as others wove their arms together, shifting to follow the arc of a young man's fall.

My heart slammed against the walls of my chest as a lanky boy fell from the crow's nest. His arms flailed, his mouth opened, though no sound reached the deck. Every muscle in my body tensed. He fell against the netting half-way down—one foot caught up in the ropes, one leg hanging out at an odd angle.

Shrieks and hollers cascaded in waves from the deck as those few brave souls spread out along the lower rigging, and methodically climbed toward the boy. Even from where I sat, I could see his chest heave. The ropes wavered with the extra bodyweight from below. My gaze darted from him, dangling head first toward the solid deck, to the climbers, to the net of arms.

"—we rise as his steadfast glow climbs the skies and leads us safely back home." I repeated the last stanza of the Rising Prayer, the tune gone. But over and over again my shaky voice said the words even as the rest of my body froze under the blazing suns and sweat beaded on my forehead. I squinted, holding a hand to shade my eyes. The only people who moved were those brave souls being careful not to shake the rigging as they climbed. Two of the five held the boy as one directed the others to manoeuver the ropes and shift his foot.

He was free!

I gasped. The Sisters and I tapped our eyelids and nose— two fingers spread wide, then one—giving thanks to the Sun Gods. Sighing, I rubbed the back of my neck and stretched it. The boy shifted, putting his foot down on a cross-brace. His leg wobbled, then collapsed.

I shrieked! Launching forward, I felt the Sisters' hands clamp down on my arms.

The people whose web of arms had linked below the rigging scrambled to reform as he crashed down several yards, toppling everyone into a heap. The look of pure fear etched on his face drove shards of ice into my heart, regardless of the high heat of the day. Eena grabbed two random bystanders. With a sweep of her arms, the three removed fallen comrades with surgical precision.

I leaned forward, every muscle taut; the damp seawater cloth forgotten. More people came to help. Concerned voices filled the salt-laced air. Then a wiry body, held aloft with his arms over two sets of shoulders and sitting in a cradle of hands, emerged from beneath the pile. They followed Eena off to one side. As the boy disappeared into the crowd, my shoulders remained hunched as my hands fisted around my clothes. *Calm down, Satie!* I inhaled a shuddering breath. Then my leg cramped.

I pitched forward grabbing the offending limb, beating the muscle flat. Ella tried to help but only got in my way. I waved her hands aside and bit my lip to keep from crying out. *Stupid muscle.*

When it finally relented to a dull ache, I snatched my sea-soaked cloth from the deck, grabbed the rail, and hauled myself up. The Sisters' voices raised in concern as they spoke different, discordant prayers. I waved them off and hobbled along the side of the ship to stretch my leg. In all my three years of dedicating myself to the Light, I hadn't once experienced the severity of today's emotional stresses. My thoughts scrambled to follow my first Observance as a Devout—follow my sworn duty to act as a conduit. I looked around for the boy, the one who'd defied logic and pushed himself to help fix the sails of this ship. *That* was true worth. But he and those who carried them had been swallowed by the crowd.

What is the worth of a prayer?

Stop it, Satie.

No. Sister Venra now.

I sighed. How could *I* be a conduit for our child-god? It all seemed so easy until today.

As I neared the quarterdeck I noticed several people, including the Magistrate, standing and staring at the door leading to the lower decks. Their rigid postures and frowns gave me the impression they waited for something, or someone. People doing things, *real* things, to help. My Observances stated that my entire being had to focus on becoming a Guardian for Zerameteth, a channel for his voice.

I turned away from them to look out to sea and did as I was supposed to do—prayed. As I leaned against the side of the ship, I stared at the endless green water and stretched out my calf muscles.

A woman grasped the rail next to me and leaned forward to stretch her back. My eyes flickered across her pale-grey skin, following her thin, red coliths as they swept 'round her arms. Her father was obviously a Shimug and her mother a Matin. But as rare and unlikely as her mixed heritage was, that wasn't what drew my gaze—it was the round ball of her stomach. *Pregnant? How in Xannia did she end up here?*

A screech echoed up the stairwell as the Nirian woman who'd helped me aboard, stumbled up onto the deck. Absolute terror etched every line of her fine features. I turned as she careened around the corner and landed in a heap at Delenon's feet, blubbering and sputtering.

The Magistrate and a man with a Resistance patch dropped to their knees as well, one righting her fallen lantern. I inched closer to the opening she'd stumbled from and leaned against the wall, straining to hear what had happened, my prayers forgotten.

The woman's words spilled out jumbled and incoherent. The Leader snapped his fingers at the Balanis boy who immediately crouched down, wrapped one of the woman's arms around his shoulders, and helped her stand. He guided her over to the edge, holding her until the shaking lessened. The men stood.

"—not possible," said the Resistance Leader.

"She wouldn't lie. I don't understand it though," Delenon said, running a hand over his dark hair.

"Chained up? What could that mean?" The woman with the short, strawberry-blonde hair asked.

"It's not something we can deal with right now." Delenon placed his hands on his hips. "Jip, Reena, find our specialists. I'll speak to the people." He looked to the sails, taut and holding the wind. As he climbed to the packed quarterdeck I saw him nod to the Matin farmer who'd organized the small sail crew before joining him on the poop deck above.

My gaze tracked back to the stairs leading to the lower decks. *I wonder what's down there?*

"There you are, Sister."

Eena bustled over, parting the crowds of people as she moved. She took the cloth from me but I grabbed her wrist. I wanted to ask about the boy; tell her about the woman ...

She locked her gaze with mine.

I nodded over my shoulder.

She glanced to the woman stretching her back, flicked her gaze back to me and then stared at the obviously pregnant lady, mouth agape. But before she could move or even speak, Delenon's deep, resonating voice drew everyone's attention.

"Children of the Suns, I have news." The crowd hushed. "We have food and verrin!" A cheer rose. "Animals in the cargo hold, supplies to cook with, and beds to sleep on." Another cheer and the rising murmur of excited voices. Delenon held his hands up and motioned for quiet. The throng obeyed.

"We have need of *specialists* to prepare key areas of the ship before you can explore the lower decks and find much needed relief from the heat. They, and the Leaders with me, will help organise our living spaces. Right now, though, I need willing sailors, hunters, and farmers to meet with Jippon at the front of the ship. Doctors, mechanics, and chefs come and join Reena here at the back, on the quarterdeck. Soon, we will have food in our bellies and a place to rest. Then, we can plot our course to follow in the wake of the great Captain Darius and find his distant island."

As Delenon turned to confer with the farmer, Marxx, Eena's wrist shifted beneath my hand. I looked at her and released my grip. She glanced from the pregnant woman to Reena and back.

Delenon had asked for doctors; clearly she had training. I stepped toward the stretching woman and nodded to Eena. She gave a curt nod back with a grim smile and turned to join Reena. But before I could give the woman my full attention, the Magistrate hurried down to the lower decks, lantern in hand, brows furrowed—toward whatever was chained up down there.

Daria

Ship's Cook

My hands shook or was it my whole body? I couldn't keep track. Cam's arm felt like a hot, limp noodle across my back and shoulders. I shrugged him off after the speech.

"I'm fine."

"You sure?"

I leaned my forehead against the rail and closed my eyes, gripping the wood tight with my hands. "Go help Jip."

"But—"

"Now, Camdin, before I throw you overboard," I grated between my teeth.

He stumbled back and then disappeared into the mass of people stuck on this Gods Forsaken ship. I shifted my head and rested my chin on crossed arms over the rail. The heat of the suns beat down on my hunched back as the front of my shirt clung to the sticky mess of my chest. I stared out at the green nothingness to the point where it turned white-blue on the horizon, where the sky sat on the sea.

"What happened, Brid? What the hell happened?" I whispered. We were supposed to be a happy family. *We* were supposed to win.

The quick lapping of water against the lower hull muted most of the noise on deck. I could hear Reena calling people over, but nothing else. The cascading ripples of the waves caused small crests of foam before churning under and down beneath the cold sea below. That rolling surf could wash away the sweat, the dirt, the sticky milk, and the dried blood. It could also wash away the memories …

I leaned forward, stretching my arms out over the edge, pressing my stomach against the rail—feeling it dig into my ribs and bite flesh. What did I care? The pain in my heart, the ache of memories and a forfeited future made me recognise the limitations of my weakened body. The weight of my limbs urged me down. Rest.

"What's that? No one can cook?" Reena's shrill voice broke through my thoughts.

"Of course, I can cook. But I'm no specialist," one man said.

"Me neither. A meal for five sure—ten when the in-laws came over, maybe. I came because I volunteered at the local clinic. Helped the nurses," a woman said.

"I'm good with building things," the man said. "Not a mechanical expert but I can handle a lot."

"Well, I'm a trained nurse. Have been for thirty years. I don't cook well, even for m' self." A set of heavy footsteps marched toward me. "You okay, Missy?" The nurse said, as she leaned into the railing beside me. I turned my head to look at her but never really focused my eyes. Her stature changed, became more angular as she placed her hands on either side of my arms and turned me toward Reena's group.

"Daria, do you have an expertise?" Reena asked. Again, I looked at her but couldn't focus my eyes. I could sense only a few other people standing around us. I blinked, and the image of the sea washed from my mind.

"No one here cooks?" I asked, not wanting to be a part of the conversation. Not wanting to be here at all. *Just let me find a bed and sleep forever.*

Six different heads shook. Most gazes faltered and lowered to the deck. I sighed.

"I run, *ran,* a café in the Underground."

Reena's eyes widened as an impossibly large grin transformed her, the gold of the coliths framing her moss-coloured face glistened, probably with sweat—still, at that moment, she shone. I crossed my arms and frowned. The nurse gave me a pat then waved at the bronze-skinned woman standing beside Reena.

"Come on then, Farrah, and help me take stock of the Med-bay."

"Bottom of the stairs, first level," Reena called after them.

I glared at Jippon's perky, blonde Second in Command wondering what she had to be so happy about. Even if I *didn't* know how to cook for hordes of people, someone else would've figured it out. I couldn't believe how little it took for her and the others to push aside news of the abomination chained and hidden down in the hold. "We'll deal with it later" Delenon had said, as if it weren't a black omen cursing our very existence.

"Daria, can you organize the galley for water rations? We don't want people getting dehydrated. Save the verrin for extreme cases. Grab a few volunteers to help you. Kitchen's on the second lower deck at the front, just past the staircase to the hold."

I sighed and ran my hands over my face as I dragged my body to the door leading down. *Water. Right. To meeka with helpers. I'll do it myself.* I stopped and froze, thinking of the possibility of needing supplies from the hold. *I'm not going down there alone.* But I still didn't bother to recruit anyone.

I grabbed a lantern at the bottom of the stairs, turned left and went down to the galley. Several lamps hung from the ceiling, now giving the mess a warm glow. Rows of wooden tables with four stools at each, stood off to the side of the stairs to the hold. I passed a hip-wall with serving counter and entered the kitchen.

Two pot-bellied stoves vented up through the ceiling. On either side of them were open fire-pits with large cast-iron drum-pots. To my right stood a prep counter with cupboards above and below and, on my left, *thank the suns*, three large barrel-sized containers. Two were clear and one a rich orange-pink—verrin. Sure, the water would take care of mild dehydration and help with cooking, but it was our verrin stocks that would either keep us alive or doom us for eternity.

I turned to look out over the mess, wondering where all the dishes and cutlery were. More cupboards lined the hip-wall under the counter. I opened one and found not only stacks of bowl-plates, but the other doors revealed tin cups, cutlery, pots and baking trays. As I suspected, the cupboards on the right held tins of spice, flour, sugar, and various other cooking necessities.

"First things first, take out the cups," my voice echoed through the expansive space, anchoring me to a new goal. I reached for a set of cupboard doors beneath the serving counter and recoiled at the sight of my arms; voided finger marks separated the sections of pale dust on black sleeves as dark blood splatters clung like dried paint. My hands shook, still raised as if to grasp the nobs. I looked at my hands. The intricate black Binding tattoo Brid had designed for my left index finger only brought back the image of his arms being flung wide as his body collapsed—not the playful smile from our wedding day that it used to.

My legs wavered and collapsed. I landed on the floor a quivering lump, squeezing my eyes shut. Instead of blessed darkness, the image of Gelden, my beautiful baby boy, waved his tiny hand over my neighbour's shoulder as I ran to catch up with the rest of my family.

"Why!" The word tore from my throat.

Heavy boot-falls echoed through the galley, scuffing the wooden floorboards in haste. I curled in on myself, my body still vibrating.

"Hello?" An older man's voice called out. "Hello? Is anyone hurt?"

Go away. Go. Away.

My teeth chattered as the chill seeped further into my soul.

"Hello?" The voice came from above on the other side of the counter.

Don't look down. Don't look down.

"Sweet Zera—you alright?" Boot-steps scrambled around the hip-wall and into the kitchen. Warmth hovered over my shoulder before a hesitant hand came to rest there. The voice was familiar. I wiped my eyes before pushing up onto shaky arms. He helped me lean back against the cupboards.

"What happened? Are you hurt?"

I shook my head but looked at my lap, willing the tears to stop falling. The old Shimug, who'd remembered about the mizzen mast, sat down on the floor in front of me.

"Are you Daria, the cook?"

I nodded.

"Nurse Eena sent me for fresh water. The boy what got caught in the rigging and fell scraped the skin off his ankle somethin' bad. She needs to clean the wound."

I held my shaking arms out, palms up and said, "I'm filthy. I can't touch anything without contaminating it. Can't— can't prep the water. Can't do anything ..."

"Now, don't you fret. I'll get a bowl of water from the jug over there 'n be back to help ya in a cricket. Sit tight." He patted my shoulder, then worked to his feet in stages before using the counter top to rise completely.

He rummaged around for a mixing bowl, released a small amount of water from the jug, and then left—boots clomping across the mess and back up the stairs. I don't know how long I sat there staring at my hands and arms thinking, *filthy, filthy, absolutely filthy*, over and over again. Some logical corner of my brain knew Delenon would be sending people down soon, but still I didn't move. What could I do? I was filthy.

Part of me was glad when I heard those boots clomp back down the stairs, but another part wished he'd mind his own damn business. The boots didn't come over to me though, they turned to one side. He grunted, and a hinge squeaked as something opened. A bang against the hull made me sit up straighter. Two minutes later, the man walked around and knelt beside me.

"Now, it's not much—got no soap—but it'll help." He set the mixing bowl down on the floor, removed a cloth from his back pocket and laid it over the edge.

I sniffled and looked up, flinching at the salty water.

"Eena assures me it won't hurt for washing. Get yourself tidied an' you'll feel better." He stood and opened a bunch of the cupboards. "Here they are. I'll take the mugs out while you wash." The clatter of tin made me jump.

I grabbed the cloth, rinsed it, and washed my face. Scrubbing in front of an invisible mirror, I following the contour of my eyes, nose, mouth, and ears. After rubbing my dark-grey hands nearly pink, I slipped the damp rag up the front of my shirt to remove the worst of the sticky milk from around my breasts and my stomach. The cold water brought with it raised flesh but also a lightness. By the time I'd wiped down the front of my shirt, the water had turned black.

"Where do I ..." I stood and held the bowl up.

"There's a wash station on either side of the mess near the first oar-port. Give the hatch a good shove then dump the water over the side."

I nodded and handed him his cloth before walking around the counter. The hatch didn't squeak so bad this time, and I used some left-over sea water from the winch bucket to rinse the bowl. A metal tub with a crude drain sat to one side, but I figured that was for washing dishes and not bodies.

At the sounds of multiple footsteps overhead, I hurried back to the galley and grabbed a mug from the far side of the counter just as the old man closed the cupboard doors. There were maybe fifty cups and over a hundred people on board.

He followed my gaze and said, "They'll just have to take turns."

I nodded and filled the mug halfway before turning back. He took it and passed me another.

"What's your name?"

"Neldek Denton. Most just call me Tony."

We swapped two more cups.

"Thank you, Tony."

"No worries, darlin'. They don't need me with the sails right now anyway. Glad to help."

"Thanks for staying, but also for the wash water and cloth.

It's … today …"

"I understand. Today was never meant to end this way." The hard edge to his voice contradicted the man's softened expression, saying more than any words could.

Satie

Finding Equilibrium

Not everyone rushed for the stairs leading to the lower levels, but the stream of people disappearing through that doorway was enough to keep Mateena (*Matty*), the Sisters, and me complacent for the time being. The pregnant woman liked confined spaces about as much as her given name; so, when the line across the main deck eventually thinned, only the Sisters and I ventured over. From the looks given me, and the tender nature of my flesh, I knew my face must be purple and black. Eena never did bring me a second cold cloth. But who could blame her? That boy was probably worse off.

Delenon remained up on the quarterdeck with Marxx, the two books resting open on a map table between them. The furrow in the Magistrate's brow, after returning from below decks, only grew deeper as the two men argued. Marxx did not wear a Leader patch on his arm, and yet Delenon treated this farmer-turned-Resistance Fighter as an equal.

I walked down the steep stairs, one hand on either wall. Somehow, since we were dragged from the Temple two hours ago, I had become First Walker—a position usually sought after by the long-standing Devout. But Meg and Ella only drew further into themselves, repeating prayer after prayer under breath. The fresh scent of the wooden walls cleared my sinuses of the sea-soaked cloth. I spoke the Prayer for Light as my eyes failed to adjust in the dim corridor. *Though my eyes be blind, I ask thee to show me the way. Though my heart beats in the dark, I ask thee shine thy warmth within* ...

I heard, more than saw, Nurse Eena tending to the boy who fell—the room at the bottom of the stairs a medicinal haven. Turning left, I glanced through an open door partway down the hall. Portals cast beams of light on cots lined against the far wall. Other than walking space, the room towered with bunkbeds.

Ella tapped my shoulder. I glanced back at her as she pointed to the room, and shook my head. She wanted the bunk closest to the door, but these were the crew quarters the Magistrate wanted them saved for those who would be helping sail the ship. The general sleeping quarters were on the next level down.

Ella leaned her head against the door frame and swallowed several times, her tanned skin now clammy and yellow. Meg fared no better as her eyes seemed almost to float in the sockets of their own accord, looking this way and that without purpose.

I kept walking until a thump and startled cries made me spin back.

"Sister, are you okay?" a woman asked, leaning over Meg slumped against the wall across from the bunk room. Clutching at the panelling for non-existent handholds, she pressed her face into the wood, mouth gaping as if she might throw up. Ella glanced at Meg and clutched the door frame to keep from joining her on the floor. I hurried back.

"Are you ill? Do you need help outside?" a man asked, kneeling beside her.

Gingerly, I pried one bystander's shoulder back while slipping between Meg and the man trying to yank her up from the floor.

Stop! I wanted to shout. As it was, my prayers faltered. I closed Meg's eyes as she rocked, still hugging the wall. I thought if she could block these people out, I might stand a chance of getting her topside again.

"What's wrong with her?" The woman asked, stepping away.

I shrugged my shoulders.

"Can we help?" A man interjected.

I shook my head.

"But—"

I held my hands over my heart, then over his and the woman's, urging them with a pleading look and a wave of my arms to keep heading to the galley. Then I pointed at my Sisters, myself, and back up the stairs.

"You can't carry them alone," he said, reaching for Meg. I placed my hands on his arm and shook my head. *How can I tell him she doesn't trust him?* I blinked hard, then pointed from Ella and Meg to me and made an X with my arms bringing them close to my chest. Then I pointed to him and the others wanting to help and tried to push my palms together—showing the air between them pushing back, resisting.

Loud footfalls banged up the lower stairs as two men, holding their stomachs and their mouths crashed through the hall, flattening all of us to the walls. Bile spewed between fingers and trailed down their arms onto the floor. Ella's voice grew loud with fevered prayer. Meg clamped her mouth shut, her body shuddering. More people tried to enter the passageway, complaining of the mess on the stairs. I had to save my Sisters' dignity before they ended up the same way.

Dropping to the floor, I grabbed Meg's free hand, still grasping at nothing, and drew her body next to mine. With her arm firmly wrapped around my neck, I staggered under her dead weight, glaring at the people trying to help. *Just back off! Let me through!* Meg found her feet and stumbled with me around the corner and back up the stairs. Above, her legs steadied some, but I still had to half-drag her over to our spot by the hull.

I moved to set her down, but she pitched forward, heaving her breakfast over the side of the ship. Her hands gripped the rail without mercy. Pressure from a hand squeezed my shoulder. I glanced up at Matty rubbing her round belly.

"I'll stay with her."

An understanding passed between us. I ran back across the deck and down the stairs slipping past more people looking for water and bedding.

"Hey!"

"Wait your tur—" Their words halted when they saw me. Someone gasped, then groaned in acknowledgement when they turned the corner and saw the reason for my haste. Ella's knees quivered only inches above the floor as her white-knuckled fingers clutched at the doorframe, her nose pushed flat against the jamb. I grabbed her wrist and pulled, staggering back alone as she clung to the wood. Two new people tried to help by prying her away from the opening. One slipped on spent bile and looked up at me. I shook my head at her, frowned and pointed down to the next level.

"I'm just trying to help."

I shook my head *no* and jabbed my finger to the galley again.

Flicking her hands up in defeat she shook her head, sidestepped another line of bile, and left.

"Come on, Sister. Let go. You have to let go," the man kept repeating as he tried to lift Ella's fingers one at a time, each one snapping back the moment he let go.

"Come on!" His hand smashed the wall above her head. She dropped to her knees, screaming behind compressed lips. Grabbing his tall frame, I pushed him toward the galley stairs. He walked backwards as I stood with my arms wide, protecting Ella with the only shield I had—my own body. He dismissed me with a wave of both hands.

Dropping down to my knees, I hugged Ella and placed my cheek against hers, absorbing her body's shudders through my own wounds. *Suns Above—What am I going to do!* I could only glare at the steady trickle of newcomers. No one else tried to help.

The longer I leaned into Ella, the more I focused on the highs and lows of her whimpers—but *not* whimpers. A familiar pattern emerged: Zita's Prayer. Sister Ella was praying to her Goddess for strength.

With care, I shifted away from her cheek and placed my forehead just above her ear, whispering the words in time with her.

> *"Lend me your ear, lend me your hand.*
> *Together we'll face all life's demands.*
> *Lend me your heart, lend me your smile.*
> *Share with me warmth and wisdom a while."*

Ella's knuckles looked less like exposed bone as the natural rhythm of the words swayed our bodies. *It's working!* I let the song grow in my heart as a proper melody drew my voice and spirit into the next verse and the refrain.

> *"Lend me your strength, your soul burning bright.*
> *Love me forever through each shadowed night.*

Tell me your stories—tales long ago.
Histories and mysteries of triumph and woe."

It was too soon to prod her to stand, but the prayer helped peel away some of her stress. As I launched into the last verse and refrain, I couldn't help but wonder if it would be enough.

"Stand by my side as each cycle forms
and I'll hold you forever to weather life's storms.
Tell me your stories—tales long ago.
Histories and mysteries of triumph—"

Another voice joined mine from the lower stairs, "—and woe. Lend me—"

Then two more from the upper ones, "—your ear, lend me your hand. Together we'll face all life's demands."

As the chorus of voices grew, we started the prayer again. Ella's body fell slack against mine. I guided her hands away from the doorjamb, slipping one arm around my neck. We stood together in time to the rhythm of the song as the voices joining us rose in exclamation, still praying. And together, Ella, the voices, and I rose up to the open deck.

Guiding my Sister over to Meg, who now stood with her eyes closed, back to the wall of the forecastle, I knew there was no way either woman would ever be able to go below deck. For anything.

Matty waddled over and helped me lower Ella to the floor. Sweat beaded on her forehead. Late afternoon was always the worst when all three suns looked down from above. Zola had begun to set when the Talian's launched the ship, but her crown still breached the horizon. I shielded my eyes and looked up. The sails were taunt with wind as those brave, intuitive individuals climbed the rigging and sat on the cross-bracings—*yardarms*.

I motioned drinking from a cup to Matty.

"I'll watch over them," she said.

I nodded, closed my right fist over my heart in silent thanks, and then hurried across the mostly empty deck. Groups of people huddled by the railing on either side, but the bulk of the passengers were below. I tried to swallow but couldn't. If it wasn't for the need of water, I wouldn't have bothered going down again.

The scent of sour bile clung to the hall. Eena continued to bustle in the Med-bay, and several women lounged on bunks in the crew quarters. Likely the room along the other hall was for the men.

A haze of voices floated up the steps. Anyone who could stomach being down here was—to get out of the heat of the day. The stench of sweat hung heavy in the air, growing thicker the farther down I ventured. I breathed through my mouth to bypass some of the ripeness, joining the back of a small crowd standing amongst a grouping of tables.

I turned a full circle, taking in the lower deck; rows of benches and oars resting on the floor lined the hull to either side. Netting and fishing gear hung overhead, and a double-wide door between the two staircases showed more beds and a few tables— passenger sleeping quarters. But several people lay on the rowing benches. *Guess we're kinda crowded.*

"No. You have to wait," a familiar female voice carried above the din.

"Give me some water," a man demanded, with a metallic crack echoing his command. The people ahead of me shifted and murmured. Some even stepped back. I shuffled to avoid being trampled on.

"I remember ya gettin' your first cup, Trezzen. No seconds till everyone's had a first," another man drawled as if they were doing nothing more than chatting at the park.

"I helped rescue that kid from the netting and set the sails right. What has he done?" The mask of bodies ahead cracked open to reveal a bald, robust, Danieth man rounding the counter into the kitchen. The woman who'd helped me onto the ship blocked something with her body, arms planted on her hips. The lanky old Shimug, who had also fixed the sails, grabbed the cup from his aggressor with one hand, then turned and hugged the man's arm into his own body. Baldy cried out, collapsing to his knees. The old Shimug leaned over and whispered something into his ear before letting him go.

"Thanks, Tony, but I could've handled him."

"No doubt, my dear. I juss happened to be closer." He winked and passed her the tin cup.

As the crowd reconvened before the counter, I somehow ended up closer than before. When I found my stomach leaning against the edge of the servery, the old Shimug—*Tony*—smiled at me.

"Here you go, Sister." He passed me a half-full mug. "Where are the other ladies?"

I didn't take the water but pointed up.

He glanced at my Luma.

I held up two fingers then motioned for a full cup, raising one finger against the side.

"Who's the third?"

I smiled sadly then motioned a round belly atop my own.

"A pregnant woman on board? How on Xannia— Right. Just bring back the cups as soon as you're done. Not enough t' go 'round." He turned back to the woman waiting with the next half-cup. "Daria, fill these two up. The Sister has other charges above."

Daria didn't question him, even as baldy glared at us from a nearby table. I whispered a quick prayer for truth, accepted the two full mugs, turned and walked back to the stairs. It felt as if every gaze followed me from the counter as the din dropped by half. The force of my heart beating against my chest threatened to jolt my hands. Somehow, I manage not to spill.

Not two paces from the top of the main deck stairs, Marxx launches himself overhead, landing with a thud to my right. I stutter-stepped, sloshing water. Licking the drops from my wrist and arm, I watched the bronzed-skinned Matin barrel across the deck. My heart constricted. *What now?* As I followed in his wake, I heard another set of footsteps scrambled down the ladder behind me.

"Put it back! Put all of it back!" the farmer yelled.

That's when I noticed the deck wasn't as empty as it had been fifteen minutes ago. Giant lengths of sail cloth stretched along the hull's rail as men and women unwound coils of rope between them. And there, in the mouth of the sail hold beneath the forecastle were Meg and Ella—overseeing the others pass out supplies to eager hands and grateful smiles.

Marxx shouldered his way through the small crowd as *yips* from the sailors in the rigging above refracted against the deck. The group surrounding the hold's door backed off, but not far.

"Drop it!" Marxx commanded, drawing himself up to his full height, placing hands on hips adding mass to his bearing.

My Sisters crossed their arms too. Part of me wanted to grin but the other part, the one that spoke common sense, forced me to frown. This was out of character, even for them.

"Put it all back. NOW. These supplies are not to be trifled with. You"—he whipped an arm out and pointed at the nearest man slinging a hammock from the cloth—"take that down and bring it over. There's plenty of beds bel—"

"Well, now. Let's consider our options a minute, Marxx."

We turned at Delenon's deep, calm voice. He did not need to draw himself up, as his height easily reflected his status. He stood beside me and, rather than crane my neck, I focused instead on his first mate. A wild look slipped across the farmer's face as a red hue crept up his neck, *not* caused by the sun.

"We have no idea how long we're going to be out here. Darius was gone for over a month before he returned home. If the sails rip or the rigging falters, we'll lose precious time undoing whatever knots they make. And what about wear?" He grabbed the corner of cloth a woman clung to, jerking it from her grip. "The elements will weaken the fabric where it's been tied. You don't have to be a sailor to know the kind of damage our suns can do to cloth. Add salt water to that and you're asking for the Gods to curse us, if they haven't all ready."

Marxx stood face to face with the Magistrate, fury flashing across his face in the wake of Delenon's cool gaze and business-like stance: two men on opposite ends of the social ladder who were supposed to be on the same side.

Delenon's gaze fell first to my Sisters, then Matty. "And what do you think?"

"Who, me?" Matty faltered, looking from side to side as the Sisters curled in on themselves and tried to disappear. Whatever moment of inspiration they'd embodied, disintegrated.

"Yes. Marxx is right—" Delenon swept his arm toward the stairwell opening—"there's plenty of room below to accommodate everyone, cramped though you might be."

Meg and Ella paled. Matty's gaze flicked to them and back before looking past Delenon and me to the others surrounding us.

"I— we … I'm sure I speak for everyone sharing my circumstance"—her hands fluttered from resting on her belly, to her hips, hair, neck, and back to her belly—"when I say that as much as we'd like to go below, we *can't.*"

"That's ridicu–"

"Marxx. Let her finish."

The farmer pressed his already thin lips together. I didn't like the look of fire burning from his soul up into his eyes.

"Sir, we suffer a number of maladies from motion-sickness to claustrophobia and will cause more disruption if forced to go below than simply being able to use these stored materials for bedding and shelter on deck. We are *all* brothers and sisters of the Resistance and don't want to ruin these items, just borrow them. We promise to hand over what is needed for repairs during the voyage."

Matty's hands finally settled clasped below her belly. Regardless of what they did during her speech, her gaze never once left the Magistrate's. Feet shuffled, waves slapped, and cloth rustled as more than one person standing on that deck held their breath. Delenon turned, ever so slightly, toward Marxx.

"Stand down. Let them do what they must to find some modicum of comfort under the circumstances."

Marxx opened his mouth to retort, but the Captain had spoken.

Daria

When Nature Calls

I rolled onto my back, the width of my shoulders touched either side of the cot under the bank of windows. The absolute black of the sleeping cabin gave way only to starlight. I crossed my ankles, pinching my thighs together. Staring out at those tiny pin-pricks of light was better than tossing and turning, trying to sleep but dreading its coming. Soft snores from many of my fellow Resistance Fighters blanketed the close quarters. The room looked large enough during the day, but now that it was full—bunks and single cots sometimes with two bodies—it felt no bigger than a broom closet with living, breathing walls.

I turned on my side from the sharp, knife-pierce of a full bladder, and curled in on myself. But it was nothing compared to the jagged shards of memory picking open the fresh scab from the day's wounds. I held my hand out to catch the faint starlight, wiggling my fingers as if the ghost of his tiny palm were there to caress, helping send him back to dreamland. My baby boy …

Biting my lip, I swung my feet from the cot, and walked between the rows of bunks to the door. One woman nodded at me. A couple of men lay staring at the ceiling. I picked up one of two pails on my way out. I'd have no privacy here.

Dim lantern-light scattered strange webbed shadows across the lower deck as stacks of chairs loomed undefined along with even darker shapes in the absence of familiarity. *The kitchen?* I looked to the black cavern waiting to consume me. *No. Unsanitary.* I turned to the hull first one way, then the other, and only found more people wishing for that illusive oblivion. I sighed and walked up the closest set of stairs to the Med deck above.

The groan of the wood beneath my steps blended with the other creeks and moans of the ship giving me anonymity. More of the same greeted me on the next level up as the crew quarters, though half-full of women, were no different than below—maybe a touch warmer. I passed right by the Med-bay, relieving myself there would be no different than the galley, and forced my lagging muscles to climb the last set of stairs to the main deck where I would surely find respite.

Above, the noises of the ship were twice as loud. Since the setting of our second son, Zita, the winds had lessened even as the creaking timber magnified. Without the breeze making me half-deaf, the ship's complaints echoed loud and clear. And yet, not loud enough to completely mask the snatches of conversation from the rigging high above:

"—one better! I birthed a radder one summer when I worked at a farm near the Expanse."

"The Expanse! How could you stand it?"

"I was young enough to think I was invincible and foolish enough not to care."

"—bought up our land for high-rise development."

"Damn shame, that."

"The Kronik stopped buying our grain, and when word got out they wanted our land, well, it was sell or get appropriated."

"—kid sister!"

"Yeah, suspended clear-wrap across my bedroom door. I think I still have whiplash," he laughed.

Glancing up, I didn't see much. Half a silhouette here, a pair of feet dangling there as most of the night crew relaxed in the rigging—waiting for something to happen. I scanned the hull rail looking for a secluded spot to relieve myself but found only lumps and layers of shadows. Nearing one, the bulbous shape formed into a hammock swaying with each crest of the ship. Two sets of arms flopped at irregular angles beyond its confines. Maybe the sail hold?

I crossed my legs and fought off another urge. The sound of footsteps climbing down the ladder from the quarterdeck overrode the distant chatter above. I stared up at the billowing night-darkened sails blocking out the stars, causing giant voids in the sky like an eclipse or black hole. We knew so much about outer space, and yet only satellites had ever breached our skies. Space travel was not a priority. Any kind of technological advancement was limited to the Kronik and his own purposes.

"Strange, isn't it?" Tony asked.

I turned my head as he came up beside me. "We shouldn't be here. We don't belong here." I hardly knew this man, and yet some part of me felt compelled to talk to him.

"Ain't that the truth. But we're managing."

"I suppose."

"It's a new beginning, Daria. We've been given a second chance."

"We've been given a slow death with no hope of a proper cremation. We will starve. Drown. Whatever. But we *will* die."

"Bet-cha breakfast, ya live till t'marrow."

I snorted. "Not if my bladder bursts on me tonight."

He chucked low and slow.

"Yep, that's one thing we men needn't worry too much about—so long as no one's watchin'."

"That's the problem. I'm not exactly partial to peeing in public." I waved the small pail. "And privacy is a premium commodity."

"It t'is." He looked down at me, hooking his thumbs into the holes where the arms of his shirt used to be, like a farmer might with a pair of suspenders. "Something tells me that's not all that's weighing on ya t' night."

I pursed my lips before answering, "They're hungry. You know how I know that? Because *I'm* hungry. And somehow I got roped into feeding over a hundred mouths twice a day. Zola's gonna rise soon."

" 'Bout an hour."

"And the day crew will want breakfast. The night crew will want supper. And everyone else will want to eat too." I set my fists on my hips; the pail bumped into my leg. "I don't have a staff, and I'm certainly not setting foot back down in that cargo hold."

"Why ever not?"

I opened my mouth then shut it. Delenon didn't want rumours spreading about that monster in the ship's belly. "It's too much," I said, and left it at that. I let my arms slump to my sides and sighed. "I'll try the sail hold."

"Don't think that'll work either. The Sisters have rigged something with the door and their hammock. Can only go in and out if'n ya wake 'em."

Suddenly the weight of my body became too much to bear. *I should just piss myself.* Instead, I shook my drooping head.

"Have'n ya tried the mop closet?"

"What's that now?" I perked up.

"On t' other side of the stairs by the Med-bay. 'Cross from the men's quarters."

"Haven't been down that side yet."

"Go n' check it out. Might be just what yer lookin' for."

I nodded. "Thanks."

" 'Course."

He stayed in the middle of the deck, looking up at the shadowed sails, rocking back and forth on his heels, whistling softly between his teeth. I turned and went back below deck in search of the closet. Walking to the right at the bottom of the first set of stairs, instead of left, I made sure to keep to the middle of the hall to avoid smashing my head into the hanging lanterns—and there it was, just askew from the open men's quarters. Yanking the panelled door wide, I slipped inside.

My foot hit something soft, and a hard piece attached to it clattered against the wall. The black swallowed me whole. Stepping back out into the hall, I snagged one of the solar lanterns hanging to one side of the Med-bay. It clinked against the small bucket; I cringed. Somehow, I managed to manoeuvre myself back into the closet and shut the door.

The dim light illuminated a number of mops in one corner, one knocked on an angle. Layered shadows highlighted several buckets and hand scrubbers, jugs of cleaning fluid, rags, cans of rope and oil. I set down the lantern and pail then moved what I could to the periphery. The room was only a bit larger than my arm span. If I stood in the middle and tilted my upper body from side to side, I could touch the walls with the tips of my fingers. But it was big enough.

I wedged an empty metal mop-head holder between the door and the jamb, dropped my filthy pants, and squatted low over the bucket. I wanted to simply let go of it all, but the pail was shallow and a heavy stream would splash back. Not knowing how or when I'd be able to properly clean my clothes, I wasn't going to risk adding urine to the sweat, dust, and blood. *Brid's blood.*

I squeezed my eyes shut, trying to erase that image. Tears leaked from the corners. With shaky hands I righted my pants before my knees gave way. I fell sobbing against the door. I don't know how long I stayed there—a minute? Forever? What did it matter?

I was supposed to be home with Brid taking care of Gelden; helping run the café. Being stranded on a ship in the middle of the nine seas with over a hundred mouths to feed, and that chained curse the Talians left us was never the plan. Winning had been the plan and we failed. Somehow, after the gates were breached, the Kronik's numbers had tripled, overwhelming us. *Where had they come from? None of our intel had even suggested the possibility ...*

Prying myself from the shield of the closet door, I removed my lock, grabbed the lamp and bucket, and headed for the galley. The snores and whispered night-noises from the men's crew-cabin mingled with similar sounds below. The number of dark shapes lying prone along the rowing benches made me shudder as an after-image of the pyre on Capitol Street burned atop them. I pulled my gaze away and opened the trap to the side of the wash station and chucked the contents of my bucket out.

After washing my hands with sea water in a trough large enough to fit a small child, I let them air dry as I turned and stared past the tables into the kitchen. A deep ache spider-webbed out from my chest. My shoulders slumped. Too much. Just too much to handle—to think about—to do. My legs wobbled. *I can't do this.* I collapsed into a chair.

Then the sounds of footsteps, many of them, shuffled up the stairs from the hold. I looked over just as two women and one man appeared with supplies.

"What? I don't understand?" I whispered, grabbing my lantern and meeting them by the serving counter.

"Tony said you needed help. Suggested a simple porridge for our first meal since—"

"—since so many stomachs aren't used sailing. Of course. What have we got?" I leaned over the counter as they shared their findings.

Satie

Spirit's Wake

I stretched my neck from side to side, trying to ease the kink from staring up at the day crew fight with non-responsive sails. Marxx stomped across the deck to the mainmast and shouted up at the workers.

"Wrap your foot into the rigging already!"

"Can't!" More than one voice shouted back.

My heart leapt into my throat as cold-bumps rose across my arms. Meg clutched my arm and echoed my Prayer for Guidance, "Give me the strength to see when blind, and act as you doth heed…" Several men and women fought to untangle lengths of rope meant to raise the sails—leaning on their stomachs, they dangled across a single beam of wood. The creaking of the taut ropes and groan of the ship sounded like painful wails.

Delenon rushed over just as Marxx and five other crew worked to release a series of ties at the base of the mainmast.

"What's the plan?" he hollered.

Marxx ignored him.

Delenon grabbed his shoulder. "What are you doing?"

"To hell if I know! But we have to try something. That book's useless for troubleshooting and the crew only remember so much."

"But there are people up there! Try one thing at a time."

"This is the same thing! Follow the rope lines. If we can shift the angle of the sail, we might be able to catch the breeze."

"We don't have to do everything at once, Marxx. We have time."

"No, we don't. The longer we stay dead in the water, the farther off course we'll drift. Has anyone found a compass yet? No. I didn't think so. If we want to stand half a chance at keeping Darius' course, we"—he yanked on the binding—"have. To. Be. Pro. Active." He grit his teeth. "Camdin!" The boy leader joined Marxx to slowly release the tension from the line.

The Magistrate closed his eyes and ran a black hand over his face; it shook slightly. From stress? Exhaustion? He shifted his stance, somewhat unsteady, before turning and walking back to the map table on the quarterdeck.

Meg laid her forehead on my shoulder, whispering the end of the prayer a second time, "Bring me the peace to wrap clarity in mind, and strive for the light through the grey." She sighed. I patted her hand then helped her sit beneath the hammock in our corner. Matty smiled at me as she rubbed her belly.

"He's active today."

I smiled back. I wanted to ask her how she knew it was a boy, how she got mixed up with the Resistance and stuck on this boat… but I couldn't voice any of it.

"Ready! Heave. Heave. Heave." Marxx called. I jumped a little at his voice and shook my head. Matty laughed.

"You'll get used to it. As a farmer's wife, I've heard similar during the baling season when the crew brings the straw in for the rainy months."

I turned and sat down beside her, wondering where Ella had gotten to. I gave a cursory glance around the mostly barren deck. Not many people came top-side after breakfast. I scowled.

Matty laughed again. "What's gotten under your skin? I've never seen you so riled."

I gave her a weak smile, wishing I could answer—tell her what happened this morning. *Maybe I can ...* I spoke sections of the Rising Prayer aloud, keeping other parts silent.

"... open our eyes ... a new day's dawn ... wisdom denies the... forlorn ..." and I motioned eating.

Matty squinted at me. "Something happened at breakfast?"

I nodded.

"Denies the forlorn ... you almost didn't get to eat?"

I nodded again.

"But why? Who would do that?"

I glanced at Marxx.

"But you ate, yes? You and the Sisters?"

I nodded and spoke excerpts from the Solemn Prayer, "... my soul and its worth ... forsaken ... Trinity's Light ... uniting ... wisdom."

She frowned and bit her lip as she tried to decipher my message, but the length of the pauses to allow for the prayer to be spoken in its entirety made it difficult—for both of us. I closed my eyes and screamed, *help me, oh, Child of the Light!* But I couldn't break my vows. I had to hold on to the beliefs I dedicated my life to, especially during times of trial. *I don't think the gods ever saw this coming, though.*

"Marxx 'forsake' you. Didn't let you eat? And then ... 'uniting wisdom' ... Delenon? Daria the cook? Stepped in on your behalf?"

I nodded from side to side, trying to show her she was mostly right.

"Why wouldn't Marxx let you eat? That's crazy."

I pointed to the crew in front of us and dangling over the beams above and flexed my muscles. Then I dropped my arms and pointed to my chest and shook my head.

Dawning flashed across her face. "Just because your vows demand that you devote yourself to prayers and *not* manual labour, he'd refuse to feed you?"

I shrugged my shoulders then mimed counting on my fingers over and over again.

"I don't care if there are too many mouths to feed. This isn't survival of the fittest. I'm going to give that man a piece of my mind!" Matty struggled to stand. I grabbed her arm, shaking my head.

"… wisdom denies the dark and forlorn …"

A sudden gust forced us both to sit. Sharp yells rose from the crew on deck—the men and women yanked from their feet, collapsed on top of each other as a mass of arms and legs. And then two people fell from the mast above! A man crashed to the floor right in front of us.

Matty shrieked.

I felt Meg collapse beside me just as Ella slipped out of the sail hold with a metal bucket in her hands. She froze.

I saw all of that in my peripheral vision—my gaze locked on the eyes staring at me from the flat of the deck at my feet. Fear twisted through my chest.

Matty wailed, gasping for breath as she hyperventilated and grabbed at the rail behind her. I tried to swallow, but my heart blocked my throat, warm and pliable—maybe it was the back of my tongue … Then his hand twitched and the world ricocheted back to life.

Two swarms of people split toward either side of the mainmast. I leaned forward and crawled toward the broken man.

He blinked and groaned a muffled, halting cry—breath hitching and wet.

I reached out to touch his face, just on the other side of his backward arm, when Eena burst through the ring of onlookers followed by Delenon. His charcoal complexion spoke of the pain and horror in his heart. Eena dropped to her knees and reached for the man's neck, splotchy dark-orange where blisters from the last three days of sunlight cursed him for volunteering as a sailor.

"Is he alive?" She whispered, searching for a pulse.

He blinked again.

I nodded, whispering the Prayer for Guidance, "... bring me the strength to see when blind, and act as you doth heed ..."

"Dear Zola," her whisper more of a curse. Delenon broke through the crowd and dropped down beside Eena. "Flat board. Get a flat board!" she yelled to no one in particular, then whispered in the broken man's ear, "We've got you. Hold on." But the look in her eyes said something very different. Her hands lightly assessed every inch of his exposed body.

Two people split the ring of the crowd with a long board suspended between them. Eena stepped back and pointed to the deck near the Danieth man's back. A loud crack made everyone jump as the stretcher fell. The man moaned, the jolt aggravating his injuries. Eena stuck the toe of her shoe under the upper edge of the board. I mirrored her with the bottom as she gradually rolled the man over amidst wordless cries—my heart breaking more with each.

Eena nodded to Delenon as she grabbed the front of the stretcher. The Magistrate lifted the back.

"Sister."

I stood and looked at her.

"Make sure he doesn't fall off."

I nodded, then gingerly lifted his dangling arm and crossed it over his chest. Afraid I might hurt him, I clutched his clothing as I walked with the make-shift stretcher and its bearers across the main deck. The circle of onlookers broke open when we approached, dispersing to the edges of the ship. No one wanted to stand where the Danieth man fell.

My gaze found Marxx on the opposite side of the mainmast. He poured water across a deep pool of red. The off-white mop head turned pink as he pushed the liquid to the edge of the ship where segmented slats were missing from the lower edge of the hull. Fuchsia bubbles clung to the stained boards. Tearing my gaze away, I looked up. No one remained in the rigging or dangling from the yardarm. Loose ropes and one cock-eyed sail fluttered aimlessly in the breeze. The ship moved again, but at what price?

As we manoeuvred down to the stairs, the injured man's body nearly slipped from the board. I flinched, pushing down on his shoulders to pin him in place. But he didn't wail—he was unconscious. In the Med-bay, Eena and Delenon shifted the stretcher onto its lower frame; whoever had retrieved it had known to grab it from here. I wouldn't have.

The boy who'd fallen several days ago had been moved to the men's crew quarters, but in his place, a long black cloth covered a stretcher by the wall.

"She didn't make it," Delenon whispered. The other person who fell ... the patch of red we passed ...

Both horrified and duty-bound, I let my feet propel me over to the body shroud in death's embrace. I held a hand out—

"Don't." Delenon sighed then moved to stand beside me as Eena took control of the man still living, if barely.

"As Zola kisses your last breath,

wrapping you in eternal warmth's embrace—
Love's bonds cradle you
as suns' light breaches the darkness
and returns you to everlasting bliss."

My hand hovered over the dead woman's head, then heart, before I kissed my central fingertips and touched my forehead and heart. It was all I could do without fire for the Ceremony of Release.

"Thank you, Sister. But you should go." Delenon guided me by my shoulders around the broken Danieth man and to the door. On my way up the stairs I heard him ask Eena, "Will he survive?" If she spoke, I never heard.

Early the next morning, just as Zola breached the black of twilight, the entirety of those aboard stood once again on the upper decks. Two bodies, naked as the day they were born, lay atop the Med-bay's mobile stretchers—feet to the dawn; the Sisters and I stood in a semi-circle at their heads. Reverent silence strained by broken whispers and thinly-veiled hostility, floated on a discordant breeze threatening to strand us dead in the water again.

"It's not right. I tell you. Their souls will be trapped without the cleansing fire," a woman behind me growled.

"You heard the Magistrate. We'd risk setting the ship on fire."

"Then light their pyres at sea," a different voice countered.

"With what? The decking? Our extra sailcloth?" another admonished.

Delenon had explained all this, but the decision to release the bodies without flame was unprecedented and tantamount to heresy. Still, what choice did we have?

I reached for Ella and Meg's hands as we raised our arms to sing The Release. But even as our words rose above the restless voices behind us, I couldn't help but wonder if we condemned these brave souls to eternal restlessness. Their flesh needed to burn to be claimed by Zola and made one with the light.

Meg, Ella, and I began the hum following the lilt of the prayer's song over and over until the voices stopped. Then Meg's voice soared for love of her goddess and our worldly mother.

"Zola's loving embrace burns through the binds of flesh and bone,
Setting free your grace from sinew and soul, releasing spirit from stone.
Sister Zita, Brother -Teth, guide these spirits on Zola's breath ..."

At the final chorus of the short prayer, every single voice on the ship rose unified:

"Rise up, rise up; rise up to the new day.
Rise up, rise up; rise up—be on your way."

The Magistrate lifted the foot of the man's stretcher; Eena lifted the foot of the woman's as the Sisters and I tilted the heads higher and their bodies slid from the ship, plunging to the waters below. The salt waters. It was like killing them twice. I shivered then moved forward to watch their husks sink into the waves— but that never happened.

Ella fainted into Delenon. Eena gripped my arm like a vice, and Meg froze in a silent scream, witnessing vicious sea creatures rip and tear at the earthly remains of those poor, deprived souls. Row upon row of sharp teeth flashed from pointed snouts as blood boiled in the froth of the waves—until nothing remained.

The Turquoise Sea

Distant Coastal,
After several days at sea the men are feeling the
weight of isolation, even as their fear of the
water decreases—so long as they're on deck! We
have a schedule for the day and night crew as the
galley staff work wonders to make sure the fifty
of us remain fed and hydrated.
We've set up the desalinization device on the
poop deck, out of the way, and it's steadily
generating clean water. The verrin casks we've
brought along are many, but without knowing the
number of days it will take us to find land—if
it's out there—mean ingesting only the minimum
amount to keep our bodies functioning out here.
The beauty of these waters belies the troubles
within. After two days' steady sailing through
the turquoise sea we became low on fresh fish and
sent a party out in the rowboat. The nets caught
an assortment of rainbow fish but we also snagged
a larger creature. Its narrow, almost pointed
snout contains a maw of multi-layered teeth as
sharp as knives—Sharpteeth. The body of the
beast spanned the length of the rowboat. The
boys had trouble getting it onto the ship ... a
curse that stayed with us until we breached the
third sea several days later.

Captain Darius

Daria

Fresh Meat

I made a sour face and spat my mouthful into the fire at the base of the cauldron. The young man chopping vegetables glanced at me from the corner of his eye but said nothing. He'd learned fast. Marxx had set up a galley rotation to allow more people to be useful; Delenon had agreed that everyone needed something to look forward to each day, even if it was kitchen duty. My second helper immerged from the cargo hold empty-handed.

"None of the other ganoo are lame or injured, and I'd hate to lose a goat," she said, crossing her arms.

"Goat's out of the question. Need it for dairy. I'll find the Magistrate." I slipped out from behind the counter, changing places with the pale, blue-skinned girl who lifted the ladle and stirred the salted gelluf.

"It's getting kinda rank down there. Might want to mention that too."

"Didn't the animal tenders just change the straw?"

"I wasn't on shift if they did. Doesn't *look* dirty, but in the dim light, what can you really expect to see?"

I shuddered. I *knew* what else was down there, and if one of the Leaders hadn't taken care of it, they were going to have to— soon. Setting my apron across one of the mess tables, I climbed the stairs in search of Marxx instead. Delenon had waved me off the last three times I tried to tell him—about both situations: the meat and the monster. I wasn't wasting my time anymore.

The upper deck was eerily quiet, save the constant creak and groan of the ship and its sails. The crew rested and chatted with those civilians who lived above deck. Marxx stood at the wheel, a length of cloth, the same shade of green as his missing sleeves, wrapped his head protecting him from the suns—somewhat. I watched him watching me make the climb up to the quarterdeck. He leaned his forearms between the spokes and let his hands droop.

"Daria."

"Have you been to the cargo hold lately?"

"I'm fine, thanks for asking." He stared at me through lazy eyes that were anything but. I scowled. I liked dealing with him even less than Delenon, but at least he didn't ignore me.

"Has anyone seen to that chained monstrosity? Neeka says there's a bad stench down there, and the straws were changed this morning."

"Hmm ... good point. Delenon sent Camdin down yesterday with food—don't think anything's been done about waste, though." He squinted at me and shifted his mouth to the side releasing a high-pitched noise as he sucked air in. I frowned and scrunched my nose. My hand itched to smack him for it, but I still needed him.

"Something else on your mind?" The weight of his voice pulled at my patience and my self-esteem. But I wouldn't let this self-proclaimed farmer-turned-Quartermaster undermine me.

"We need fresh meat. Fish. Today. I've been asking Delenon for two days now, and no one has bothered to take the rowboat out."

He squinted one eye at me and sniffed. "He's tried. No one will volunteer. We've got a ton of supplies in the hold. Darius' Journal says we'll transition out of the Turquoise Sea in another four days or so. We'll go fishing then."

"You want your crew to stay strong, right?"

"Of course. We all do." *Are you daft?* Was left unspoken, though implied in his tone.

"If I keep serving the salted and dried meats, we'll run out and then be at the mercy of the seas. Didn't that little book also warn us to fish when we can because so often we can't? And by eating the salted meats our bodies use more water to process them, which in turn depletes those supplies. See? I know what's in those waters just as much as the next person"—I glanced at the belied calm of the sea—"but if Darius' crew did it, so can we. Now figure it out. At least *you've* got a backbone."

He smirked and stood straighter. I hated complimenting him, but it worked. I turned to leave.

"Where do you think you're going?"

I frowned at him. "The galley."

"Oh, no, you don't. If you want people to fish, *you're* going to help me collect them."

Well, that backfired.

The pullies suspending the rowboat rocked and swayed as Reena loaded fishing gear with three other anglers. Jip stood beside Marxx reading from a textbook on how to fish—the second of the two tomes left us by the Talian Curators.

I walked over to Reena just as Jip handed the book back to Marxx and joined us. My foot slipped on the slimy deck boards. Jip tried to grab my elbow to help steady me, but lost his footing too. We crashed down at Reena's feet. The slime coated down one side of my arm, pant leg and hip.

"Disgusting," I spat.

"What do you expect," one of the anglers said. "It's not like we can do anything about it."

Jip helped me up as Reena said, "Actually, in the passages of Darius's Journal that I've read, he's mentioned a boatswain who regularly got his men to wash the deck. Has that even been done in the past four days?" She looked from Jip and me to Marxx. I shook my head and shrugged my shoulders. It would make sense as to why we had a mop closet. The fact that it was now the go-to spot for privacy when relieving yourself made the mops a little difficult to access regularly—but they were still there.

"It would certainly give the other passengers another job to add to their rotation—though I doubt they'd look forward to this one!" Jip laughed, then motioned for the others to get into the rowboat. No one moved, or rather no one moved *forward*. Those who'd offered their services back on day one were anything but eager now. But they were hungry.

"I thought we'd be hauling nets from the deck, not sea level," the green-toned, Metek man wiped sweat from his brow with the back of his arm. He glanced over the rail and shook his head.

"The fish won't swim that close to the ship," Jip said. Reena jumped into the boat. Her body language shouted, *come on!* but her eyes reflected just how scared she really was. Jip held her gaze then moved to usher the others aboard, keeping a wide stance so as not to fall a second time.

When everyone was aboard, Marxx and one of the day crew winched the boat down. I shaded my eyes and glanced at the position of the suns before turning to leave.

"Not so fast, Daria."

"What now?" I openly scowled at Marxx.

"We need a scout. And that's you." The sound of the rowboat splashing into the waves punctuated his words. I crossed my arms.

"I'm the cook, not the scout."

He turned and walked back to the wheel to relieve the woman holding it steady in his absence. The other guy released the tension on the pully then returned to monitoring the sails or whatever sailors do.

"You wanted fish, you can wait for it. Shouldn't take long, right? Book said the waters are ripe." He tipped his chin down like a gentleman might had he been wearing a hat. But Marxx was no gentleman, and the action came loud and clear as the snub it was meant to be. I turned away from him then leaned on my hands over the rail to watch the progress below.

One hook had been detached as the other kept the boat, which now looking tiny as it bobbed on the waves, connected to the ship. The four people in that small craft looked so out of place among all that greeny-blue *salt*water. Ten minutes submersed in that death liquid and any Xannian would go into sodium shock. Ninety percent of all victims died within an hour. There was a reason modern ships were basically large plastic bubbles with nets.

I shuddered as my thoughts flashed to days-old images of pink foam and sharp teeth. My gaze flicked to a dark patch under the water. *Is that*— but then it was gone. *Stop imagining things and concentrate.*

The group tossed a large net into the sea, anchoring one portion to the side of the boat. More and more dark patches came and went in the water—just shadows. I wouldn't let my mind trick me. There were no bodies in the water to call the sharp-teeth, just wood and rope.

A figure walked toward me from the back of the ship. I ignored her, like I did everyone, until she leaned against the rail beside me, whispering a prayer. The young Sun Guardian. I still didn't look at her, but my mind flashed images of that fateful day as we walked along the wharf to the ship, and then climbed aboard to our doom. Her porcelain-pink skin made her look fragile and delicate. I couldn't help but wonder how she managed to avoid getting sunburned while living on deck with her other Sisters and the pregnant woman.

My baby's face blossomed in my mind: his perfect little nose and big bright eyes. I blinked back surprise tears as my glands excreted more milk. The Sister placed a hand on my shoulder, her touch radiating a calming heat I wanted no part of. I shrugged her off, pushed the wet from my eyes with the side of my hands and turned to face her.

A shout from below cut off whatever stupid thing I was about to say. Reena fell back into Jip, the two of them landing in the bottom of the boat between the seats. I couldn't make out what they were saying, but fear didn't need a voice.

Those dark shapes hadn't been a figment of my imagination. Dozens of them surrounded the little craft, churning the water and making the boat spin. One of those shadows rammed the bow causing the craft to keel toward the weighted netting; the other two citizens fell into each other and onto the side of the tipped boat. Jip and Reena scrambled to climb the high side, slipping on the smooth wooden seats.

"Great Trinity!" the Sister cried. Throwing her arms in the air, she raced through the Rising Prayer over and over again, as if pleading to all three gods might stop the madness.

"Marxx!" I shouted, launching over to the pully to release more and more rope as the craft turned and got shoved farther and farther away. I slipped as I fought to catch my balance and the wild pull of the rope.

I grabbed the reel handle attached to the pully. My knuckles jammed against the mechanism. I cried out. The rope dug into my palms as the Sister reached up beside me and, between the two of us, forced the rope to wind. Marxx and several crew members leaned over the rail and grasped the taut rope, hauling back in synchronized heaves. The Sister and I reeled the loose rope up through the pully as the rowboat slowly pulled back toward the ship.

Her hands fell away as she cried out, covering her mouth. I looked past the gaps in the haulers' frames to the sea below. Jip and Reena counterbalanced the rise of the rowboat, but their bodies leaned out over the still high edge. A sharpteeth launched from the water straight toward them.

Jip shouted. Pulling Reena into him, they ducked. A seven-foot-long beast arced over their heads, teeth gnashing, body thrashing in the air—just missing them.

The hull keeled again. A scream pierced my dulled senses. As the rowboat drew into the air, dangling from only one rope, a full net of fish yanked it back toward the frothing *pink* waves, a river of red poured down the female angler's body from her shoulder, where her arm used to be. More crew grabbed what they could of the rope, the pulley forgotten. Feet fought for purchase on the slick deck.

Delenon appeared suddenly, trying to swing the end of the other rope-hook toward the suspended boat. But each toss fell just short. Then Reena wrapped Jip's arms around her waist, and she was in the air, above the churning sea and the monsters. She caught Delenon's next swing and slid awkwardly back into the vertical craft, Jip's gip never failing as Reena tried once, twice, then three times to attach the hook.

I cried out when it latched, and shifted to help Delenon reel in the dangling portion of the rowboat. It still leaned dangerously to one side. Other, stronger, crew members brushed me aside to help bring the craft home to dock. They reached for the anglers, hauling them back on board; I staggered back out of the way. Nurse Eena and her helper wheeled a stretcher over for the poor woman, no longer conscious—*at least I hope she's not.*

Then the net of silvery-rainbow fish dropped onto the deck, spilling out at my feet. I dropped to my knees amidst the fresh meat. Tracts of tears scalded my cheeks. I didn't look at the price of my insistence—instead, I stared at the smear of red on the rail and followed the crimson drips across the deck to the stairs.

Small arms wrapped tight around me, rocking me … trying to soothe my broken soul.

Satie

The Burden of Choice

I lingered in the cabin doorway of the general quarters, but I didn't consciously acknowledge those few people already in the room; lounging, napping. Poor Daria lay as still as those crewmembers during the Ceremony of Release. Her already ashen skin darkened in the long shadows of the space as she stared unseeing at the ceiling, a perpetual film of tears glinting but not releasing.

I did what I could to make her more comfortable: wiped the deck slime from her clothes, the bloody rope burns on her palms—praying silently to ease her mental flinches. The words soothed only my soul, but even then I was certain I could do more even if I wasn't sure what. I slipped away, turning to face the galley and mount one of the sets of stairs flanking me to the deck above. Although the next meal wasn't for another few hours, the chairs were full as every person present chatted on, oblivious to the sacrifice made.

The scent of simmering soup soured when it reached the back of my throat. I turned and climbed the stairs lifting one weighted foot after the other. The night crew slept as I shuffled past the men's bunk. I averted my eyes from the Med-bay door. Nothing clattered or crashed, but the flurry of movement from Eena and her helper drew from my lips another prayer. Using the railing, I hauled myself step-by-step up the last steep staircase to the main deck.

A mound of sleek, twitching, rainbow fish lay abandoned on the deck near the starboard side. The crew worked to correct the sails, manoeuvring around the pile when necessary. All four mops and buckets from the privy were in use by non-sailing volunteers. The red spatters were gone, but my eyes followed their invisible trail past the Daria-sized void in the fish, all the way over to Magistrate Delenon.

I could not walk past this man to sit quietly and pray like a proper Devout in the midst of her Observances. I could not ignore the slant of his shoulders, the dark stain of sweat tracing a V down the back of his cotton suit-shirt, or the drooping of his head as he looked out to sea standing beside a darkening smear of red. My feet took me to stand by him, opposite the blood.

I had no words to speak, nor did I risk praying aloud. I understood the need for silence better now. Instead, I rested my hand on his shoulder. His body shuddered beneath my touch, but he did not shake me off. He did not turn away.

Following his gaze to the waters below, I expected to see nothing but vivid, turquoise waves. I was wrong. He felt me stiffen as I watched maddened sharp-tooth fish shadow the waters surrounding the ship, several rammed the hull over and over again. Small vortexes swirled as hordes of them paced beneath the waves.

"I told them not to …"

He'd known about the vicious fish? I squeezed his shoulder.

"Marxx ... but then Daria ..." he sighed. "Her interpretation of the Journal was different. Marxx was indifferent. I suppose it was only a matter of time."

One of the sharpteeth below smashed into the hull so hard it drew blood. The other beasts attacked, ripping the bloodied one to pieces.

I gasped, covering my mouth with both hands. Delenon shuddered then collapsed at my feet. My heart splintered as I dropped to the deck beside him. He tried to look up at me, but another jolt quaked his body. I cupped his face with my hands then let go. *Hot!* This wasn't a weak constitution; he was sick.

Slipping his arm across my shoulders, I slowly manoeuvred him to stand with me as his crutch. No one else came to help or even approached, the severity of the situation lost on them. His legs trembled as we shuffled across to the stairs. Snatches of different prayers all related to strength and fortitude flipped about in my mind.

We teetered at the top of the stairway. Delenon tried to hold the rail, but his hand was useless. My foot slipped off the edge of the step and we tumble-jogged down to the bottom. If Eena hadn't already been busy, she'd have hollered and come running to help. As it was, the only shouts were from the crew trying to sleep. I limped to the door, Delenon staggering beside me.

Eena and her helper didn't look up. They still leaned over the woman's shredded shoulder, her body spasming even in its unconscious state. I helped Delenon around the operating table to one of the few remaining empty cots. Most of the other patients lay with their backs to the mess or kept their eyes closed. I rotated and allowed us to flop down on a bed by the far wall.

"Check the supply cabinet," Eena barked in concentration.

"We've used it all."

"We need more or infection is sure to set in."

Bottles and cans rattled and clanked. "There's no more."

Eena swore.

I signed to the Trinity.

Delenon groaned. I helped him lay down. He was burning up, shaking and shuddering. His teeth chattered.

"Use the ale."

"What?" her helper asked.

"In the cargo hold, Daria mentioned there were three casks of cooking ale. Get a bucket of it. Now, Farrah!"

The helper wiped red hands on her already bloodied apron, then tossed the garment at a hook on the wall before careening around the corner and racing downstairs, leaving a clear sightline to the metal operating table and the woman's gaping wound. Eena carefully twisted and knotted the end of a piece of fleshy string. My stomach clenched.

The nurse swore again. I closed my eyes.

"Sister. Sister!"

I opened them.

"She's stopped breathing. Help me so I can do CPR without her arteries spurting blood all over the place."

I thought I started to rise, but my grip on the edge of the cot held firm.

Get up and help, Satie!

A Devout in Observance doesn't work!

She's dying—

My vows—

What good are they if you're not helping people?

What happens to my soul if I break them? My connection to Zerameteth? My life?

"Sister!"

Daria

Compulsions

I stared at the ceiling in the dark. Zerameteth sat at his zenith, casting a pale white-yellow ghost of light over everything.

Mostly everyone was asleep, with steady snores and sighs from people unafflicted by guilt.

My stomach grumbled, pinching my insides, but I didn't care. I *did* care about the mounting pressure in my bladder, though. Rising, I pushed my stiff body off the cot and over to the door. Turning left, I mounted the stairs to the men's hall and took a moment to relieve myself in the mop room. Instead of returning below to toss my urine from the waste shoot, I continued climbing. Too many bodies below; too many ignorant, sleeping fools.

Above, the breeze shifted loose strands of hair across my face as I stood framed in the doorway. I pushed at them, crushing the palm of my hand into my face and forcing them away. The weight of my bun, half-undone, tapped against the nape of my neck. Turning starboard, I emptied the contents of my bucket at one of the notches along the rail. The wind took most of it; the sea would slap against the hull and take care of the rest. *Maybe it should take care of me too?*

I moved away from the edge, not trusting myself. Turning back to face the main deck, I shuffled forward. Necessity dictated I return the bucket, but my feet moved me toward the middle of the deck. An invisible stain on the port-side hull drew me. But I stopped exactly where I'd collapsed among the fish mid-day. I saw them wriggle and squirm, their black beady eyes staring at me everywhere I looked. Though the clean deck belied their earlier presence, their heavy scent lingered.

A good woman nearly died today because of me—might still. Eena had come to visit me not long before the sleep rush. She'd knelt by my head and said a bunch of stuff I mostly ignored. What I did hear was something about the potential for infection and severe nerve damage. That brave woman lost her arm because I couldn't leave well enough alone. Even if she survived, she'd never be whole again … I'd lost my heart and my soul for a cause that never stood a chance of winning. I'd deluded myself then, and I was still doing it now. *I'm dangerous—shouldn't be in charge of people, feeding them—*

A wall of heat suddenly radiated beside me.

"Yer awfully quiet t' night," Tony drawled.

I couldn't pull my gaze away from the memory of what was—both today and a week ago.

"Looks like ya could use a distraction. Come on."

As my body cooled, I found myself following his warmth, walking beside him across the deck. He climbed to the quarterdeck, around a crewmember steadying the ship's wheel, and over to a door beneath the poop deck. A line of light glowed at the base of the closed door—one of only a few on this ship. Crass laughter and banging buffeted the inside of the door.

I looked at Tony. "I don't want to be around people right now."

"S'not like that. In there, no 'un knows yer name."

I frowned at him. He gave a low chuckle.

"Can you keep a secret?" the night quartermaster whispered, a twinkle of conspiracy in his eyes.

I felt myself nod, though I don't know why. Everyone knew my name—ship's cook. How could such anonymity exist in a close-knit, floating town?

He opened the door and guided me in.

Soft light from four oil lamps hung from the ceiling in the centre of the small room causing half-shadowed faces and dark figures in duplicate and triplicate to waver on the walls. The map table, for during the day this is where they stored Delenon's books and the star chart from the Journal, was pushed to the back of the tapered room. Men and women sat on stools borrowed from the mess in small circles about the space.

A pair of dice clanked against one of my tin cups from the kitchen—*who had dice on them during the battle?* Two other groups tossed drezeks of various currency, the coins pinging and whirling against the wooden floorboards. Another group had liberated a set of measuring cups and proceeded to move them around, open-side down, on one of the smoother planks.

"But, Ton—"

"No names, now." He winked.

"Does the Magistrate know?" The dice group yelled, some pleased, some not.

"No. Nor should he."

"But he trusts you—"

"To do my job and keep the people on this ship safe. You feed 'em, Nurse heals 'em, Day-watch disciplines 'em, Magistrate inspires 'em, and I let 'em play. Without balance in life, what kinda life is 't? Besides, I know people's nature; this would've happened with or without me." He sauntered over to a group with piles of simple items before them, no physical game like the hand-symbols happening over in the opposite corner. The piles were made up of nuts, rings, lengths of cloth torn from clothing, hair pins, buttons, and other random stuff.

"What's it doin'?" Tony crouched on the edge of the circle. "We find any joy on the Sister's name?"

Various participants responded:

"Not yet."

"Still doin' her Observances."

"How 'bout Day-watch? How many times he rub his nose t' day?" Tony prodded.

"Twenty-seven."

"Ah, ha! I called twenty-nine. Any one closer?" Tony asked.

"Na, you got it, DM." Tony collected one nut from each participant then looked a young man in the eyes as Tony touched his own nose.

The young guy nodded. Then Tony stood and swept me over to the map table at the back. He held out his hand to me, palm up, "Nut?"

The simple food had likely been in various people's pockets, hands, and on the floor, but my stomach growled again. I reached to pluck one from his palm when he turned my hand over and gave me the lot of them.

"I couldn't. It's your currency."

"You haven't eaten yet, have ya?"

I shook my head then popped them in my mouth.

"Stay as long as ya like. We shut down juss afore twilight 'n tidy up. Juss don't wager somethin' ya can't bear to part with, or something ya can't follow through on—like taking someone's mop duty when you're on animal duty. Consider how much something is worth to ya before uppin' a wager. Always start small."

He bumped shoulders with me. "Relax."

I took a deep breath and stared around the simple room.

"Any questions?"

Not really. Maybe one. "What's DM stand for?"

He leaned over and whispered in my ear, "Den Master." Then he chuckled and wove his way back through the circles of games and out the door to fulfil his night duties. Leaning back against the map table, I let the wash of fevered voices pull me into a completely different reality.

Sometime later, I left the Den and walked out to a star-smeared sky. Little Zerameteth hung low with twilight only a couple hours away. I didn't gamble that night, just observed and let myself get lost in the wagers and the games. I breathed in the sharp, cool sea air and listened to the rush of the waves. Footsteps on the deck above caught my attention. I didn't see Tony at the wheel or out and about checking in with his crew, so I turned and climbed up to the poop deck. His frame crouched low to the deck as he examined one of two distillation devices set up by our resident "builder/fixer" several days ago.

"Amazing, aren't they?"

He looked up at me and smiled. "That they are. I've been studying how they're put together."

"So you know how to store them in case of bad weather?"

"No. I was shown that."

"What for then?"

Tony rose to his full height and stretched his scrunched limbs. "I heard we had some extra pieces. Wanted t' put somethin' together to offer as extra incentive in the Den."

"What do you mean? If they had enough spare parts, they would have put a third one together, right?"

"Yep, but there's some pieces missin'—pieces that won't break if dropped."

"And you want to put these extra pieces together with ... with other found items to make a third still?"

"Exactly."

I had a feeling I knew where he was going with this.

"Okay. I'm in. Tell me what you need."

Satie

Delirium

Fresh water dripped from the cloth as I wrung it into the basin on Eena's portable trolley. It rolled away slightly, but I caught it with my foot, held it steady with my forearms, and then set the wheel lock. I soaked Petra's neck and chest as her eyes moved erratically beneath closed lids. Re-dunking and then wringing the cloth again, this time I laid it over those fevered eyes. I peeked beneath the dry bandage where her arm used to be, whispered the Prayer for Light, and noted that the irritated flesh Eena had stitched over the wound looked more pink than red today. She might yet survive.

Eena bustled around the Med-bay rubbing ointment on severely blistered skin, changing bandages on rope burns: hands, arms, legs—whatever happened to get in the path of a rope's trajectory, and cream on dry, cracked joints. We had ten patients, not including our two special guests.

I released the wheel lock and pushed the cart over to Delenon's cot at the back. The stark, near nakedness of this great man wrung my heart every time I looked at him. Sweat glistened everywhere on his ebony body, even as the gold ribbons of his coliths dulled, showing the truth of his condition. I moved the water basin to the centre shelf, checked that the wheel was locked, and proceeded to wipe down this once great man's weakened body.

As was my ritual for the past three days, I began at his feet and worked my way up, past his britches to his stomach and chest. I recited prayers, sometimes the same one over and over again. As the cool cloth slid across the hollow of his neck, the man's eyes opened. I jumped slightly, startled. This wasn't the first time the unseeing orbs sought to focus.

I spoke aloud the prayer I'd been repeating in my head, the Song for Spring—I needed something positive as a counterbalance to working with Eena and Farrah, who was currently on break. *Though I guess I'm technically helping now too.*

But with the sound of my voice, Delenon grabbed my wrist and stared at me—as if looking straight through my eyes to the back of my skull and beyond.

He muttered something around a thick tongue.

"Mag—?" The partial word slipped. I bit my bottom lip and shut my eyes, silently cursing myself. I'd compromised on so much since this voyage began, I couldn't afford to destroy *everything* I'd worked for. *I am Devout.*

I opened my eyes.

His gaze focused for a split-second. "Feed ... feed him," he rasped barely above a whisper.

I leaned my ear closer.

"Hold ... down in basement ... chained ..." Then his eyes rolled back and his body spasmed.

"Eena!" I cried, yelling at myself to shut up at the same time. Tears wet my cheeks. *Stop it, Satie! Pull yourself together.* I launched into the Prayer for Guidance, begging appeasement from my god.

She rushed over, grabbing a mug of broth from the counter on the way.

"Hold him still."

I grabbed his arms but his body writhed.

"*Hold* him, Sister," she commanded.

I draped my body across his chest and hugged him to the cot, grabbing the steel legs beneath. My head lay on his heaving chest as his heart hammered the cavity within. Eena drizzled the broth into his mouth and massaged his throat. Half a cup later, he fainted. I released him when his heart rate returned to normal.

Eena sighed. "Ya did good, child. I know how it cost ya, but ya did good all the same."

Farrah chose that moment to breeze in through the door.

"Your turn, Sister," she said and relieved me of my duties.

Hanging my smock up on a peg by the door, I went down to the galley to see what was left of breakfast. I repeated the Redeemer's Prayer to the point where I hardly registered walking past tables of people on my way over to the serving counter.

Daria nodded at me, collected a single serving of eggs, toast, and re-hydrated meat on a plate with half a cup of verrin. The poor woman's gaze spoke of sorrow an ocean deep. The dark rings hailed sleepless nights, and the droop of her shoulders echoed the broken woman on the inside. I gave my usual slow-blink of thanks and nod, now fully back in control of my senses.

On my way back to the stairs, my gaze lingered on the steep stairwell leading down to the cargo hold as Delenon's fevered words "feed him" over-rode my prayers. *Was he fevered? Or was that really a moment of clarity?*

I recalled Daria's haste that first day on board, as she burst from the stairs onto the main deck ranting about a "monster chained in the hold" … Then Delenon's determined look as he later went down—likely to check for himself.

What's down in the hold?

A blast of salty air hit me as I breached the main deck. I stuffed three mouthfuls of eggs into me, half a slice of toast, and one bite of meat, washing it all down with two sips of verrin. My stomach begged for more, but I just swallowed air as I hurried across the deck to the sail hold and my Sisters' place of residence.

Neither would look at me.

I set the remainder of the meal down at their feet, spoke a prayer for thanks, turned and left. I glared up at Marxx on the quarterdeck behind the wheel. Since Delenon became ill, Marxx had superseded both Jip and Reena, naming himself "Acting Captain". That also meant Acting *Dictator* as he decried that only those citizens who "worked" got fed. He didn't equate prayer to work the same way Delenon had, and the Sisters were either too stubborn or too devoted to their goddesses to break their vows as I had—or both. *But I'm just bending the rules … someone has to.*

Heading back down the stairs, I didn't return to the Medbay early, like I usually did. Instead, I grabbed a lantern, walked down to the galley, and then on to the hold as if I had every right in the world to do so. And no one questioned me.

I wasn't alone. Three other people were in the cargo hold with me: one cleaned out the ganoo roosts and collected eggs; one changed the goats' straw and filled their troughs; and one pumped disgusting bilge water from a recently discovered cavity between the bottom of the ship and the floor. Breathing through my mouth, I skirted the workers and inspected the space behind the wall of ganoo.

Just a mechanical room—nothing out of the ordinary.

I circled back just as the guy collecting eggs set them in an empty crate near the bottom of the wall in neat trays of egg holders, before returning to the galley with several in a basket.

Probably for baking. Walking over to the closest pen, I stepped inside to pet the two goats. Doing this for each animal, I paced myself to remain three stalls back of the cleaner at any given time. Luckily, three pens later, she set the crates of spent straw along the throughway from the stairs to the wall of ganoo and then left. *I guess someone else lugs them upstairs and tosses them overboard.*

I finished patting the last of the animals, just to make sure no one else dropped by. My hands reeked of goat, so I kept them away from my clothes as much as possible, grabbing a lantern as I walked behind the hold stairs. It was darker back here since fewer lights were kept on—no animals to care for supposedly. Row upon row of barrels and crates held a variety of food staples. It looked massive, but I knew that with over a hundred mouths to feed twice a day, and a hydration stop mid-day, these supplies wouldn't last forever.

The creak and groan of the wood was more apparent now that I had nothing to focus on except the small cast my light made before me. Footfalls overhead were sparse and muted even in the cavernous space. Then a different kind of wall blocked access to the bow. The flesh on my arms pimpled as I shook off a chill. If this end of the ship mirrored the other, the space behind would be relatively small. It was far enough away from the main action with the animals that it made sense if something was chained up down here—a something that needed to be fed—it would be hidden behind that wall. But I had no food. I'd given everything I could to Meg and Ella. Still, the Leaders seemed to know about what was down here, so I could get food if Delenon's concern was valid. Right?

Taking a deep breath, I peeked around the edge of the wall and into the confines beyond and saw ... *nothing.* Just a ring of boxes and an old pile of rags heaped in the middle of some straw. Whatever had been down here, wasn't here anymore.

"Sweet Zerameteth—" but whatever prayer I was about to utter erased from my brain as the clump of rags shifted, shuttered, and rose ever higher. I pressed my back to the wall. *The monster!*

Chains rattled and slid over the straw, clanking against the boxes of its nest. My heart threatened to smash my chest to pieces, but I couldn't move. Delenon had sent me here to feed it—with me? *No, that's ridiculous. Get your head on straight.*

As it turned, an act so slow and methodical, I couldn't help but wonder what beast moved with such aching deliberateness.

A pile of the rags dropped from the peak and revealed—

A man.

But not just any man.

A Talian.

"Holy Mother, Sister, 'n Brother …"

He tilted his shaggy, filthy head. His eye sockets and cheekbones protruded almost as significantly as his collar bones. Scowling at me, he turned away and sat on a box with his back to me.

What could I say? What could I do? I had nothing for him. *But you can find something.*

I ran back around the side of the wall. *The water troughs were just filled,* a bucket hung from the closest one on either side of the walkway. I grabbed both and raced back to the rows of supplies. Crates and barrels with white chalk marks on the lids likely meant they were the ones currently being used. I collected two handfuls of nuts, an elppa fruit (fresh), a piece of dried gelluf, and, in the other bucket, a skimming of verrin—maybe two cups worth. He needed it. The tinge to his lips showed it had been some time before he last had a sip of the vital liquid.

Hurrying back to the hidden room, I slid on some scattered straw and skidded to a stop just shy of the main pile. The Talian still sat with his back to me. I walked to the closest crate and set the two buckets down.

His chains shifted. Before I could even think to scurry back, he had his arms around me—chain links pressing into my throat.

I squeaked. *What's he going to do!* Trembling uncontrollably, I tried to pry his hands away.

He attempted to yell but couldn't with such a hoarse voice.

"No. Body. Down. Here," I gasped, scrambling to yank the chain from my neck, shattering a vow only ten days old. I breathed in the layered scent of sweat, urine, and feces, gagging doubly.

"Free me," he growled into my ear.

"No. Key ... please ..." Pin pricks of light flashed behind my eyes seconds before the world disappeared.

Daria

Side Ventures

"I'll get it," I said. Not that I was in a particularly positive frame of mind or anything. I just wanted out of the kitchen. I left my apron on a peg by the serving counter's opening, grabbed a small pail and headed for the stairs—the hold's stairs.

I hadn't set foot down there since that first day, but between Tony's idea floating around in my brain and the nearness of so many people, it really was the only way to find a quiet moment—and check for a spot to hide a makeshift still. Yet, as I stepped down the stairs, a chill etched down my spine—and not because of the temperature change.

Turning to face the cargo portion of the hold, my feet suddenly refused to take me where I needed to go. I inhaled and exhaled, but the calming technique lasted all of two seconds. *You're not going anywhere near the back. Just the side. Shift over that way—that's right. Now twenty steps more.*

I talked myself over to the casket of sand and cracked the lid with a nearby crowbar. The fine, coarse grains were ideal for scouring pots and pans; and the eggs this morning had left every one of them a mess. I scooped a quarter of a bucket; a little went a long way. As I reached down to grab the heavy wooden lid, a high-pitched squeal made me jolt straight up.

That was no mouse.

My body shivered and my teeth chattered. *Run!* I dropped the lid and the bucket, but instead of running up out of the hold, the way I wanted to, I ran for that back wall and that terrified sound.

Multiple feet scuffing over straw confirmed my worst fear. Grabbing a prybar from a nearby crate, I whipped around the corner, arms raised.

Her face was purple; her mouth opened in a silent scream seconds before her entire body collapsed. The sudden dead-weight pulled the monster forward. Yelling, with every fibre of hurt, every death, and abandoned child back in the Prime, I smashed that Talian's head.

He dropped.

The crowbar's momentum dragged it from my fingers, and it clattered against the wall. *Take that you evil piece of meeka!* Shoving him off the Sister, I grabbed her under the arms and pulled her beyond the reach of that animal's leash, and into my lap. Red, chain-shaped welts encircled her neck.

"Sister. Sister, wake up." I patted her cheek with a slight slap. "Sister!"

She coughed and groaned, curling her body in on itself. I leaned back against the wall and sighed, absently smoothing hair back from her forehead as I stared at her white Luma cap scrunched under that thing's arm. Her body quaked, then she sighed—a sound that mingled defeat and perseverance at the same time. She struggled to sit up. I helped as best I could until she rested beside me, gingerly massaging her throat.

"Thank you," she rasped. Tears welled in her eyes, cascading over her cheeks in silent agony.

I jolted back in surprise. I got the impression her tears weren't for her injuries. She smiled wearily then swallowed with a grimace.

"So— so much for vows," she shook her head gently, then closed her eyes and leaned back against the wall. She didn't wipe her face, but I was transfixed by the struggles wrought over her brow, across her nose, along the line of her lip ... she fought with a million demons—or maybe just three very silent gods—until her muscles went limp and the life drained from her.

"Sister?" She opened her eyes but stared only at something past the ceiling, perhaps as far as the sky and the stars beyond our little world. "What are you doing down here? I thought you worked with Eena?"

She licked her lips and her gaze focused on the beams of the ceiling. "I do. I was tending to Delenon— said *he* needed food." She inclined her chin toward the unconscious beast on the floor and winced. "I didn't realize he was that dangerous—that *fast*."

"He can damn well starve for all I care. We should've dumped him overboard that first night." She frowned at me and tilted her head, grimacing and touching her swollen neck.

"Why should we kill a man we don't even know?"

"Case in point." I motioned to the results of her attempted aid with both hands. "The Kronik chained him down here for some reason. If they don't want him, why should we? What has a Talian ever done for the other races? For us *commoners*? Nothing. The Kronik doesn't care and by extension, neither do any of the Talians whether they're behind the Compound wall or a ship's wall of crates—they're one and the same." She pursed her lips and frowned. "Don't tell me you feel sorry for him? That monster just tried to kill you."

She tilted her head to the side then turned a bit to look at me. "I don't think he meant to."

"What?"

She sighed. "He wanted a key I didn't have. He wanted to escape—to where? I don't know. Maybe to hide down here somewhere instead of being caged like an animal. Treat someone like that long enough and they begin to believe it."

"Broken vow or no, there's too much kindness in your heart, Sister. The wrong people will take advantage of that. You need to start looking out for number one."

"If I did that, Daria, I don't think we'd stand even a chance of finding Darius' island."

I stood up and offered the Sister my hand, then pulled her to her feet. She didn't let go right away.

"Really, thank you for rescuing me. If you'd only been thinking of yourself, things might have turned out very differently. Don't lose that compassion; it makes you beautiful, not weak."

I scrunched my lips together, not wanting to hear her words, then said, "Don't stay here alone. Tell Jip or Reena what happened." I brushed off my clothes, collected the crowbar and her Luma, kicking the Talian in the gut to move him aside.

"*Sister* ...?"

"Venra. I chose Third Guardian Venra's name during the *Third* Rite of Passage. I don't know that I deserve to keep it, seeing how thoroughly I've shattered my vows—"

"Sister Venra, I won't tell the others you spoke—if that'll help."

She gave me a sad smile. "That's very kind of you, but *I* will still know what I did—as will my god Zerameteth and the goddesses. I— I just don't know what to do."

"I don't think any of us do." I patted the side of her arm, then left. Oh, to only have a crisis of conscience to worry about. But even that simple, fleeting thought of Gelden made my milk release and with it the tears.

Satie

Prison Ship

Folding my hands over my lower stomach, I waited patiently on the other side of the wall of crates. When Jip walked around to the cargo side, he grimaced when his gaze fell across my neck. I'd promised to check in with Nurse Eena while the prisoner was re-orchestrated, but other than prescribing a cold, sea-dampened cloth for the swelling, she'd just told me to see her if it hurt too much to swallow—then she'd give me something for the pain.

"I don't like this, Sister."

"He needs medical attention." I cringed internally, still not comfortable with speaking—and not just because my throat hurt. "He's been bludgeoned, is malnourished, and dehydrated. Look at his lips for Gods' Sake. It's not our job to kill him. He might know things."

Jip raised his eyebrows, then shook his head and sighed. "He's secure now. Let me know when you're done."

"I will. Oh, and—"

"Yeah?"

"Who's supposed to be feeding him?"

He blushed. "Delenon took care of that. Delegated to Camdin occasionally but Camdin usually just cleans the straw and empties the waste bucket."

"The Magistrate's been in Med-bay for *three* days. It's no wonder he attacked me. I'll take care of his meals until Delenon recovers."

"All right." He turned to leave.

"And how exactly do I do that?" I coughed, the strain of raising my voice put too much pressure on my throat. "What will *Marxx* say? What will anyone say if they see me leave the galley with two servings of food every meal?"

"Delenon had been giving him the scrapings, once everyone ate. Those who cared figured he was feeding it to the goats."

"Scrapings?"

"He *is* a prisoner."

"Of what crime?"

"Never said."

"Then how do you know he's guilty?"

"Sister, if the Kronik left him chained on *this* ship, there was probably a darn good reason. That's enough for me." He took a few steps down the closest cargo aisle then turned back. "Be careful. He can still bite."

I picked up the satchel of medical supplies Eena instructed me to bring, as well as a large pail of saltwater and a rag before stretching my neck and walking back around to the Talian's cell. He lay spread out on his back, on the floor; the chains on his wrists and ankles were now nailed to the deck. His head rested to the side, facing away from me, giving the welt on his head freedom from further impact.

I stood there a moment, frozen, mouth open to speak but not sure if I should. *A prayer maybe? No, he'd think I'm an idiot ... or would he? What does it matter, Satie? Help the man already.*

"Hello. I'm Sister Venra, Guardian to Zerameteth. Until Magistrate Delenon is feeling better, I will be your liaison." I knelt by his side, just below his outstretched arm. I knew he was lucid as I'd heard him bark and struggle with the others as they worked to nail him down.

"If you had remained calm earlier, neither of us would have gotten hurt. Now, I'm going to check your wound." He stiffened when my hands touched his head to either side of the lump. I pushed his greasy hair back and moistened the rag with the cold seawater. Eena had said there wasn't much to be done for a strike to the head except keep the swelling down.

Gently, I pressed the cloth to his wound. He flinched and his body shuddered. After five minutes, I removed the cloth and used it to wipe down his forehead, drawing the water back through his hair like I had done with several dehydrated patients in the Med-bay.

"What are you doing?" He growled.

"Bathing you."

"Forget it. Leave."

"No. Not only are you dehydrated, but we've had a couple of cases of Typhus recently. With your state of uncleanliness and close proximity to the animals, I want to make sure you don't become ill."

"What's Typhus?"

"A type of infection due to body lice."

"I don't have lice. Now leave me alone."

"I want to make sure you don't get it, either. It's awful: high fever, muscle pain, and severe headaches. Nurse Eena says those symptoms lead to a rash and then delirium. The two animal workers up in Med-bay have a less than fifty-percent chance of survival. I wouldn't wish death on anyone, least of all one that painful." The image of the two naked bodies sliding into the sea without the touch of cleansing fire flashed behind my eyes.

I shook my head to clear the image, then found the small piece of anti-bacterial soap that had broken off the brick we used. Eena had said I could have it. Dropping it in the water, I let it soften slightly at the bottom of the pail before applying the cold cloth to his head again. With each fresh application, I worked a little more soap into his hair and over his pale silvery-white face.

Layers of grime forced me to leave, toss out the dirty water, and then return with a fresh batch several times. He didn't speak to me again. Still, I took the time to scrub his eyebrows and the low scruff of a budding beard. Few citizens were known to grow facial hair, and those that did usually shaved so as not to look beyond the norm. Now, the norm on board simply showed the trace of a shadow or not. This man's beard clearly spoke of more than just a week at sea with us.

Once his hair was clean, I removed a pair of scissors from my pack.

"I'm going to cut your hair. It won't be even, but I'll do my best. Shorter hair will be easier for you to manage while you're here." He didn't say anything, nor did he bother to look at me; so I did my best to trim his mane, careful not to rest his wound on the floor. I wasn't permitted to leave anything behind that he might turn into a weapon or use as a lock pick, so if this man was going to get clean, it was up to me … although even I would only go so far. I could help with his torso and lift his loose pant legs, but that was the extent my modesty would permit. He did not wear the clothes of an unkempt man. In fact, with a closer look I could see a faint pin-stripe to his slacks—he'd been considered a gentleman and maybe even a businessman … *what is he doing here?*

After washing his feet, and legs to the knee, I dumped the water and returned with fresh for one final round. This would be the most difficult task as his wrists were pinned to the floor and he still wore a shirt—his patchwork cloak was discarded over a crate before they'd pinned him down.

I started, as I usually did with my patients, by unbuttoning his shirt. The fact that it had a collar struck me as odd. *Since when do prisoners wear button-up business shirts?*

I paused before pushing the fabric aside. For a woman who had devoted herself to the gods, helping Eena had brought me into such intimate contact with men. First, holding Delenon down in his delirium, helping rehydrate the ill, and now bathing a Talian prisoner.

What are you doing, Satie? My Venra tone demanded. *Saving a man's life?*

The stark contrast of Delenon's midnight skin to the Talian's pale, shimmering canvas made me shiver a little. I couldn't help but wonder how the elite Talian race got to be so different from the rest of us—when had brother turned against brother? Become ruler instead of friend?

After treating his wound with another dose of cold liquid, I used the last of the soap to froth the rag and the water. As I scrubbed and swept the cloth across his chest and abdomen, I couldn't stop myself from following the thin lines of his empty coliths—just simple black *tracings*.

Focus on the task, Satie—not the man.

I bit my lower lip to keep me present and aware of the true nature of my task. *This man strangled and nearly killed you—follow Daria's advice about limiting your kindness.*

"Arch your back best as you can."

Surprisingly, he complied. Not a simple task while your wrists and ankles are chained to the floor.

I pulled his thin shirt up so that it bunched just above his shoulders, then set to washing his back, blind to my work but not to his taut chest only an inch or more away from my nose. I blinked rapidly—the tingling of my nerves sent a new sensation through me. *He's a Talian. I've just never been this close to one before … has any commoner?*

As I reached under him, my arm brushed against his skin and several raised portions. I doubted they were layers of crusted dirt but I had to be sure. So, I slid dampened fingers across the contours of his back—*scar tissue*. I dropped my head to the deck and tried to catch of glimpse of what I'd felt. Long, thin welts, still bright pink with healing, crisscrossed this man's back.

I rose to my knees again and leaned over him, questions burning my lips. He dropped back down to the floor and then opened his eyes, staring right at me. His anger and the fear churned as they screamed silently, alternating between *leave me alone* and *help*.

Daria

Tiny Holes

The steady chop, chop, chop of tubers and other root vegetables dulled my senses and lulled me into automatic pilot, freeing my mind. But my mind wasn't free. The flashing memory of the mass-pyre of dead rebels returned time and again, whether my eyes were open or closed. My family hadn't survived: not the storming of the gates or the Collection. My younger siblings, and most especially my son, only knew they'd been abandoned. Still, they were alive. I wouldn't wish them here even if I could.

The repetition and staccato of chopping morphed into bullet spray from Brid's semi-automatic as the black-clad Contractors, mostly sexless in their attire, betrayed their kindred to work as mercenaries for the Kronik—*Talian bastard*. They were all alike: proof in point down in the hold.

Laser fire burned holes into the brick of the old buildings, weakening mortar, spraying fragments onto my face—the pain as sharp as it was that day, piercing pinpricks into my skin. Then Brid, the other half of my soul, ripped from me in the space of a heartbeat. The heat of his blood on my face and hands searing like a razor's burn—

"Daria!"

I blinked, the sharp burn persisted even as my eyes cleared. Or had they? Red painted my vision.

"Daria, stop!" Neeka pulled the knife from my hands. The wet, red of Brid's life covered the counter and the vegetables; it's sting persistent.

"What?"

"Your hand! What did you do?"

I glanced down, seeing but not seeing—one finger red instead of grey; sliced roots stained with *my* blood as a flap of skin hung exposing bone. I gasped. Pain stole my breath, slamming me back to the present.

Cupping my good hand under the maimed one, I scurried from behind the counter, and up the stairs to the Med-bay. Stumbling from one wall to the other, small white spots flashed behind my eyes. Blinking only made them worse.

"Nurse!" I staggered through the door and onto a stool by the operating table. "Eena!"

"Suns Above!" a clear, youthful voice exclaimed—not the Sister's. *Saw her go down to the hold anyway* ... Farrah then. I grimaced then swooned. Firm hands caught my shoulders and leaned me toward the table.

"Where's the blood coming from?"

Where do you think? From me.

"Daria," her voice sharpened. "Where are you hurt?"

I lifted my hands to the table as if in prayer, one folded over the other, then let my good hand drop to the side.

"Sweet Zerameteth," she whispered, then proceeded to talk to herself. "Stop the bleeding. Stop the blee—tourniquet!" Sharp scissors sliced the air nearby seconds before she grabbed my hand.

"AHH!" An electric jolt bolted up my arm as she wrapped something white around my finger just below the second knuckle. Pulling my good hand forward, she used it to prop the maimed one up in the air with my elbow on the table.

"Breathe slow and steady."

I nodded, gritting my teeth. The white pain sparked and flashed through my brain, consuming all thought. Something sharp pierced the flesh around my wound. I screamed again, opening my eyes. Between the bright flashes, I watched, as if removed from my body, as Farrah inflicted sting after sting with a tiny needle.

"Slow and steady," she said, dropping the device into a jar with yellowish liquid.

"Wha—"

"Remember to breathe, Daria. The solution shouldn't take long to numb your finger ... and most of your hand. I used extra," then she started talking to herself again. "Eena wouldn't approve. Eena's not here, you are. Do what you have to. Make the patient comfortable—Ha. Impossible." Twice she struggled to thread a curved sewing needle before crying out, "finally!"

"Where's Eena?" I managed to force past clenched teeth.

"Main deck. Making the rounds. Can't wait. Can't risk more blood loss." She tied off the thread then sat down opposite me, pulling my hand toward the table. She slammed a black rubber cuff over my forearm.

"What the—" It suctioned to the cold, metal table.

"Can't have you squirming." The woman's pale blue skin blanched even more, if that was possible, making her look grey. Farrah's small, purple coliths popped like bruises along the side of her face and up the length of her shaking arms. *Shaking? Gods help me.*

She moved to raise the inch-long flap of skin back toward my knuckle and wiped the excess blood with a cloth. I closed my eyes and dropped my head across the forearm of my good hand, resting on the table. The chill of the metal seeped into my body or was that the blood loss?

I felt pressure on my finger but nothing specific as I followed the random streaks of light behind my eyes. Short, sharp footfalls added an echo of sky-blue fireworks in my head. The sound stopped with an intake of breath, then scurrying around the table. It wasn't Eena.

"Can I get you anything?" Sister Venra asked.

I was about to reply when Farrah said, "Hot water. And verrin for Daria. Maybe a bun from breakfast if there are any left. She's woozy."

The bright flashes of blue diminished with the fading of the Sister's footsteps even as Farrah pushed more tiny holes into my skin, trying to put me back together—*impossible. Too many pieces missing.*

When Sister Venra returned, I opened my eyes and watched as she set the small pot of hot water on the operating table along with a mug and scone—those she slid over to me. She must have wiped the table down. Not nearly so much blood now. My stomach revolted even as it complained of hunger. I grabbed the mug and drank—not what my taste buds wanted, but I drank it anyway. Farrah paused in her knot-tying to stare at me, so I knew drinking it wasn't optional.

As she bathed my numb hand with the hot water, now warm, I watched the Sister quickly visit the half-dozen or so patients who'd been subjected to my screaming. Then, she settled down on a stool next to Delenon's cot. As Farrah splashed water over my hand, the dips echoed in the Sister's bowl as she refreshed the cloth covering the Magistrate's forehead.

His eyes fluttered open. She smiled down at him as he gradually registered her gaze. Whispering something, he smiled back at her before taking a few mouthfuls of porridge. I stared at her perfect pink hands as they fed and caressed our Leader. Hands that had likely, only minutes before, worked to feed the beast in the basement.

A hot flush crept up the back of my neck and into my cheeks.

"I'm going to rub antiseptic over the wound now. Daria? Daria."

I nodded, still watching Venra with the Magistrate—only a day later—that purple and black chain link bruise ringing her throat. Hearing her insistence to try again with the prisoner. *Talian filth.*

The sharp sting radiating from my newly sewn finger jolted me back to Farrah. Grabbing a length of gauze, she wrapped it around with mind-numbing slowness. Venra's gentle voice grated against my already frayed nerves. *Those same hands cared for the enemy.*

"Enough." I snatched the strip of gauze from Farrah, overturning the stool in my haste.

"Wait!" She followed me into the hall as I leaned against the wall with my shoulder and marched toward the stairs. The nurse's helper said something about keeping the wound dry and changing the bandage regularly—eating ... I waved her off.

The sharp smack of the sea air and constant roaring of the waves cleared my head. I breathed in deep lungfuls of it before staggering with the roll of the ship. Catching my bearings, I walked to the port side and leaned against the rail on my forearms. Not really watching what I did, I wrapped the trail of gauze around my finger while staring out at the rich turquoise sea. But my gaze refused to hold the horizon where blue met blue and instead, fell short as white-capped and frothing waves churned the water around and around. *Are the sharpteeth still following us?*

Whirlpools of varying sizes pock-marked the sea, vast distances apart. And yet, the change in the water's consistency was clear enough. I shook my head then focused on tying the bit of gauze. My finger throbbed, reminding me of the blood that still pumped through my veins, of Gelden's pulsing fingers, waving at me when I left him to fight—and Brid … no longer of flesh and blood; no longer able to hug my fears away as I lay ear to his chest, listening to the steady beat of his heart.

Pushing off from the rail, I turned with sure-feet and strode back downstairs: past the Med-bay and crew quarters, down through the galley and into the bowels of the ship; past the baying animals and roosting ganoo into the maintenance hub. And there, tucked into the bow was exactly what I needed.

I shifted the length of sailcloth and let it fall to one side before double checking the delicate apparatus Tony and I had constructed. The portable burner still gave off heat from the solar recharger we'd rigged together four days ago. Moving to the catch basin, I checked on the levels. We'd tossed the first batch overboard last night. Tony said it would kill a man. But the second batch was nearly ready.

I didn't care for *nearly* and changed out the collector right then, pouring a sample of the spirits into the mug with a busted handle we kept for just such an occasion. Blasting back a shot of choking turpentine-smelling liquid, I grimaced as it burned the whole way down—radiating a warmth throughout my entire body. Sitting on a nearby crate, I took another shot and closed my eyes.

Satie

Night and Day

Delenon's fever broke two days later, but with it came vomiting … and diarrhea—cleaning the blood, pus, and mucus destroyed any chance at enjoying my dinner. Thank the Gods Farrah took the next shift.

Eena called it Dysentery. She said Captain Darius had spoken of it to the Elders after he'd returned home; a disease mentioned in the medical texts but very rarely seen. An amoeba affected the large intestines due to poor hygiene and sanitization—we were all at risk but Delenon had it bad and would be laid up for weeks. The man kept putting everything and everyone ahead of himself, and now he paid the price for it.

Walking past the invisible barrier between below and above decks, a brisk wind swirled around me as the sails flapped and snapped overhead. Carrying a full dinner, save half a mug of citrus-infused water, I skirted around task-oriented and single-minded workers trying to adjust the sails. The wind refused to cooperate, continuing to swirl, speed up, and then die off. Large dark clouds blocked much of the sunlight, but rain didn't appear to be an immediate threat. Still, many of the upper deck inhabitants did what they could to reconfigure their hammocks into shelters.

Meg and Ella had a good location. Their hammock, now attached to a new hook on the wall, instead of the handle of the sail hold's door, protected them from above; and two walls sheltered them to either side. As I approached their nook by the forecastle, they kept their gazes averted—same as this morning, and yesterday, and days before that. But when I set the meal down by their feet, their gazes whipped up to my grimy Luma— the symbol of what should have been my Devout status and Observance … except that I wasn't, and they knew that.

I'd been careful not to speak outright when at all possible and limited my use of prayer vocabulary whenever I drew near them, but the simple fact that I chose to "work" instead of remain one-hundred percent in my Observances destroyed us.

"You might as well stop trying, Sister," Matty's voice rose from the adjoining hammock, her arm draped over the side with her wrist and hand buffering the erratic breeze, the only sign that she was awake. I walked over to her and looked down at her still body, her round baby-bump cradled and snug.

I started into a choppy version of the Solemn Prayer, "… illuminate my soul—"

Matty held up her dancing hand for me to stop. "They know." She looked to my Luma. "We all know. They won't eat what you bring, they feed it to me—for the baby. But then, they won't eat what's brought to me either for the same reason, and no one else cares. Well … Nurse Eena does, but she can't ask someone to share their food with—"

"Non-workers," I finished, glancing over at Marxx struggling with the ship's wheel. Struggling? I looked up and nearly fainted. So many sailors balanced on their stomachs trying to find the right sail height to catch the wind ... it made me nauseous. But the wind wasn't the only problem. I'd learned to ignore the constant white-noise the sea made—I had to if I wanted to sleep at night. But looking out beyond the rail, the once small, widely dispersed whirlpools were now bigger and closer.

I leaned over Matty to get a better look just as the ship lurched. I tumbled against her. We both struggled to rise. The back of the ship listed toward the large, swirling mass. Matty and I locked gazes. Why hadn't Marxx sounded the alarm? Just then, the night crew, led by Neldek Denton—*Tony*—spilled out onto the main deck.

Their presence refreshed overtaxed spirits as men and women alike worked harder than ever to catch the wind. But Tony didn't take over for Marxx. No, on the quarterdeck the two men argued: hands raised, holding defensive postures. I shifted to a better vantage point and leaned over the rail. The back of the ship drifted farther and farther toward the edge of the spinning water, close enough to breach ... *and what if it does?* Fortitude or fear gave me the certainty that if we were pulled into the swirling vortex, we wouldn't get back out.

Movement by the ship's wheel drew my gaze. Marxx waved a book in front of Tony's face. But Tony just shook his head and turned away. He studied the sails, and the water even, as the ship drifted closer to the swirling edge of the pool. Someone had to do something...

You know he knows.

I've no proof.

Ask him anyway.

Even as I argued with myself, my feet took over, leading me faster and faster around men and women hauling sail lines, fighting with the choppy wind. On the other side of the frantic workers, Tony disappeared down the stairs seconds before I reached them. Careening around the corner, past the Med-bay and the women's crew quarters, I saw his head bob down to the mess.

Nearly falling head-long down the staircase, I raced past Tony—standing still and rubbing his chin by the closest table—and down into the hold. I didn't need to think about what to do next. I *knew*. I had to talk to the Talian.

Whipping past the towering rows of food crates I burst, gasping, around the prison wall to the back of the boat. Resting my hands on my knees, I gulped air into my lungs. He sat on the crate farthest from me. I shuffled toward him, heart hammering my chest.

What do I say?

"Please—" I panted, pushing myself up to my full five feet two inches. "Please. We need. Your help. The ship—The water—Massive whirlpools …" He still didn't move, didn't even twitch at the impending danger. *Am I wrong? No! He* knows *what to do.*

"How do we move the ship away from the danger when the wind is inconsistent and the sails won't catch?"

Silence.

"I *know* you're not here by chance. There's a reason the Kronik is torturing you this way. He and the Council don't do anything on a whim. You're connected to this boat."

Nothing.

"Please! There's over a hundred people on board who don't want to die. Even if you're not one of them, help me save the others. Help me give them a fighting ch—"

He whispered something.

"What?" I stepped closer.

Nothing again.

"What did you say? I couldn't—" My pounding heart suddenly swelled with hope.

"Go."

"I don't understand ..."

"I said GO! Go away and leave me alone," he managed to both yell and growl at the same time.

"No. You didn't. You said someth—"

He whirled around and came at me hollering, "GO!"

I scrambled back out of his reach, then turned and ran back to the stairs. Hot tears stung my eyes but didn't fall. *What had he said? It was only one word ... it sounded like "go" but wasn't.* My feet tromped back up the hold's stairs heavy as wet sandbags. *What was it? You heard it. What did he say!*

And then it didn't matter anymore.

Tony encouraged anyone and everyone in the galley and the general quarters to grab an oar and *row*. Three to five people sat on each bench to either side of the ship, rowing to the steady stomp of his boot against the deck boards. He'd figured it out on his own.

"I'll check on the progress!" I called over to him as I ran up the next two flights of stairs. My heart felt lighter, but not just from the return of hope that we'd get out of this alive.

Above, I scurried to the port side and looked over the edge. A myriad of oars rose and plunged in perfect time. The ship no longer slipped backward, but it didn't gain much momentum either. The sails snapped and the wooden masts creaked as the ship groaned with the competing efforts of the Acting Captain above and the Night Quartermaster below.

I looked at Marxx, struggling to keep the wheel steady as he signalled every so often to one section of the crew or another. The ship tilted more and more toward the spinning pool. If he hadn't listened to Tony, he wouldn't even give me, a small, insignificant *Sister,* half a chance at an explanation. Deck dwellers and crew alike struggled to keep their footing as the tilt of the ship increased. Shouts and hollers weren't just for direction now.

"Look out!"

"Get out of the way!"

I staggered toward the stern, clutching the rail. A mass of bodies huddled in amongst the draped sailcloth in the Sisters' corner.

What do I do? What do I do ...

A familiar growl whispered a word in my head—*Mutiny.*

I don't know why the thought came to me, but suddenly I knew what to do. One-by-one, I hurried to the night crew, scrambling for leverage, reminding myself not to stare at the numbing tilt of the mainmast.

Tony has a plan, I said. That got their attention ... *the gods approve...* sealed the deal.

And one-by-one, they disobeyed the Captain's orders and disappeared below deck. I did my best to hide amongst the rigging as the still-working crew spreading the word. The Talian had said "row". Tony knew it too—so mutiny we did.

Daria

Rotgut

I tried to keep the two tin serving jugs from banging against the stair treads as the weight of the hooch pulled my arms lower and lower. The jugs were supposed to hold verrin or water, allowing a server to walk amongst the tables in the mess without spilling. The rudimentary design helped conceal what they held, and I didn't need them for serving meals—we had to watch carefully just how much liquid each person received ... not including the fiery-sweet nectar we'd distilled from rotting tubers and mouldy corn.

A choir of snores echoed on the Med-deck. No one here was awake, or at least no one wanted to admit it. I turned the corner and lifted the jugs—*not high enough!* The clang rang clear into the Med-bay and down the hall. Heaving the liquor as high as my aching arms could manage, I jogged up the stairs then rested to the side of the doorframe in the damp, cool blast of air.

Releasing the jugs, I crossed my arms and rubbed my throbbing shoulders. I couldn't understand why my body ached all the time now. *Thirteen days at sea, that's why.* Had it really been that long? It seemed only yesterday ...

Cool flecks of misty rain tapped my face. I swept a stray, moist strand from my eyes around to my ear. My hand shook— *not* from the chill.

Tony paced himself as he walked down the far set of stairs from the quarterdeck glancing from the frothing clouds above, back-lit by the faint glow of Zerameteth, to the book in his hand. The solar lantern he held cast an equally gloomy light across his page. He didn't look at me until he stopped a hand's breadth away. Worry lines marred his usually clear brow, but his smile reached his eyes—*is he happy to see me or the hooch?*

"Let me help you with that." He passed me the lantern and Journal before grabbing the two jugs by my feet. Glancing at the mottled sky, he frowned again before climbing up to the Gambler's Den below the poop deck. White-caped waves frothed in the depthless dark beyond the weak glow of the deck lanterns as I followed him. On the quarterdeck, I glanced at the open Journal in my hand and blinked from it to the sea and back before saying, "I wasn't sure if I should bring both tonight."

"I know just the lad to mete it out. Anythin' left over, and there should be—don't want anyone blind drunk in the morning—we'll store in a crate in the back."

"Won't people be tempted to ..."

"Probably. But I'll put somethin' heavy on 't to deter skimmin'," he laughed.

I opened the door to the Den, and he ducked inside as light spilled across the slick deck, flickering like fire on water. Stepping inside, the warmth wrapped around my chilled body. Tony held the jugs aloft, and a chorus of cheers filled the air, but no mad rush. I was surprised.

As he set up a drink station on the map table with several pilfered mugs for the night's entertainment, a few gamblers drifted away from their circles. They passed him scraps of cloth that looked suspiciously like the remnants of the sleeves from his shirt. Then he left a young man in charge of collection and distribution. I eyed the flow of liquor before allowing the conversation from a nearby group to distract me.

I hovered around the circle of verbal bar-bets: general trivia, historical facts, feats of skill and the like. You could learn a lot about the nature of people here; probably why Tony preferred it to the others. He sauntered over and the group welcomed him with a chorus of hails.

"Toe!"

"T-Man!"

"DM!"

"Tone-Tee!" Never the man's given name or even his full nick-name.

"What do we have tonight, friends?" he asked.

"Shoe thinks there's something happening between Red and Crester on day shift." The middle-aged Matin flashed a smile and a wink, rubbing his hands together.

"What are the fors?"

"Simple stuff. Talkin' more, smilin' more, and one lingering glance just before start of shift this mornin'."

"Put me down for first kiss in two days, end-a shift. Two tabs." Two small squares of fabric floated to the floor in front of the speaker. "Any news on the younger Sister?" Tony asked.

I stood a little straighter. *That's right; they're trying to see who can figure out her name.*

"I'll get in on that action."

Maybe I shouldn't.

Why not? It's out there now. She may have told others.

133

She hasn't spoken much and only does so under extreme duress.

"What's your wager?" the speaker asked.

I glanced at the hooch and the Tabs on the floor. If I wanted more than one cup of the anti-memory nectar, I'd have to win it. "An extra scoop of food with first-meal …" The group looked at me, quiet, expecting. I glanced at Tony; his gaze flicked to the ceiling and he lifted an eyebrow. *Raise the stakes.* "For three days."

"What's your wager?"

I looked at him questioningly.

"When do you think you'll find out? That she'll reveal?"

"Oh. I'd like to put my guess in now."

They all shifted to look at me, or rather gawk. "You have a guess and a date for the reveal?"

"I do."

Everyone leaned forward. Tony and I crouched at the same time for a more intimate connection with the group.

"She introduced herself to me three days ago"—gazes shifted, tracked, acknowledge the time stamp—"as Sister Venra."

"Witnesses? Anyone to validate, corroborate?"

The Talian monster. I shook my head no. Suddenly revealing the name of a woman who placed the enemy on the same level as our Magistrate didn't concern me in the slightest.

"Who's up to verify authenticity?"

"I will," Tony rumbled and gave me a wink. "It makes the most sense that the lass 'ed tell me 'n any ah you."

The group went on to betting who in the circle had the longest colith as Tony and I stood up. I leaned over and spoke into his ear, "So, do I get a free mug since I made the stuff or do I have to figure out how to win a cloth tab?"

He smiled. "First ah the night'll always be on the house for the Cook."

I didn't need to be told twice. The boy knew who I was and poured a little extra into my mug. I nodded my thanks and took a swig before turning back to Tony. The fireball exploded first in my mouth, scorching my throat all the way down, past my chest and into my gut where it just kept expanding until the heat slowed my pulse and my thoughts. I squinted with the mug resting against my bottom lip, seeing yet not seeing.

"Ya know"—I startled a little at Tony's sudden nearness— "settin' yer mind to puttin' t'gether the still and usin' yer wits gave ya purpose. Was sumpthin' interestin' t' focus on. The Den's a great distraction, but not so much when yer try'n t' rebuild."

"I don't want to rebuild. I don't want to be here at all."

"I know. But here ya are. An ifn' yer lucky, ya might juss live long enough 't get back home one day."

"Darius was the sole survivor of a crew of fifty. What makes you think an untrained, ragtag crew stand—" The ship shuddered. Tony looked up, side-to-side, then grabbed the Journal and lantern before making for the door.

I'd seen the page he'd been studying. I knew what he suspected and tossed back another scalding, teeth-gritting mouthful of forget-me-sauce.

The White Sea

Gale Waters.
Night and day we row against the frothing white
caps, unable to unfurl the sails in the constant
rain and bursts of swirling wind. Everything on
deck was either strapped down or brought into the
sail hold or map room. Even the sturdiest of my
men are becoming weak-of-knee and stomach with
the upheaval of these waters.
One of the men has a theory about alternating
currents and atmospheric pressure but without
any practical instrumentation we have no way of
knowing for sure. Tales are already spinning
about these seas mirroring the trials our ancestors
faced when crossing the Deserts all those
centuries ago. Though few stories remain of those
harrowing travels, I cannot help but concur with
the crew's assessment—I only hope that we are
able to brave these trials as well as they did.
I've had to alternate the crews every four hours
to keep exhaustion from setting in. The constant
gloom of twilight in a starless, cloud-riddled sky
drains one's soul faster than the physical strain of
constant rowing. Navigation is sketchy at best and
I worry that we've been sailing in circles.

Captain Darius

Satie

Brother and Sisters

Soaked through, I sat cross-legged on the deck with barely a canopy to keep the steady rain from hitting me directly. This morning's breakfast lay on a scrap of cloth—someone's kerchief by the look of it—just as drenched and unappreciated as I was. I finished the last of the Redeemer's Prayer with my Sisters. This was their only acknowledgment of my presence, of my connection to them and our gods; traditionally, the prayer was only said in groups of three in the Temple in times of great need. Not only had my Sisters accepted this corner of the ship as "Temple" but their desperation permitted them to pray with the Broken One … *me*.

Matty smiled at me from between the two women and shivered. Meg and Ella pulled the section of sailcloth more tightly around the three of them. She thought the Sisters were starting to come around, but I knew better—they were just desperate. Back home we were lucky to see this much rain in a month let alone over *two* days.

"This is ridiculous, Matty," I said as the Sisters murmured different prayers to themselves, ignoring me once again. Their dark, sunken eyes and overly sharp features shouted my failures at me: failure to keep my Observances; failure to keep them safe ...

"I can't. I tried." She turned her head and stared at the door to the sail hold. The look in her eyes, the set of her jaw, said it all. "I'd rather be damp and awake with all my faculties than dry and virtually unconscious in there. The rise in my blood pressure alone would be bad for the baby."

Few people remained to battle the incessant mist and wind—only those, like Matty, who couldn't stand to be in confined spaces for long. And for all their misguided beliefs, Meg and Ella refused to leave Matty out here alone. My heart ached with love for them at the same time as it screamed with the pain of having lost them. I tried to breathe deep enough to dilute the emotion, but Matty still saw my struggle and frowned. Her gaze flickered away from mine, somewhere over my shoulder. I turned to look.

Eena charged through the erratic gale winds, one hand protecting her eyes from the slant of the sharp drops of rain, the other gripping her black medical bag. Ducking under the makeshift canopy, she crouched beside me and smiled at Matty.

"Sorry to be checkin' on ya so late today, Mamma. Shall we see how the bun's a doin'?"

Matty nodded. Meg and Ella shifted forward off the excess tarp and sat huddled close to Matty's head as she lay down next to the hull. Eena knelt beside her legs as I took up the dominant position by her belly. Eena passed me the stethoscope.

"Sister Venra will run the check today."

"I have complete faith in her," Matty said

Following Eena's instructions over the past several days, I shifted Matty's shirt to the top of her belly and listened for the baby's heartbeat. I located it near the bottom of her belly off to the left.

"He's been active. Have you been able to sleep much between him moving and the weather?" I asked.

"Some. The Sisters keep us warm, but sometimes I just can't turn my brain off to rest. I've taken to dozing on one woman's shoulder or the other when the wind dies down a bit."

I nodded then checked her blood pressure: slightly high but still within the normal range.

"Have you been eating?"

"Some. It's hard with the anxiety."

"I understand, but keep trying. Now is not the time to be losing weight." I wanted to say the same to the Sisters, but this check-up was about Matty and her baby, not two grown women who should know better. "What about your urine?"

"Yellow."

"No other signs of bleeding?"

"No. All clear."

I smiled at Matty then looked to Eena. She patted Matty's leg then reached to help her sit up again.

"We should talk about yer birth plan. Will be a bit different now, I think." Eena winked. Matty sighed and smiled. I still hadn't rallied the courage to ask her how she ended up on this accursed barge.

"What do you suggest?" she asked, wary of the answer.

"Don't think the baby's comin' anytime soon, so hopefully the storms'll have passed. We can look at makin' plans for a temporary wall 't block pryin' eyes from above an' on deck, seein' as how you'll want 't be lucid for the birth."

Matty's eyes brightened. She likely worried Eena would try to get her down to the Med-bay or into the sail hold. As Eena chatted with her again about what to expect pain-wise, and making sure the baby had turned before active labour, I collected the soggy cloth of uneaten food and pierced the storm to return below decks. My Luma kept my hair in place, but the soggy mass of fabric was more than a little uncomfortable. Still, I was loath to part with it—the last vestige of the Guardian I'd vowed to be, and the Devout I was supposed to be.

Passing into the mess, the most current set of rowers moved in time to the beat of Marxx's boot. The ship's wheel had been tied in place with a length of rope since the crew shifted from the sails to the oars. The few people sitting around the tables were not nearly as lively as they'd been before the storm. Everyone knew what bad weather meant—especially since we could no longer see the stars to navigate.

I carried on down into the hold and emptied the scarf of food into the closest goat's trough, leaving the cloth to hang-dry off a crate by the bottom of the stairs. I didn't know how the Sisters had procured the piece, but I'd make sure they got it back with my next meal offering. The animals bleated and bayed, clearly uncomfortable with the effects of the weather on the usually calm ship. The two farmers tending the livestock paid me no mind, and I slipped behind the stairs to the food stores and beyond.

When I rounded the prison wall, I watched to see if he detected my presence. Though it remained quieter back here, a dull din lingered. He never moved, or at least I didn't see him shift or hear any scuffing of retreat. He sat on the far crate with his hood up, shoulders slumped, and back to me.

This time, I didn't hesitate. He'd been relatively docile the past two days preferring to ignore me, even when I brought him a pail of food—no wonder he acted like an animal. I sat down facing the way I'd come, one crate separating us, and just waited for the longest time. Matty's frightened gaze competed with images of Daria's frown swimming in my head, and not just from the morning she rescued me, but every time we'd crossed paths since. I had not been blamed outright for the mutiny but only because my efforts helped save the ship. Still, Marxx did more than frown whenever I met *his* gaze, and Delenon slept. Eena said his body was trying to heal itself, and without adequate antibiotics this was a struggle he had to endure alone. She had no idea if he'd pull through.

I absently whispered Zerameteth's Prayer, mindful enough to repeat it three times. The dark, skeletal features claiming my Sisters' health accentuated my own failings and inability to devote myself—martyr myself. My head lowered until my chin hovered above my chest. I pulled the once white Luma from my head and stared at it, through it.

"Have you ever committed murder? Ever hear of a Sun Guardian committing murder?" I sighed and laughed without mirth. "I have no idea why you're here, but something tells me, brother, if you'd killed someone, this would not have been your punishment." The image of a flameless cast-off and those two, brave sailors being ripped to shreds by the sharpteeth weighed my soul down nearly as much as not finding a way to remain Devout and still eat.

"Not only did I allow two souls to become trapped in these seas, never to reunite with Mother Zola, but through my own ignorance I've condemned my Sisters to the same fate." I fought with the Luma, gritting my teeth and cursing my existence, then dropped it as if burned. I stared at my hands, palms up. Hands meant to help and guide now slowly choking the life from the innocent.

I raised my head to look at the ceiling high above, but froze mid-ascent at the steady gaze of two abnormally grey eyes staring back at me.

Daria

Poisoning

Sliding the last of the chopped ganoo from the prep counter, I handed Neeka the pot to pre-heat for the meat pies to come, then leaned over the sticky surface and put my face directly in front of the sailor's. "I do know what time it is, *now*. How am I to keep track when we haven't seen light for more than three days? Dinner's coming."

I swiped a damp rag over the counter, leaving pale streaks of liquid pink behind. Dropping the cloth into the wash bucket, I cracked open the cupboard beneath and shot back a mouthful of throat-searing liquid before tucking it back into place and dumping the last of the firm veggies on the counter. I retrieved my knife from the same slop bucket. The weight of a body hovered behind me, I turned, ready to battle yet another complaint.

Hetly gasped and took a step back. I crossed my arms, the knife now hanging below my underarm.

"*What?*"

His gaze flicked left and right in rapid succession. "I—uh—how long should we wait for the gravy before filling the—"

"I told you already."

"But it's taking too long. Can we shorten the cook-time any?"

My brain buzzed as the numbing sensation spread throughout my body, creeping into my brain. Change of shift was supposed to happen in twenty minutes. It would take that long for the crusts to rise. The bang of Marxx's boot as the bass drum for the rowers, and the rise in volume as more night crew learned dinner wasn't ready yet, made it hard to think straight. The hum in my head got louder, more insistent.

"Would the ganoo cook inside the pies while we heated them?"

Yes, but—but there was a reason it had to be sautéed first.

I must have nodded because he said, "Neeka can do a quick sear, then I can fill the pies. We'll only be ten minutes behind then."

"Yeah, do that. I'll make the veggie sticks and plate everything as I make room on the counter." It took a moment for the wooden countertop to stop spinning. I blinked, grabbed hold of it and then chopped and quartered lengths of green and red crisp-veggies. But between the thwack of the knife on the counter, the stomp of the boot, and rising voices, I could barely keep my head straight. I tried to block everything out, get past the lapse in time, focus on the dinner plan and not hack off another piece of my body.

But the gentle haze that kept the memories at bay slipped back from the edges of my mind, and the shouts in this confined space sounded more like a baby wailing—laser blasts spraying brick shards...

An arm crashed onto the counter, knocking a pile of veggies to the floor at my feet. *Brid? No, not again!*

"I ain't lyin'!" a man yelled, scrambling back up to his feet. A circle of bodies penned him and his pursuer in, together with the table and a set of chairs closest to the prep area. His skin deepened to a rust orange as unbridled anger surged through the Danieth sailor. He flew at the other man screaming, "We're lost! Gods Above, we've been lost for days!"

They crashed onto the empty table as Tony broke through the outer ring, and the men beat each other senseless.

Crouching low, with one hand I gathered the stray vegetables, and with the other, I cracked open the cupboard under the counter. The handle on the second mug from the right faced toward me. I grabbed it, swallowed a shot, slid it back home and then dunked the fallen food into the wash pail. Flicking the water off them, I shut the cupboard leaving everything as it had been before—mostly—and stood up again.

I staggered back as Marxx's face swung at me over the prep counter.

"What in Xannia!" I shouted, clutching my chest over my heart.

"Where's dinner, Daria?" he growled. I still heard a boot stomping out the rowing rhythm, but it wasn't Tony's. Marxx shoved the two men over to the port-side wash station and dunked their heads in the waiting sea-filled bucket before releasing them and returning for an answer. The buzz in my head lessened, but I staggered slightly with the roll of the ship.

"It's cooking. What do ya think?" I spat back. An incessant tug came at my elbow.

"Gods, woman. You reek. What the hell do you—"

"She's ill." The tug morphed to a yank and I tumbled into Neeka. "She's pushing herself too hard and she lost track of time.

We all did. First rounds will be ready to eat in fifteen minutes." I heard chopping behind me. Orthin? No. I shook my head. Hetly. I leaned into Neeka's back as she half-dragged me to the general quarters between the stairs. The ship spun. I landed on my cot and groaned. Maybe I *was* sick.

Satie

Perfect Storm

I rolled over on my cot in the Med-may for the hundredth time. Rain lashed the windows overriding the soft snores from three of the twelve occupied beds. Warm lantern light swung back and forth across the open doorframe. Someone on the far side coughed. Delenon breathed easy. I'd chosen the cot closest to him after the Sisters refused to make room for me above. Eena didn't think he was going to make it, but over the past week, since my sleeping arrangements changed, he'd steadily improved.

Fierce winds and pebble-hardened rain rattled the windows. I sat and looked up the damp steps to the deck above. I couldn't see the sky or the storm, but in my mind's eye I could see Matty and my Sisters huddled under layers of sailcloth shivering in the mounting storm. My clothes, still damp from my last attempt to bring them inside, clung like cold hands refusing to let go. I rubbed my arms and walked into the hall, still staring up into the wet black above.

The ship shuddered. I fell into the wall. Regaining my footing, I ran my palm along the partition, around the corner, past the women's crew quarters and down the stairs to the mess. Two of Daria's staff worked toward getting the morning meal organised to the steady *thump* of Tony's boot tracking a rhythm for the tired rowers. *Do they even know which way we're headed?* Most everyone else remained in their quarters, since the sailors had taken over those benches previously used as extra beds.

I grabbed a soft elppa fruit and a pocket full of nuts, nodding to the guy organising the baskets of ingredients.

"Elppa nut bread this morning—I hope." He gave me a tired grin.

"A bit more spice this time, if you have it, and it'll be perfect."

"That's the plan." He tossed me another elppa, a golden one not quite so soft as the red one I'd snagged. "You're up early."

I shrugged. "The storm. Might as well make myself useful. Thanks," I said, and headed down to the hold. The cooking staff had been made aware of the situation below in the most general of terms. They knew someone was being held prisoner, and they were forbidden to see him. Only the Leaders and I knew the specifics, and only I was interested in knowing more.

Nabbing the water pail by the trough, I cracked the verrin cask with a crowbar and gathered enough of the thick, orange-y liquid to cover the bottom. The rest of us were served a half-cup every other day; I made sure the Talian got the same. It wasn't our job to torture the poor man; the Kronik had clearly done that aplenty.

As I walked around the corner of the prison wall it was all I could do not to stagger or slow down—and not because of the ship being tossed about on the waves. Today the Talian sat facing me: his hood down, arms resting on his thighs, and looking straight at me. I sat down on the crate nearest him, a body's breadth away, as if it were the most natural thing in the world to do.

I held the golden piece of fruit over to him as I rested the pail between us, nestled in the straw. He accepted it, fingers lightly brushing mine—the first time he'd dared touch me since the strangling. I mentally rubbed my neck. The bruises were gone now, but only recently. Instead, I emptied my pockets and set the rest of the food on the wedge of crate beside his leg.

His eyebrows rose at the sight of the second elppa.

I smiled, unable to break away from his pale gaze. "Guess I should accost the galley staff this early every day."

He snorted then bit into the fruit, glancing away. I sighed, then leaned back on my hands, holding the back edge of my crate and crossing one leg over the other. I hadn't planned on it— opening myself up like this—but the calm of his presence almost dictated it. If I remained closed, so would he.

"The storm is worse and I still can't get Matty or my Sisters to come inside or even move to the sail hold with most of the others. They're not the only ones still on deck in this wicked weather, but they are the most vulnerable ..."

The silence between us remained comfortable. I'd spoken of this to him yesterday too, to his back, but nonetheless he'd heard. I heaved a weary sigh, ready to launch into a morning prayer when the words caught in my throat.

"Why are they more vulnerable than anyone else?" he spoke, conversing for the first time.

I leaned forward; this was not a casual topic. "Matty's pregnant."

He coughed on his bite of fruit.

"And the Sisters are dying. Starving themselves. They're too weak to survive this kind of weather much longer."

"Your Sisters are ignorant and deserve their fate. But a pregnant woman? On *this* ship?"

"Yes. I don't know her story. But the Sisters, they're far from ignorant. They might be loyal, to a fault, but that just shows the depth of their devotion to their goddesses. I have no doubt that they believe *I'm* the one who's contributed to this foul turn of events." I pulled the Luma from my head and stared at it in my hands.

"If you've given up, why still wear it?" His voice was steady, non-judgemental.

"Because I do still believe in it. I *don't* want to give it up. Don't want to break my vows … but isn't that exactly what I've done? And in abandoning my Observances, I've abandoned my Sisters, my duty to Zerameteth, and in turn condemned everyone on this ship?"

"Whoa, whoa, there, Sister. Remember, you're not the one responsible for the monstrosity that is this ship," he spat the last two words and kicked at the straw.

Some crazy asinine part of me desperately wanted to hold his hand, just as I'd walked through the rumbling and confused crowd the day we were abandoned. The day I'd been punched. I didn't want to get punched again. Instead, I waited for him to look up. Waited for nearly five minutes as he finished the golden elppa and guzzled back the verrin. Then he wiped his mouth on his arm and turned his head to look at me.

His gaze startled me. Only his eyes shifted in their dark, hollowed-out orbits, the rest of him stiffened.

I wanted to ask him a million things, starting with what happened to him. Clearly, he braced for this question and more. Instead I asked, "What's your name?"

He studied me, eyes narrowed slightly, lips pursed. His pale skin shone, as if damp, in the dim light cast by two lanterns affixed to the wall of crates.

"Andraxis. Andraxix Riggen."

I smiled.

"But call me Drax."

I held my hand out to him, "Satie—I mean, Sister Venra."

He shook my hand. "I remember. Nice to meet you, Sister Satie." And he returned my smile.

I laughed, "It truly is Sister *Venra*. During my Ceremony of Rebirth, the day the Resistance fell, I shed my given name and took on the first Child Guardian's name as homage to Zerameteth. I'm just not used to it yet." My voice faltered. I swallowed then put the Luma back on. Perhaps I didn't deserve the name now.

"I'm familiar with the rites. Within the Talian Compound we follow the same Observances. Give respect to the gods in the same way. A cousin of mine is a Guardian to Zita. He loves being intimately connected to the goddess."

"Yes, as do I with Zerameteth. But ..."

"But what?"

I blew air. "But I can't stop questioning ... everything. Why must we conform to our Observances in a situation we've never faced before? Shouldn't we adapt to new situations? Crazy situations that no one could have foreseen? But then maybe this is a test, like Meg and Ella think. Maybe only by being fully Devout will we get through this, save everyone's souls. But I want to help the living, not just coddle the dead." I cringed, even at my own words.

"They're dying because I broke my vows. Matty is trying to share her food with them. If I'd only remained faithful and followed my Observances, someone else like Matty would have taken pity on us, right? Would have fed us even when the Acting Captain restricted food for workers only? That's what my Sisters believe. But now, they won't even accept Matty's food because she needs to keep the baby healthy, and no one else is stepping forward to help. Oh, Drax," I buried my face in my hands. "What have I done?"

The warmth of his tentative hand on my shoulder went from consoling to urgent as crates beyond the wall smashed against the floor. I fell into him. The tilt of the ship, frantic bleating of animals, erratic footfalls and shouts from above made my heart jump into my throat.

"We're capsizing!" Drax shouted.

"What do we do?"

He grabbed my shoulders, and this man of bony flesh hauled me to my feet as though I were an overturned chair needing righting.

"Get everyone off the main deck."

"But—"

"And over to the opposite side of the list."

"But—"

"Go, Satie! I'm not ready to go down with my ship."

Scrabbling over slippery straw, crushed crates, spilled grains, and shattered casks, I heaved my body up skewed steps to the mess. Terrified shrieks clashed with ignored or unheard orders. A burly man knocked me down as he raced toward the upper stairs. Someone crushed my hand. I screamed, clutching it to my chest as I gripped an upside-down table leg and launched toward the tallest man in the room; the one shouting the only orders that made sense.

"TONY!"

He looked down at me as I fell into him with another shudder from the ship. I held his head, ear to my mouth, and told him what Drax said. He picked me up and tossed me into a clearing by the stairs. I missed my footing, landing hard on my knees, losing all breath. Gasping, I clung to the rail and dragged my body up the stairs even as the first wet souls tumbled down past me.

My breath rushed back into my lungs as I pushed past everyone, yelling, "Starboard! Get starboard!" Delenon stood braced in the Med-bay doorway, face ashen but determined, body trembling. "Get them starboard, Magistrate! Starboard!" Grim determination ignited the man as he took up my cry, shifting past me in the opposite direction.

Rain lashed my face and hands as I climbed the slanted stairs. Several people slipped and struggled across the blackened, wave-soaked deck reaching for help. *I can't do this alone. I'm too small!* I looked behind me. A length of rope hung beside the cache of lanterns on the outer Med-bay wall.

I jumped down the stairs, crashing into the wall with my shoulder, and grabbed the cording. Wrapping the end around my waist, pain shot through my crushed hand as I fought to secure the knot before launching myself at the stairs. Another vicious wave crashed down, soaking me through. I coughed and sputtered as I scrambled back up.

Wedging myself in the crook of the stairs and the wall, I tossed the rope out. Two deck-dwellers latched on. I cried out, the strain of their weight on the line disfigured my body. They crawled down the stairs past me. I heaved and sucked in breath after breath. The tilt of the ship lessened. I looked up, squinting against the razor rain. Two bodies moved as one toward me. Coiling the rope back up, I hollered at them then threw it out on a better angle. The wind caught it. *Need to weigh it down.* But there was nothing around. *Nothing but me ... my shoes!*

Whipping the line back in, I knotted my shoes together with the end of the rope and tried again. My body smashed into the V of the wall and stairs—they caught the rope! Eena and Matty materialised fully. Steps away, Eena gave Matty a push and she fell into my arms. Sitting her down on the stairs, I looked away as she scuttled down the steps. I held my hand out to Eena.

"Can't! Marxx lost the books! I saw them! Going back!"

"No, Eena! It's not worth it!"

I lost sight of her within seconds, but the steady tug, tug, of the rope marked her progress ... until it didn't. A giant wave crashed onto the deck, flinging me back down the stairs, the loose rope sliding down with me.

Daria

Damages

The scent of sour bile weighed down the air. I collected mugs, strewn about the kitchen, placing them into the biggest pot I could carry. Bending down to snatch two more by the base of the spice cupboard, I bumped into Hetly.

"Hey! Watch ou—Oh. Daria." He went back to salvaging what he could from various up-ended canisters at the smaller counter under the raised cabinets. My heel connected with another mug, sending it clattering across the floor.

"Whoa! *Trinity*," Neeka swore. She wobbled and kicked the mug away as she and another occasional staff member tried to right the heavy cauldron at the back of the cookery. I snagged the offending mug, but elbowed someone else when I stood up again.

"Why don't you just leave this to us," Neeka said. It wasn't a question. She took the mug-filled pot from me and passed it to her helper.

I blinked and staggered slightly, gripping the edge of the prep counter behind me. "What?" I asked.

She crossed her arms and just stared at me. I blinked again, twice, then glanced over my shoulder. The tables and chairs littered the mess. I pointed, arm wavering, over my shoulder and swallowed the bile threatening to spew from my mouth. Using the counter for support, I walked out of the kitchen taking small steps. No one else seemed affected by the roll of the ship, but then most people were either sitting with their back to the hull or lying on the floor between the few rowers who remained.

Two women carried a third's body. I scrambled to right a fallen chair in their path only to get a hip slammed into my shoulder for the effort.

"Watch out!" the woman walking backwards yelled. I sat down on the chair and watched the limp arm of the woman being carried up the stairs sway without restraint—back and forth, and back and forth until she disappeared. Then the boy who'd tumbled from the crow's nest the day we launched, puked into the wash station before tumbling down and holding himself, shivering. I looked around—he wasn't the only one. *Sea sickness from the violent storm* came into my hazy mind, but that didn't seem right ... not for everyone.

My gaze lingered on the stairs to the hold. I licked my lips and rose to venture down but veered from the stairs when frantic bleating and the shriek of a goat shot up toward me. Too many people. Too much damage. I'd have to check on the still later.

I steadied myself on the wall as I climbed to the Med-deck. Trails of puke hastily splashed with seawater mingled with pink rivers. *I could mop the deck* ... but closed my eyes at the thought of all that back and forth sweeping. Someone else would do it.

Glancing in the women's crew quarters, a few beds were filled with bodies curled in on themselves, shaking. *Guess the others are topside helping with the clean-up.* I turned the corner, but a flash of white in the Med-bay caught my eye. Sister Venra held a woman by the shoulders and walked her backward until she collapsed onto a cot. They disappeared from sight, but the Sister's voice broke through the white noise of the rain above.

"No, Farrah. Stop pretending there's nothing wrong. You're sick," her voice wavered. My heart ached at the desperation-laced tone. The afterimage of my brother Gerrund, silhouetted on the rooftop watching our family burn; my baby's hand reaching for me around my neighbour's shoulder, flooded my mind.

"You can't do this alone. You can't go back up there ..." Farrah wheezed.

The Sister gave a heavy sigh, "No. Not yet. I'll sit with you a minute, then I'll check below." I cringed, certain she'd emphasised the word "below". *Cares more about that damn prisoner than her own kind.* Pushing off the wall, I made my way up to the steady drizzle above. Two more people supporting the ill and wounded slipped past me down the stairs.

Above, the sharp, salty smell of the sea clung to the back of my throat. I coughed then wiped the wet from my face. The cool air chased the buzzing in my head away. Mostly. Bright globules of light strained to be seen from behind indefinable clouds as the misty rain clung to everything. My gaze lowered back to the deck and the carnage left by the storm.

Few people remained on deck—standing. A row of bodies lined each side of the hull, feet toward mid-deck. Not one of them moved. Angry voices carried down from the quarterdeck. I didn't have to look to know who spoke.

"There's no sense, lad. We need t' take care of the dead firs', then look t' navigatin' outa here."

"The dead aren't going anywhere and neither are we. Who knows how much farther off course we'll get if we don't rally whoever is left to row? We can't afford—"

"We can't afford t' damage our souls *or* theirs. Rights need sayin'. Respect needs payin'. Civility is t' only thing left separatin' us from animals."

Dead. I looked at the rows of bodies and trembled. Stumbling along at their feet, my gaze clung to them: each pair of arms rested crossed over still chests, eyes closed. Grief made my legs wobble. *So many dead …*

"Almost there!" Delenon's deep voice boomed, drawing me away from the sea of corpses to the sail hold. Straining against the drag of mangled rope and sail the Magistrate, ill for so long and looking to be half the man he was, heaved the mess out into the open with three others. In the tangle, two familiar bodies lay twisted. Falling to my knees, a sob forced it way out as I watched, helpless.

With careful precision, Delenon instructed the others which way to pull or lift or slide. Their grim faces set, determined to find every last soul that hadn't been swept out to sea, revealed none of the turmoil I knew shredded their hearts. The gentle macabre that played out in front of me obliterated any remaining desire hidden within my soul. I was the one who'd prayed for death. The one who—then it struck me why so many had taken ill.

Two days ago. The ganoo pot pies … *undercooked.* The veggies chopped on a blood smeared prep counter …

I don't know how I got to my feet, but they knew what to do—where to take me. Straight past Delenon and his team to the port rail. I collapsed over it, leaning on my stomach, arms stretched to the white-caped sea churning and crashing against the lower hull. One foot then the other slipped away from the deck, un-anchoring me from everything.

Then a shout—

"They're alive! By the Suns! The Sisters are alive!"

My body balanced on the rail, ready to slide into the sea, but I hesitated.

Is it true?

Then a strong hand clamped around my ankle as a familiar voice drawled, "No ya don', Daria."

Satie

Survival of the Fittest

The moment Farrah allowed her eyes to close, she fell into a fitful sleep. Tears brimming, I checked on the other patients, most of whom were feverish and vomiting—but this wasn't sea sickness. Eena ... I'd been taught to spot the signs, and while nausea was one of them, the fevers and diarrhea were not. Something else was wrong. It was like they'd been poisoned.

Two sets of heavy footsteps echoed down the stairs in rapid succession. I turned from bathing a young man's forehead as Delenon and a day-shift sailor carried two bodies into the room; but not just any bodies—

"Meg! Ella!" I searched the room—no free beds. "Seddrik, I need you up. Take Zethra to the women's quarters then go rest in the men's."

He nodded, holding the worst of his rope burned hands to his shoulder as he hugged Zethra and helped her off the cot. Her fever wasn't as bad as the others, and I'd already given her verrin and a soak-down. Delenon and his man cradled my Sisters as they laid them on the now empty cots. Meg clutched a leather-bound book in a death grip—except she wasn't dead.

The Magistrate turned to me. "We'll need another cot. Denton is bringing Daria." *Denton? Oh, Tony.* He knelt beside Meg and gently removed from her comatose grasp Darius' Journal, one of the books Eena had been so desperate to save. I tried to shake my head clear.

"Daria's hurt?" I froze between the Sisters' beds, not sure who to check first. Both remained unconscious. Only the steady rise and fall of their chests kept me from completely falling apart.

"Not physically, but she needs supervision," he said.

My brain sizzled with too much information. I glanced from my Sisters to Farrah and then randomly around the room not really seeing the others but knowing they were there.

"What about him?" Delenon asked of the bandaged man with severe sunburn who'd been brought in only hours before the misting rains started who knew how many days ago now.

"Okay. He's stable. Put him in the men's quarters." *There's certainly enough room for everyone now … everyone left that is …* I squeezed my eyes shut and pushed my palms against them, trying to breathe without a shuddering hitch. Eena's face, wet with rain and her hair knotted and dripping as she thrust Matty at me, kept hovering in my mind. *What do I do, Eena? I don't know. I don't know what to do.*

A firm but bony hand gripped my shoulder. I looked up into Delenon's deep black face, gaunt but determined. I nodded, not trusting myself to speak, and dropped down next to Meg. He escorted the burned man from the room, the damp book firmly clasped in one hand.

With care, I felt for every bone I could and laid my lips upon her forehead for a fast temperature assessment. I vaguely registered another set of footsteps entering the Med-bay.

"Sister?" Tony asked. I jumped a little, then turned and stood, the metal assessment table stark and barren between us—and Daria, who he carried in his arms. Her eyes were open but her stare blank. "Where can I place her?"

"Over there." I pointed. "What's wrong? I don't understand why she needs supervision." I glanced at the catatonic woman he lay on the cot, then turned to Ella and began my assessment of her condition.

"She juss tried t' kill herself." The matter-of-fact way he said this made me stand up again.

"What?"

"I've bin worrin' 'bout her fer some time now. Make sure she doesn't try anythin' else." He turned to leave.

"Wait."

He turned back, confused.

"I can't watch her that closely. Send someone else. Put her in the women's quart—"

"T'ain't anyone else." The weight of those words reflected the rows of bodies I'd checked for any signs of life not half an hour earlier—too many familiar faces ... too many faces period.

"Then strap her down," Delenon said, coming back into the room.

I balked at the idea, but Tony just nodded and grabbed the rope on the floor I'd tried to kick under the examination table. The rope that lost me Eena.

By the time I finished checking over Ella, Tony had left. I stood and looked down at my Sisters. Delenon shifted around the table and stood beside me. I'd forgotten he was there.

"Are they hurt?" He leaned forward, and I watched as he studied the reflection of himself in their features—gaunt, frail ...

"No. Yes."

He stood tall and looked at me.

"Starved."

"What? I don't understand."

I lifted my face and looked back. "Marxx."

"Marxx? But— He didn't? He couldn't have? While I was ill?"

I nodded. "Are you taking back command? Now that you're on the mend?"

His eyes shadowed over, and the faint wisp of hope that I might yet save them snuffed out.

"No."

I asked every question I could think of, but each one died before the next could slip past my lips. *No, of course not.* He'd been out of commission for too long. He had the respect for who he used to be, but Marxx had the power now. He and Tony—

"What about Tony? Could he challenge ..." but the Magistrate's look countered that as well. If Tony could challenge Marxx's ruling, he would have by now. They shared responsibility for the crew, but it was Marxx who'd stepped forward right from ground zero to take the reins.

"Can you save them?" he asked.

Should I? "They need water and verrin. Maybe once they're rehydrated they'll be able to stomach some toast or hot cereal." I looked around the room. The water pail was half-full and the verrin one empty. *But then what?*

"I need more supplies."

"I'll collect—"

"No. You've overexerted yourself helping after the storm. I can't have you collapsing on the stairs carrying water and verrin we can't afford to waste ..." My words echoed in my head: can't afford to waste, to *waste* ... "Bathe their foreheads, necks and chests for me."

"What's wrong with the others? Nearly half those remaining are ill. Is it serious?"

"I don't know. I hope not." I stole a glance at Farrah. "Maybe…" I shook my head. "I'll be back soon." Sharing suspicions I couldn't guarantee, would only cause greater panic. I glanced at Daria: still, eyes staring up at the ceiling but not seeing. Then I jogged through the doorway and down, down into the hold, my tears flowing freely, searing my cheeks with their hot tracks.

I bi-passed the few surviving casks of water and verrin, blindly running toward the wall of crates. Most of the broken ones and resulting mess had been cleaned, leaving gaping holes and a fine layer of flour and grain on the floor, but the floor-to-ceiling prison wall remained mostly intact.

Drax rose the second he saw me. I stumbled forward, no longer able to hold myself up. His thin arms wrapped around me, supporting me like steel gridwork. Burying my face into the thin shirt-folds at his chest, I fully gave over to my emotions.

He didn't shush me or rock back and forth, just stood there as my soul bled. Once spent, I sniffled as he led me to the semi-circle of crates, and sat across from me, knee-to-knee, holding my hands in his. He didn't say anything. He didn't have to.

I inhaled a shuddering breath. "They survived."

He nodded. I didn't have to explain who.

"They're unhurt but nothing's changed, even with Magistrate Delenon back on his feet."

"What do you mean nothing's changed?" his deep, even voice wrapped like a hug around my frayed nerves.

"They're still dying."

"Can you save them?"

I met his eyes and spoke my fears aloud, "Should I?"

He squinted at me, concern written across his brow.

"I *might* be able to if I can get them rehydrated and eating. But…"

"What?"

"Once they recover, Marxx will only allow them to starve again. They won't break their vows, and that means they won't work to earn food to eat. They refuse my charity. And no one else, other than Matty, the pregnant woman, has come forward to share their meals. Why … why should I …"

"Save them only to watch them slowly die all over again?" he growled. Not at me. No. At Marxx and Delenon and Tony and the rest of the ship who cared more about themselves than being charitable and helping keep alive the embodiment of our spirituality. Marxx wasn't the only one who favoured that the strong would survive and those who contributed would be rewarded.

"No one with any power believes that spiritual work is worthy." I dropped my gaze down to our clasped hands resting on our knees. The man before me knew all too well of the debilitating prejudices that ruled the treatment of anyone "other" or "non-conforming". He'd been left on this ship to rot by both the government, *his* people, and the rebels, *my* people? *No. I might be a commoner who believes in the cause, but I am not like them.*

"Do you know why I'm here, Satie?" His hands tightened around mine. I looked up into troubled eyes that only looked through me. "When I learned the Kronik meant to strand any surviving Resistance members on board and set you adrift with no training or experience—as a false symbol of compassion—I set fire to the ship. *My* ship. Based on the original blueprints for Darius' craft, I thought to celebrate his sacrifice for all Xannian's with a memorial museum. But the Kronik knew I was angry with his ruling and had me watched."

I could figure out the rest. Not wanting a traitor with sympathies of any kind for non-Talians they'd tortured him to make sure he wasn't a spy and then left him with us to die. His team was likely the reason this floating tub came as well-stocked as it had, but they hadn't been able to save him.

His eyes refocused and his gaze burned into mine.

But I'd had a choice, and I hadn't let him die. Suddenly, I knew the answer I sought. I hadn't "wasted" resources on this man. I'd helped him—just as I'd find a way to help my Sisters.

"Thank you," I whispered, then ran to get my supplies.

Daria

The Damned

"WEll, Daria?" Sister Venra asked. I pulled my gaze from the ceiling and turned my throbbing head to look at her, still bound as I was to the cot.

"I *promise*."

She gave me a grim smile, nodded, and then worked to untie my bonds—no mean feat since Tony had secured them. In the past two days, they were certain to have tightened more as I tossed and turned with fevered dreams, sweating the alcohol from my system.

I watched as she tugged and pulled at the rope holding me to the frame of the bed. My mouth felt dry, my tongue thick. She worked steadily even as her gaze flicked over to the cot behind my head. I knew who and what lay there. Really, the only reason I readily made the promise—to get away.

As the rope slipped over my chest and the Sister, turned *only-nurse-left,* loosened the wraps around my left wrist, a knock sounded on the door frame. Venra jolted up to see past the examination table, her insecurity about letting me loose written in her stiff stance.

"There you are," rang Reena's voice across the room. I groaned and shut my eyes, loud anything still didn't sit well with me, but I kept worrying my wrist in its binds, loosening it more and more regardless of how I felt.

"There are two bodies now," the Sister said, voice choked. From my peripheral vision, I saw her wave at the bed near me and one across the room.

"I'm not here for the dead. I'm sorry, Sister. I need to speak with you if I may."

Venra walked around the table, and both women took a few steps into the hall. One wrist now out, I worked on freeing the other before tackling my feet. The conversation from the hall easily carried into the room.

"It was brought to our attention that the illness sweeping the ship might be due to food poisoning. What's your take on the situation?"

"I'm hardly qualified to—"

"Just do your best. Based on what you've dealt with so far on the voyage, what's your opinion?"

"I knew right away that it wasn't severe sea sickness and the fish we've been eating is the same as the fish Darius caught. I was assured that there were no adverse effects to his crew, that were recorded anyway. The diseases and illnesses we've dealt with to date reflect hygiene and exposure. Though some symptoms were similar to the Dysentery the Magistrate fought, and luckily survived, these deaths are happening so fast in comparison to the initial signs he faced that it makes sense to question everything— even our food."

"Is Daria lucid enough to speak with me?"

"Yes."

They walked back into the Med-bay and around the table to where I sat, elbows on knees breathing past the small fit of nausea. Reena stepped back, clearly shocked at seeing me untied and rubbing my sore appendages. Sister Venra's face blanched, not at my escapism but from catching sight of the dead body on the cot next to mine. I glanced over. It was Farrah, the other nurse's helper. *No wonder she's so stressed. First Eena now this ...* Venra dropped to her knees at my feet and studied the rope marks on my wrists and ankles as Reena sat beside me on the cot, blocking the dead woman from view.

"How are you feeling?" Reena asked, avoiding the obvious. I coughed then stared at her for the audacity of asking. She reached for a mug of water sitting on the table and looked at Venra, who nodded. Reena passed it to me and clarified, "All things considered, that is."

I shrugged and swished the water around my rancid mouth before swallowing. "I'm ready to return to my duties if that's what you mean." Not really. I didn't want them to begin with, and if I caused the poisoning, it was the last place I wanted to go back to. Still, I wouldn't try to jump overboard again ... for whatever that was worth. *They* might toss me over, though.

"Tell me about your kitchen staff."

"What do you want to know?"

"Are they competent? Do you have concerns?"

"Why?" I knew why, but I didn't want to show my hand. Instead, I took another swig of water and cringed inwardly—it just wasn't doin' it for me.

"We think the deaths might be associated to a severe case of food poisoning. We're checking all possibilities, but *I* was given this lead to follow. So, tell me about your staff."

Venra bustled off to check on her Sisters, briefly stopping at the other cots of invalids along the way, offering a gentle caress or kind words. Setting the mug between my knees, I rubbed my face with a hand then tried to work both of them through my unruly mass of hair. Rank BO made me cringe, so I gave up on it and let my arms drop to my lap.

"They listen well and learn fast. I've left them on their own during prep several times when I've gone to gather supplies." *Check on the still.* "They are efficient and work well together. At this point I'd say they really only need me as a source for recipes, figuring out quantities, and balancing the meals, but I'm sure they'll have the hang of that soon too."

"You've never had to reprimand one of them for being careless or unobservant?"

The image of the diluted, pink trail of ganoo blood on the work surface and then me plunging fallen veggie sticks into tainted wash water to rinse them hazed at the back of my mind.

"No. They're good workers."

"Okay, then." She stood up. "Thank you. I'll let you know if we discover anything." I was going to ask "why" but I was the Cook. It was my kitchen. My galley. *My mistake …*

Two men entered, chatting, just as Reena left.

"Completely gone," the Balanis man said.

"And the Journal? I've seen them with it since the storm," the Metek man ran his hand through short, thick black hair.

"I hear it's useless now."

"The bodies are over here," Venra interrupted. I knew the still man on the far side of the room wasn't the issue; it was her colleague's corpse. It likely served as a constant reminder of how inexperienced she was … how little she could really help anyone on this Gods-Forsaken barge.

They grabbed the man first: wrists and ankles. The body swayed heavily, suspended between them. As the Balanis man passed through the doorway walking backwards, he continued his conversation.

"I tell you, we're lost. No suns, no stars. The Kronik's finally getting his wish." He glanced at the body between them. "It won't be long, and Marxx knows it." Then they disappeared up the steps to the main deck, the Sister watching them long after they'd gone.

She was testing me, had to be. I leaned back against the mainmast between massive coils of rope with my arms crossed. Since no one had yet released Venra from babysitting duty, she'd dragged me with her up on deck as she walked amongst the dead. The mist abated but the clouds continued to roil overhead.

Maybe not. Maybe she got me out here for different reasons.

Venra didn't seem at all interested in me. Never glanced over her shoulder or even spoke to me. Several times she even closed her eyes, her lips moving in prayer. She either wasn't worried about me in the slightest (but if that were the case why didn't she just leave me unattended in the Med-bay?) or she'd forgotten I existed—either way, I meant nothing to this woman who studied the dead with more interest than she'd passed onto me since Tony left me in her care.

I shifted my weight from one foot to the other to position myself a tad more toward the quarterdeck where Marxx, Tony, and Magistrate Delenon argued. With few people on deck and nearly no wind, their voices carried beyond the confines of their position.

Without a doubt, we were lost. Just as the pallbearer had said. Their discussion looped time and time again around the same facts: if we did nothing, we risked sailing back into the White Sea storms; if we picked a random direction and rowed; we risked sailing back into the storms; if we unfurled the sails and let the wind direct our course; we … It just gave me a headache. There was no way to gain our bearings, and neither man was willing to risk siding with another for fear of being wrong.

Then Venra, who'd travelled the length of the opposite side of the ship, following the rows of the dead, bolted for the nearest staircase to the quarterdeck. I paced myself walking over to the space of wall between the stairs going up and the ones going down; not staying close to my sitter because I was on my best behaviour, but because I had a feeling this wasn't going to be about the corpses she refused to have released to the sea.

"You can end this stalemate right now," she said, no reverent greetings or half-spoken prayers.

"Excuse me?" Marxx asked, clearly perturbed that a lowly Sister would dare interrupt their empty posturing.

"Wait. Let her speak," said Tony. I'd heard how she'd rallied the night-crew to disobey Marxx and help Tony save the ship. Clearly, he hadn't forgotten, but neither had Marxx considering his tone.

"You have a valuable asset chained down in the hold."

"What the Gods—"

"Listen to her," Delenon's deep voice silenced him. *Ooo, Tony and the Magistrate* do *agree on something—Venra.* But I scowled. I knew what she referred to as well, and I sided with Marxx.

"Drax"—a long pause likely punctuated with baffled stares, I could only imagine—"the Talian in the hold, built this ship. Well, not by himself, but he was the lead Engineer. He knows it inside and out."

"We're sailing fine on our own, now," Tony said. "Why would we need a ship *builder's* help?"

"Because he knows anything and everything about how it works *and* sails. If we ask him to be our navigator, I'm certain he'll know exactly what we need to do to get back on track. He's probably memorised Darius' Journal too ... have any of you? Word is, the water damage is severe."

"He's a Talian and a criminal. He can't be trusted."

"Marxx is right," Delenon said. "He is a criminal. If the Kronik imprisoned him on a ship suspected not to make it, who's to say he won't just toss himself overboard or try to kill us?"

Mixed emotions roiled in my stomach and my head. I had done both and yet they still trusted me ...

"He's not a criminal—not really. Please, listen to me. He tried to burn down the ship when he learned the Kronik wasn't planning on a museum anymore. He's not a bad man."

"No," Marxx said. "We're not letting him up here and we are certainly not asking him to navigate for us. We've gotten this far on our own. We can figure it out."

Neither Tony or the Magistrate spoke against Marxx's decision.

"But—"

"Stand down, Sister. Go back to the dead. You only have another twelve hours to find a solution. *That* should be your main priority. That and nursing your Sisters and the others back to health." Delenon supported Marxx, though I could hear in his strained voice just how much it cost him.

The Navy Sea

Deep Waters.

Morale remains low after nearly a week without ____
Having abandoned the star charts I can only hope
that our compass still works. The constant mist ____
rain make it twice as hard to manage the sails and
even your clothes are wet. It somehow seeps into
your soul and drags you down—further each ____
We tried sending the rowboats out to collect more
fish, but the thrashing waves nearly capsized them.
Two men died today. Perhaps I should have opened
with that? They were so waterlogged even their ____
refused to burn. I told the crew I'd seen the Gods
whence them—I can only hope my prayers bound
them to me, instead of losing them to the seas.
I watch the compass now instead of the water ____
know what's out there for it lies inside me. The
ceaseless damp and misty rain cause more than just
morale problems. The incessant wet is affecting our
feet. Most of the crew have now abandoned wearing
boots and shoes, but the foot rot has taken hold. If
we cannot push past the pain and disfigurement,
there'll be no one left to sail the ship. All we can do
is follow the compass and keep going.

Captain Darius

Satie

Keep Your Enemies Closer

I scrambled to the main deck holding my short medical apron closed against my thighs.

"NO!" I screamed as two of the crew shifted to swing the boy's body, gaining momentum to toss it overboard.

"Hold up. Hold up, then!" the Magistrate's deep voice carried from the quarterdeck, reining in the workers. Clutching the spice container to my chest, I manoeuvred around deck hands and the cleaning crew, dropping to my knees beside the released corpse. Excess water swept in and around the rotting bodies of the dead, which only made their skin decay faster.

"Make it quick!" Marxx's voice cut through the air.

This was it; my last chance to save their souls. I shuddered at the thought of Eena and thirty or so others who were swept away into the chilling waters, forever bound to the physical realm—unable to rise with Sister Zola into the cleansing heavens. If I could have bound their souls to mine, I would have—but that was impossible, right?

Camdin's blotchy and bloated face was no more than a sickly washed out version of itself, even as the bands of his vibrant gold coliths spoke of the trapped soul within. I sliced his close-fitting t-shirt from chin to stomach, clipping a square of fabric from the neckline. The back of my hand nudged his chin and the clammy shift made me gag. I snatched my hand back, shaking it out.

I was not a nurse or a mortician. I was a failed Devout. *No more!* I would release these people from their mortal coils—I had to.

Using the tip of the scissors, I flipped the cut shirt to expose the young Leader's chest then unscrewed the spice jar, careful not to jostle its liquid contents. I dipped a corner of the small square into the heady aroma while saying a short prayer, then laid the fabric over the dead man's heart. Resealing the solution, I placed it on the deck and pulled the scissors and a chunk of flint from my work pouch. I struck the sharp edge against the rock twice before a small spark flicked up and landed on the cloth.

It ignited!

I watched the blue-green flame, nearly colourless at its tip, consume the Spirit Threads leaving a blackened mark the shape of a small child's hand. *Zerameteth's blessing!* I lifted my tool-filled hands into the air and sang out the prayer for the dead.

The men moved in again to take the body. I stayed them with a glance, then gathered my supplies and hurried to the quarterdeck. Half-way up the narrow staircase, a shriek of laughter echoed from the lower deck by the Med-bay. I turned mid-step as Daria, animated and boisterous, stumbled out sidestepping desperate hands from behind her. Jip and Reena scrambled up the last of the treads and spread out to either side of the twirling and laughing Cook. She took a swig from the mug she held before chucking it at Jip.

Whipping back around, Daria flew under Jip's reach and sailed past the woman mopping the deck, dancing past the feet of the dead.

"What in Xannia?" Delenon asked, leaning over the upper rail in line with my head. I glanced at Marxx; his scowl said it all.

"She's pissed."

I narrowed my eyes and watched as Daria leapt about, her full apron fluttering around her.

"She doesn't look angry," I said, more than a little confused.

"No, Sister, she's drunk," Delenon clarified.

Daria let out another cackle of false mirth as she launched herself up onto the rigging for the central mast. I gasped. She'd been out of my care for over twenty-four hours, and now she dangled herself over the edge of the ship again after she'd promised—*but wait. No, she's not jumping, she's climbing.* That is she was, until Reena caught her ankle and Jip grabbed her around the waist not even a quarter of the way up. Somehow, between the two of them, they got her wriggling body back on deck.

Then Daria punched Reena in the face. I winced. I knew what that felt like. Suddenly, everyone was on their way down. Delenon, Marxx, and I met Jip, Reena, and Daria near the top of the stairs to the lower level. Jip held Daria in a headlock with her arms trapped behind her. Noxious fumes rose from her clothes and her breath—fumes surprisingly similar to the liquid fire I clutched in the pocket of my apron. It had been left in the middle of the steel Med-bay table with the note, "try this" and nothing more. *Was it from Daria?*

"What's going on?" Marxx growled. Daria's struggling became more subdued the longer Jip held her. My gaze flicked from the rise and fall of her chest, to the arm nearly strangling her, to his face. I had to make sure he didn't go too far.

"*She* did it. She poisoned everyone," Reena snapped, waving her arm in Daria's general direction.

"You know that for sure?" Delenon asked, always the voice of reason.

"Yes," Reena and Jip said together.

"Explain," Marxx said.

The pair took turns detailing Daria's slow, debilitating decline as voiced by the kitchen staff. Ultimately, it was under Daria's order that the ganoo pies got only half their usual cooking time, and she compromised the state of the prep counter when the raw veggies were chopped on a salmonella-laced surface just prior to being served.

"None of this would have happened if she hadn't been stealing supplies to make hooch from the extra water distillation pieces," Reena said.

"Why's that?" Delenon asked.

"Dinner was late and improperly prepared because of her drinking. She put the entire ship at risk and killed—"

"Indirectly," I said.

"—over thirty people. Thirty people, Marxx! She destroyed more lives than that storm did. I say we throw her overboard."

"NO!" I shouted. Everyone looked at me. Reena scowled, Marxx was impassive, but Daria's half-suffocated body spasmed as her eyes widened.

"Sister, I don't think—" Delenon started.

"I do. Someone has to speak for her. Yes, the outcome of her escalating depression *indirectly* caused the deaths of our crew. She's not a cold-blooded killer. She's a woman consumed by the loss of her family, her baby no less. Yes, she was late with dinner, and had she been sober she might not have made those same choices. However, you"—I looked to Marxx—"would still have chastised her for being tardy and pressured her to fix the mistake faster than she would want to. And you—"I stared at Reena— "said the staff were told the proper way to make the meal, but when the pressure to perform made them anxious, they asked a woman they knew wasn't sober for cooking advice. And then, who gave her the alcohol in the first place? I know for a fact that when the water distillation units were set up, Daria was asked to help but said she didn't know how. That's when another helper stepped forward."

"What? Now you're blaming a dead man for making her drunk? That was her choice," Reena said.

"No, I'm not blaming the helper. I'm simply saying that whoever did put the still together knew more than Daria did. They enabled her, just as her staff did. Don't you see? The woman's soul-sore and trying to forget. No one, except the person or people who put that still together, bothered to help her in any way, and that was the wrong kind of help. We're *all* at fault for those deaths. She was just the instrument of our ignorance. She doesn't deserve to die. She's not a malicious person, nor is she a killer. She doesn't need incarceration. She needs help."

But just as I thought my words finally sunk in, I caught the glances to my Luma, the dead littered over the deck, the invisible sightlines to the "creature" chained below, and the pure hatred radiating off the Captain who still hadn't forgiven my mutiny. In their eyes, I was only a poor excuse for a replacement nurse; a woman who'd broken her vows, caused descent; and had a history of siding with the enemy. It didn't matter that my reasoning was flawless; because it came from me, they'd never seriously consider it.

I sighed. My heart ached for an ounce of understanding. I had only one chance left as Jip yanked Daria toward the side of the ship and everyone but me stepped forward.

"If you kill her now, you'll only be granting her the one thing she so desperately wants—to die. Keep her alive and she not only has to live with the loss of her family but the choices she's made, and her part in the deaths of thirty-four of our brothers and sisters. Kill her now, and she wins."

Everyone stopped. They didn't look at me this time but at Daria, and the wild, haunted look in her eyes. Marxx cleared his throat.

"In that case, there's really only one thing to do."

Daria

Reversal

I tried to twist, scramble back away from the stairs, but Jip tightened his grip on my neck and lifted me so only my toes scraped the deck boards. Stars flashed in front of my eyes. I tried to say, "It was my fault. Kill me," but only a strained gargle made it past my lips. I stopped struggling long enough for Jip to loosen his hold on me. At the bottom of the stairs, I smashed my heel on the top of his foot. He nearly let go.

Pushing against his weakened grip, I stumbled forward. Shouts followed me as I staggered at an alarming rate down the hall. Falling down the mess hall steps, I cried out as my back hit the treads. Scrambling forward onto my knees, I staggered past the sleeping quarters over to the opposite stairs that led back to the main deck.

The air wooshed from my lungs as a pair of arms wrapped around my waist, folding me in half. My pursuer staggered and we landed in a heap at the bottom of the other staircase. Recovering my breath, I struggled against my pursuer until pain burned across my scalp as my head was yanked back. I landed, splayed across the floor. The grip on my hair tightened as my captor wrapped another length around their hand. Then Jippon stood above me. Someone said something and he hauled me over his shoulder. Reena released my hair then bound my wrists together as Marxx folded my legs in one swift motion and tied my feet to my quads.

He yelled something to Delenon about making the speech of a lifetime before recruiting a team of men from the few still awake—still alive. He didn't have to. Four men followed Marxx, Jip, and me down the open staircase into the hold. The animals squawked and bleated; goats hit their chests and horns against the make-shift pens. I found my voice and shrieked!

Marxx smacked me across the face. "Shut it, Daria."

Blood drizzled from my nose and into my mouth. None of this made any sense until I caught sight of the wall of crates.

"NO! No you can't! Don't do this. I'd rather die! Kill me. Kill me!"

Rounding the prison wall, Jip hauled me off his shoulder, dropped me to the ground, and sat on me. Then Marxx rounded with the four men. Their wide eyes and uneasy demeanour had nothing to do with me and everything to do with monster in the corner—except, when he turned around his close-cropped hair, clean face, and confident stature revealed nothing of the haggard creature I'd discovered over twenty days ago. In fact, he looked almost *civilized*.

"Today's your lucky day," Marxx said to the Talian, who nodded slightly but did not remove his intense grey eyes from Marxx's face.

"Sister Satie mentioned she'd ... spoken with you," the monster said.

Marxx's face echoed my confusion. "You mean Sister Venra," he corrected.

The Talian gave a half-smile before saying, "We'll see."

Marxx shook his head, then motioned for the men to remove his chains. My heart tried to break free from my chest, even as the ache of my ribs from the weight of Jippon kept it prisoner … like me. With the surge of adrenaline now gone, I sank into a haze of confusion.

Two of the men walked the Talian dog out, a chained leash still attached to his leg. One man held the remaining shackle open as the other dragged me out from under Jip and into the half-ring of crates and straw. With a clang, the cold metal closed around my ankle. I squeezed my eyes shut, trying to shut out the world.

PART II

Satie

The Navigator

Chain clanking, Drax stumbled into the Med-bay directed by a burly sailor. Marxx followed, filling the doorway.

"Looks like you got your wish. Make sure he's presentable but not too pretty. I don't want a sick Talian exposed to the crew. Topside in ten for the speech."

Drax lifted his head when the sailor pushed him forward. A bright red line oozed blood from his throat. He tried to warn me with his eyes not to show compassion or concern, but I couldn't stop myself.

"What happened?" I asked, rushing over, gingerly taking his jaw into my hands. My heart pounded out of rhythm.

"The Captain had a few questions for me."

I narrowed my eyes at his simple answer, then realised we weren't alone. I turned to the man holding Drax's leg chain. "Isn't it about time for shift change? Why don't you dump that on the floor by the examination table and stand guard at the door? I'm sure Marxx won't want everyone finding out about the Talian until he's good and ready."

The man considered my request a moment, took a quick glance around the Med-bay then did exactly that—his broad shoulders and back filled most of the doorframe just as several people walked past. With his gaze trained on those heading topside, he was as preoccupied as the rest of my charges who were either asleep or struggling through the last stages of clearing the poison from their system.

"Sit." I pointed to the stool by the table.

"Must I?"

"Yes," I said, then lowered my voice. "I need to take a look at you."

"You saw me just this morning, Sister." There was no hint of malice in his voice and yet, even though he'd shared so much with me, he still didn't trust me.

"Drax …" I placed my hands on my hips. I didn't care that Marxx wanted him to look one way or another, I knew he was healthy. I wanted to keep him that way.

He sat with his hands on his knees, slightly hunched forward. I poured a fresh bowl of water from the main pail and grabbed a clean rag from the cupboard. Lifting his chin with one hand, I methodically washed the drying blood from around the cut on his throat. While there was no question that his skin had been sliced, the way it overlapped gave it more the appearance of a bad papercut than attempted murder.

"You shouldn't need stiches, but I should dress it with clean bandages."

"No. Leave it." He held my wrist, his grip firm but kind. "You need to stop fussing."

"And why exactly should I do that? I'm the nurse. You're my patient. And I was told to clean you up."

"Satie." Fireworks ignited down my spine. "I'm fine."

I raised my gaze to his stormy grey eyes that said so much more than his words ever did. I wasn't supposed to feel this way. Not for any one person; not like this. My vows … but I'd broken those so many weeks ago. Still, some part of me refused to let go of that first promise I ever made: to cherish all the brothers and sisters of Xannia and act as a conduit of light for the Sun Gods.

I blinked and took in the dark brown stain ringing the collar of his worn button-up shirt. His business pants were a stark reminder of his otherness, just as the Magistrate's suit pants set *him* apart. But this wouldn't do. I slipped my wrist from his grasp, set the bucket aside, and then riffled through the bottom cupboard before tossing a shirt and a pair of work pants at him.

"What's this for?" He caught them then squinted at me.

"You're covered in blood. You need to change." He didn't ask who the clothes had once belonged to and I didn't offer the info. We'd stripped the two sailors before releasing their bodies to the sea and kept the clothes since we had no way of manufacturing more of our own. In a way, my insistence in keeping the dead on board until I'd discovered a way to release their souls, had ruined thirty-four sets of perfectly good clothing—something I'm sure bothered Marxx more than the rot of the bodies or the state of their souls.

I turned away as Drax manoeuvred the clothing around his shackle and chain, studying the rows of medicines I still knew nothing about.

"Done."

I turned back just as he rolled the sleeves of the work shirt up over his elbows. The pants were a bit short but the frayed edges hid the discrepancy and softened him somehow. The sailor guarding the door walked in before I could do or say anything untoward. The man picked up Drax's chain, but I took the

Talian's arm first, and walked him through the door and up the stairs.

Of the remaining sixty-odd people on this ship, other than the twelve in the Med-bay too sick to stand, everyone stood looking up at Marxx and Delenon on the quarterdeck. Because their gazes focused on what was happening directly above us, it felt as though every eye locked onto Drax and me as we stepped free of the shadowed door frame into the late afternoon haze.

The skin on the back of my neck prickled as I ascended to the platform, followed by Drax and the Irons Man. The welcoming din fell silent as every man and woman took in the presence of a Talian on our ship. Before the charged air could erupt into cries of outrage, Delenon spoke to his people.

"My fellow Xannians it is time to introduce you to the windfall the Kronik's Council felt inclined to leave aboard our ship. Meet Drax, our new ship's navigator."

A swell of hostile voices rose, threatening to eclipse Delenon's. He placed both hands in the air in a silent request for peace. As the roar abated, our very black Magistrate placed a hand on the shoulder of this very white symbol of our repression.

Neither man looked at the other but kept their gazes flickering over the collected masses. Delenon exuded every inch of confidence and superiority he had when he was actually Magistrate of Darzeth, while Drax remained wholly unreadable. The clothes he had on spoke to the working folk, and the shackles to their perception of his rightful place in our presence. That moment embodied everything these people had fought for, risked their lives and the lives of their families for: the rule of the citizens over the Elite Sect.

Delenon held this peace as long as he dared, remaining silent, allowing the image to speak for itself.

"It has taken some time for me and the Leaders to fully understand Drax's presence on our ship." *Now that's a load of hooey.* "But we have come to learn that he opposed the Kronik's plan to abandon us to the Nine Seas on the very ship he built, by attempting to set fire to it and destroy his life's work. We have long known that there are sympathizers to our plight trapped behind the Compound's wall. Today, we have in our midst at least one Talian who dared oppose the Kronik, and for that, we now turn to him as an equal"—gasps exploded like fireworks— "and invite him, however tentatively, to join our crew."

The chain of Drax's shackle clattered at that moment as if to emphasise just how tenuous this peace, this *equality*, really was. And while some part of me trusted that Delenon believed his own pretty words, looking at Marxx and the others I saw the thinly veiled hostility bubbling just under the surface. They, like Daria, refused to believe.

Then Drax was pulled back away from view toward the poop deck. Marxx's rough hands gripped my shoulders, forcing me to take two steps forward. I forced a halting breath past the lump in my throat. *What now?* Delenon spoke again.

"Before we return to work or rest, we'd ask that you help us usher those loved ones and comrades now deceased, on their path into the beyond."

"It's your turn, Sister. And it better be worth the wait," Marxx growled into my ear before releasing me. I only had time to follow my instinct and raised my arms up to our gods high above and beyond the dark clouds, hidden within the molten folds of their suns.

"Join me, brothers and sisters, in singing Zola's Prayer." I took a deep breath, drew from the depth of my diaphragm and sang with all the power of my heart.

"Holy Mother, bless this day,
Wrap your warmth and with me stay
until my mortal demise,
Cradle my soul until the suns rise …"

After the first verse, every voice raised in chorus, I slipped down the stairs to the main deck and disappeared below. I had maybe two minutes until the end of the prayer; perhaps a little over one before they noticed my absence. Crashing into the Med-bay table, I banged my hip before rolling through the impact and around to the cupboards. *Where is it? Where is it? Where is it?*

The spice jar of ill-begotten liquor wasn't on the counter or in the locked cabinet. I could already hear the voices petering out above. *You're taking too long!*

I spun around and scanned the room, my gaze lingering on Meg's and Ella's gaunt faces until a slight shift in posture drew my sight to the bed just beyond them. *He's not sleeping.* The set of the sailor's face and pronounced curve of his spine as if closing around himself set alarms blaring in my head.

"Hand. It. Over," I punctuated each word with the fullness of my voice, anger and frustration fraying the forced calm. He shuddered, still fighting the poison but without the pain lines creasing his forehead. *Oh gods, please … please tell me he didn't—*

I stormed over and yanked his arm away from his coiled body.

"You'll 'pill it!" he cried, tears springing to his eyes.

I yanked the open canister from his weakened grip and cradled the small cylinder to my face. *Less than half left.* Fear stabbed at my heart. *There are over thirty bodies! I can't—I don't—* Gulping air to force down the panic, I capped the container and ran back up the stairs just as the prayer ended, climbing a couple of steps up to the quarterdeck before turning to face the unsettled crowd.

"Now, as my shipmates and I tend to the bodies before and beside and behind you, sing in round the Prayer for the Dead as I release their souls to the heavens above." At that moment, the clouds parted for the briefest of seconds, but it was enough to awe even me as that band of light struck us before dissolving into shadow.

Slipping back to the main deck, I motioned with my head for Jip and Reena to join me. They followed me over to the closest body.

"Here. Take these scissors and slit every shirt open like you see here. Quickly cut a small scrap of material and place it on the deceased's chest. I'll conduct the new Rite of Release and follow your progress." I could tell by the expression on their faces they weren't happy about having to go near, let alone touch, the dead. But I caught the glint of respect in their eyes. Even if they didn't like me, they trusted me as their Guardian in this world and the next.

As the crowd decided amongst themselves who would hum and who would sing, never letting the prayer die out, I knelt by the second body and prayed to Zerameteth to see me through this. I dipped a tiny corner of cloth into what was left of the alcohol and enacted the rite. One, two, three strikes of the flint and the Spirit Threads ignited, leaving a similar blackened hand print over her heart.

As I moved onto the next body, Tony and the Magistrate took hold of each vessel in turn and released it to the sea, grown such a dark purple it seemed as if their blood released upon impact with the waves.

The Purple Sea

Deep Waters—
When the heavens finally parted and the rains
ceased, I kept a light-duty crew on constant
rotation every two hours to allow the men time to
lie on deck in the sun and dry out. During the last
days in the dark gloom of the Navy Sea, I buried
three more souls to ———their weight a palpable
thing. Eight others had to have toes or even a foot
amputated to remove the gangrenous tissue from
the dead appendage. Who knew just how deadly
even regular water could be?
I made ready a crew to try their hand at fishing
again. Food stores are running low, even if our
fresh-water reserves now overflow. The purple
undulating forms beneath the waves have all of us
wondering what more is in store.
The men talk about turning back—not right away
but soon. Between the storms on the White Sea and
the perpetual mist lingering over the Navy Sea,
hope is all but gone that we'll find land, let alone
see it. They miss their families. Who can blame
them. Most only joined because of the extra
money promised, but even that remains to trust
until we return. With seven dead, the loss for those
families weighs even heavier than before.

Captain Darius

Satie

Finding North

There was nothing left. I'd wiped the sides of the spice jar with the second-last piece of Spirit Thread and it almost didn't ignite. *Oh, guide me, dear Child of the Light. I cannot allow even one more soul to remain trapped in these vicious waters. Please, please guide me ...*

Exhaustion pulled at my limbs and dragged my head down. The weight of expectation from those singing pressed against my chest, making it harder and harder to breathe. We'd released thirty-three spirits in the last hour. If I failed now, I'd lose all those yet living. The tears fell unbidden in giant drops, soaking my lashes and drawing my eyes closed. Tony and the Magistrate hovered nearby, blocking even the weak resonance of warmth coming from the cloud-masked setting of our second sun, Zita.

Should I fake it? Just light the cloth with a few extra sparks for a good show?

NO!

I opened my eyes and stared at the lost woman lying before me then lifted my face to the sky, unsure where Zita actually sat, and begged her to reveal the future … my destiny …

But nothing came. The magic liquid was gone and my time was up. Even if someone out there knew where I could get more, how long would that take? Had Marxx destroyed the still? Would Daria tell me if she had a hidden stash?

My eyelids fluttered as I lowered my gaze back to the empty container. Only, it wasn't empty anymore …

I gasped.

Then I took in the damp tracks conforming to the shape of my hand around the cylinder. I wiped my wet cheeks with the back of my other hand then swirled those few collected tears as an image came to mind: cleaning salad dressing residue from the server after meals at the Temple. Hope sprang through my chest as I fumbled to cap the container. I shook it for all I was worth.

Luckily my helpers crowded close enough to block any direct sightlines from the singing crowd, now wordlessly humming in anticipation of this final release. I picked up the Spirit Threads and wiped first the inside of the lid before sliding that tiny piece of cloth over every inch of the vial, and laying it with a shaking hand over the young woman's heart.

Body still vibrating with the toxic blend of hope and fear, I struck and struck and struck again the metal of my scissors against the flint. What few sparks I made landed wide of their mark. Then the Magistrate's warm, ebony hands closed over mine. He didn't try to ignite the spark himself, just held my hands and gently hummed the Prayer for the Dead.

I inhaled a shaky breath then nodded. He released me and I tried again, more focused and clear of mind than I'd ever been. I struck the flint three successive times, each spark hitting its mark.

The air fairly buzzed with tension as Jip, Reena, Delenon, and Tony leaned over just as the Spirit Threads ignited! A tiny black hand, barely an outline of a shadow, imprinted over her heart. And then she was gone.

The Leaders dispersed.

The crew changed shifts.

I knelt there staring at the empty spice container until Marxx's gruff voice cut through it all.

"About time you got those bodies off my deck. Work's not done yet. You're needed above." His boots clomped steadily toward the closest staircase up to the quarterdeck. *What now?* I rose to follow him, my knees aching in protest. *I have patients to tend to and dinner to eat ... will anyone think to feed Daria?* I shook my head and sighed. This was not how I wanted Drax's release to happen.

A clanking echoed through the air. I hurried the last few steps to the quarterdeck and watched as Jippon swung a sledgehammer one last time—nailing Drax's shackles to the boards of the deck by the map table. This wasn't a *release*, just a different form of incarceration. The Talian shipbuilder finished flipping through the leather-bound Journal and tossed it to the table.

"Useless. Absolutely useless," he said, crossing his arms.

"Sister Venra—" The Magistrate began.

"Satie," Drax countered.

Delenon coughed then continued, "The Sister said it didn't matter. That you'd memorized his writings."

"Lucky for you *she* wasn't stretching the truth for my release." He eyed the length of his chains then looked back at the three men left before him.

"I read that book too, cover to cover. Other than a compass, nothing explained about how to sail without stars," Marxx snapped.

"And that's exactly what we need." Drax narrowed his eyes at Marxx.

"Is that all you've got? We don't have one. Might as well toss both you and Daria overboard." Neither Tony nor Delenon openly disagreed with the Captain.

"I wouldn't put it past the Kronik to set you adrift with just enough hope to imagine you starving to death trapped in the White and Navy Seas without any hope of regaining your bearings."

Marxx scowled.

Delenon held up a hand to Marxx and, after a quick glance at Tony, said, "We've looked everywhere. Is there no other way?"

Marxx spat then gave me the evil eye. I stared right back at him, face blank but curious.

"That's why I asked you to bring Sister Satie along. She knows why."

I do? All four men stared at me. Then I realised what he meant.

"Drax knows how to make one, don't you?"

He gave me a half-smile before the others turned back to face him. "That I do. And it's the only way you'll ever be certain about what direction you're travellin' in. Satie, my dear, here's what I need."

I knocked on the open door of the sail hold before popping my head inside. Matty swayed back and forth in her make-shift hammock, curled into a tight ball. Eight others, who couldn't stomach being below deck or staying in enclosed spaces for long, sat on crates or folded sailcloth. Most of the spare rope and patching supplies were shoved into the point of the bow. The only reason the door actually remained on the hinges was in case the storms returned.

"Hey Matty, how are you doin'?" Both of her hands massaged her belly. I had yet to ask about her birth plans since Eena's *parting*. I just couldn't bring myself to step fully into the nurse's role. If Farrah … but even she could no longer help, and had certainly been a better assistant than me.

"I'm just glad the bodies—I mean, the souls have been released." She gave me a sad smile.

"I understand. The smell was getting to everyone. Sorry for the delay, and for being confined in here until I found a way. I hope it hasn't been too difficult."

"Some times are worse than others. I haven't fought off waves of nausea like this since my first trimester. But don't you worry. I'm better than I thought I'd be. You're here early."

"Kind of an unofficial visit, really. I was hoping to find one of those sturdy mending needles."

"Has a sail ripped?"

"I wouldn't doubt it after those storms. No, I'm working on a special project that's all."

"Here's the tin of needles," a man rattled a flat metal box attached by a small chain to a shelf board.

"I'll see you tomorrow, Matty. Thank you, sir." I made my way over and selected a needle slightly longer than my middle finger, nodded to the man, and hurried from the sail hold. The stark nature of the empty main deck hit me for the first time. Only those eight people survived that night— ten including the Sisters. Between the storm and the poisoning, we'd lost far too many lives.

Several of the crew fanned out from the stairs carrying lanterns, placing them about the ship in the gloom of yet another cloud-heavy night. I still had three more items to collect for Drax, but needed to stop by the Med-bay to check on my patients first. I crossed the deck in record time, the sail needle woven into the fabric of my half-apron.

I made a cursory assessment of my ten remaining poison victims. They were all going to make it, but needed to be kept well-hydrated. Tonight, I meant to try feeding them damp bread, but I might not get *any* supper at the rate I was going.

Settling down on my knees between Sister Megrhen and Sister Ellanir I checked their vitals. As of this morning, they'd fallen into a coma. I had no idea if that was good or bad. Eena had mentioned once that comas were the body's way of shutting down the non-essential systems to help target those that needed extra attention—but not everyone came out of them. I took ten precious minutes to moisten their faces and exposed skin before drizzling a tablespoon of verrin into their mouths, massaging their throats to encourage the swallow reflex.

After saying a quick prayer, I blessed each one with a two-finger tap to the eyelids and single to the nose before rushing out the door and down the stairs. The heady aroma of fresh bread and goat stew made me drag my feet as I stared at a mess of hungry crew. All four of Daria's helpers caused a whirlwind of activity filling bowls and mugs and portioning out morsels of bread. Without meaning to, I found my feet leading me over to the serving counter. I stood off to the side until the last five sailors were fed.

"Sister," Neeka sighed, wiping her brow with the back of her hand. "Two meals?"

"No, not yet. I'm running an errand, but I don't want to miss out. I'd like to give ten of my patients some bread tonight. I have my own supply of verrin, so don't worry about that. Also, I'll need *three* meals. Daria ..."

Neeka's eyes glazed over briefly before she blinked the tears away and nodded. She slid me a meal with some bread and a half a cup of water.

"I'll keep the rest aside for when you get back. We'll be here a while yet cleaning up."

I gave her a grim smile, collected the meal, and then disappeared down to the cargo hold. I balked at the sight of several goats suspended from the rafters, bleeding out. Only three remained alive. Most of the ganoo were fine as they managed to stay in their crates during the thrust of the storm. Rounding the back of the stairs, I inhaled sharply at the sight of our supplies: over half the crates and barrels had been knocked over and destroyed as the ship had tossed in the sea.

Those few crew who cleaned, salvaged what they could but much had been lost between the cracks in the floorboards, soaking in the bilge water. I breathed through my mouth to try and bypass the stench of the filthy water yet to be pumped out, and headed to the stern. Most of the prison wall also remained intact. It, like the coops, must have been fastened together and then anchored to both the rafters and the floor.

I slipped around the edge of the wall then froze. Daria sat where Drax had, only she didn't face the hull with her back to me as he used to. She stared right at me—no, through me. Her dishevelled hair framed red-rimmed eyes and rounded shoulders. I stepped forward, the bowl held out, but no words got past the lump in my throat. I wanted to stay, even just to sit in silence, but I had a mission to complete and hungry patients to feed. Daria, however disillusioned, was still capable of feeding herself. Still, my heart ached for this poor woman as I set the bowl down on a crate, turned and hurried away.

A stack of pails, once used for fetching grain, dried fruit, and salted or smoked meats, leaned to one side as if daring gravity to topple it. I pulled one from the top; the rest, miraculously, didn't fall. I had two items left to find.

Walking the sparse rows of crates and barrels, I tried to figure out where on this ship I might find a magnet. I mean, why would a ship this size need magnets? Was there even one on board? And without even realizing it, I aimlessly looked about at the cargo listening to the sharp clap of my shoes against the floorboards. Eventually, I found myself staring at one of only three barrels of verrin left untouched by the storm. And I couldn't look away. Finally, I stopped focusing on where to find a magnet and blinked myself back to the here and now.

Why am I standing in front of a verrin barrel?

And then I saw what I was looking at: the cork!

But I can't take this one.

There were other barrels ...

I whipped around and scanned the rest of the cargo hold. I couldn't take a cork from a sealed water barrel either, but ... Hurrying back to the pile of debris from the smashed crates, I dropped to my knees and riffled through the split wood, half boxes, and shattered barrels. A splinter jammed up under my nail.

"Ouch!" I snatched my hand away and waved it about even as I continued shoving aside what could only now be used as firewood. But no matter where I searched, I found only large chunks of broken wood. *There has to be one! One! That's all I ask.* Then, at the very bottom of the pile amidst iron hinges and nails, I found *five*. I laughed out loud and grabbed the one with the largest diameter, shoving it into my apron.

The once neat refuse pile now spread over twice the ground it had before. But there was no time to be polite and fix the mess. My stomach growled. I placed a hand over it to ease my discomfort. I wasn't the only one who still needed to eat.

I sighed, "A magnet. Right." Who might need to use a magnet on a sailing ship?

The mechanic?

Skirting behind the bloody animal mess, past the bales of straw and hay, I made my way over to the rudder room. After cracking open five different parts boxes labelled "mechanical" I was still no closer to finding a magnet. I did, however, find the still. It was smaller than I'd expected, but it looked a lot like the water distillation devices up on the poop deck. Half a jug of liquid sat beneath the condensing unit. I made a mind to come back later to refill my spice jar.

My spice jar ... Med-bay ... That's it!

I scrambled from the rudder room and hurried back up two flights of stairs to the Med-bay, panting from the effort. Sliding around the metal work table, I went to the nearest cot and grabbed the clipboard from the foot of the bed. It released with a metallic scrape. Flipping the board over I found a thick round magnet. Maiming the simple piece of equipment, I pried the disk out with the blade of my scissors, left the clipboard on the table, and raced up two more flights to the quarterdeck.

I handed Tony the pail.

"Easy now, Sister. Catch your breath."

My stomach growled again. Daria's blank stare flashed foremost in my mind before the prone forms of Meg and Ella and all my other patients overwhelmed me. I leaned against the map table as a wave of light-headedness washed over. Then a wall of warmth along my left side grounded me—Drax. Marxx and Delenon just looked at me expectantly, one with kinder eyes than the other but both demanding results.

I pulled the remaining supplies from my apron just as Tony reappeared with a nearly full pail of distilled water. We all watched as Drax slid the magnet repeatedly down the length of the needle, fifty times one way, then flip and fifty times the other way. With each stroke, the muscles in my shoulders tensed, and the men leaned forward another half-inch until we were a ring of heads above the small table.

Drax worked the needle into the middle of the cork, piercing it so that it lay parallel to the top and bottom. Then, when he placed the needled-cork into the water, we all watched it bob and twist and shiver until it moved no more.

"There," Drax said. "Due north."

Satie

Playing Nurse

I tossed and turned on my cot in the Med-bay clutching to imperfect sleep. Part of me refused to let oblivion take me and yet I didn't want to give up trying. The clanging of pots and pans in the galley below startled me fully awake. I lay there, staring at the ceiling. Shift change would happen in an hour, just after sunrise.

Pushing myself up to sitting, I rubbed my face with both hands. Muscles I didn't know I had, ached and complained. I glanced at the clock on the wall—only two hours of sleep. Using the basin of cool saltwater, which acted as my dry-sink (no actual running water with pipes), I splashed my face and tried to wipe away my need for more sleep. After visiting our make-shift privy, and then washing my hands, I returned to check on my patients. Most were still asleep, but I could judge breath sounds and assess for fever without disturbing them.

As I sat down on the short wooden stool between Meg and Ella's beds, my glutes screamed at me. I rubbed them then shoved an extra, folded apron under my tush to try and pad the stool. Both women were bathed in sweat again, but they shivered. I didn't know whether to cover them up or strip them down. It had been like this all night.

Using the Med-bay's distilled water to wipe them down, some part of me still wondered if I was wasting rations on a lost cause. The other, usually stronger part of me held firm that no life was worth losing—a sentiment Eena would surely have agreed with. But the thought of Eena disappearing in the storm, of Farrah dying from the poisoned food, my Sisters on the brink, and all those lives lost to the seas made me close my eyes and drop my head back toward my shoulders. I had felt an incredible weight on my soul since that night, one I couldn't shake.

I inhaled several wavering breaths.

Stop keeping score.

But I couldn't. It seemed every small victory became overshadowed by a terrible tragedy. And so, knowing that I'd found a way to release the souls of the dead—a not so small victory—hovered like an anvil over my head as I waited for an even bigger disaster to befall us.

It took longer than usual to clear myself of these dark thoughts. The sun was about to rise and I needed to make the rest of my rounds—topside. With the down-turn the Sisters had taken, a full three days had passed since I last saw Matty.

After seeing my Sisters settled, I collected Eena's med-kit and headed above deck.

I didn't lift my eyes to the sky until I stepped free from one set of the quarterdeck's stairs—why bother? Clouds blocked out the night's sky for weeks.

But not anymore.

"It worked," I whispered, staring at the billions of twinkling stars above. For the first time in ten days, a pale red glow lined the horizon. The homemade compass got us through the storms.

I had to be quick.

I looked around but only saw Tony standing at the wheel. He nodded. I nodded back. Then he cocked his head to the side and motioned behind the map table. I walked over and found Drax lying on the deck, staring up at the sky.

"Hey," I said, kneeling beside him.

He didn't say anything.

"How are you doing?" I tried again.

He still didn't look at me but finally said, "It was worth it, just to see the stars again."

"Thank you for helping us." I eyed the chain snaking from his ankle over to the iron stop secured to the deck. "Although, this isn't what I had in mind when I asked them to free you."

"I know."

But he was still a Talian—the enemy—and they weren't going to let him forget that. I gave what I hoped was an encouraging smile but feared it came off more as a grimace, before lightly brushing his hand with mine and standing.

I went down the other set of steps just so I could take a look at the compass again. Such a simple design and yet, if you don't know how common items can make something extraordinary— life saving … Had Drax not been abandoned with us, we might never have sailed free of the White and Navy seas. I vaguely recalled learning about magnetism and its relation to compasses in my early education, but even that vague memory would not have surfaced without Drax.

The majority of the sailors worked above to lengthen the sails just enough to catch the moderate breeze blowing through. They didn't rush or holler at one another, just did what they knew would be their last efforts before breakfast.

In the shadowed half-light before dawn, the lanterns were nearly useless, being in need of a solar recharge. Still, enough light kept me from tripping over coils of rope as I made my way across the deck to the sail hold. Odd shadows near where the hull met the deck drew my attention, but I had to wonder if I really saw anything. My sleep-deprived brain had more than enough to handle without trying to see in the dark.

Warm oil-fuelled light puddled on the deck at the door to the sail hold. I gave a quick rap before walking in. A few lazy hands waved above the edge of their hammocks, but not Matty's. I hurried over to her spot and peered in.

Her face contorted in pain as she clutched her belly.

"Matty! What is it? Has your water broke?" I looked around for signs the baby was coming.

She let out a long, haggard breath. "No."

I felt her belly as Eena taught me. "The baby hasn't turned yet. Is it your back? I could mix you—"

"No. I think it's those hiccups, the *practice* contractions Eena told might happen. Baby's not due for another three weeks."

She might as well have said the baby wasn't due for another three days! Eena said first pregnancies tended to go long, but stress and malnutrition could lead to an early delivery. And while we'd only been struggling with meals since the storm, I knew Matty's appetite had dropped even as her stresses increased.

"How often are they coming?"

"Maybe once or twice an hour."

"Since when?"

"Uh … sometime after Zita set but well before Zerameteth.

"Are they coming regularly or—"

"No. That's why I think they're the practice ones."

"I'll make sure you get verrin today. We need to keep your hydration levels up. You are drinking for two, after all." I checked her pulse now that the contraction was over. Slightly high, but still within the normal range. She wasn't fevered, and all other signs were normal. "When the kitchen staff bring you breakfast, I'll be sure they know to give you a little extra."

She struggled to sit up. I helped by keeping the hammock steady; but then she got to her feet.

"Oh, no. You need to keep elevated. If you're getting the practice hicks I don't want to be tempting fate by having you walk around."

She looked at me with wide, pleading eyes. "But the sun's rising—and we can see it!" She held her hand out to me, wiggling her fingers ever so slightly as if to entice me to reach for them. "Satie," she whispered my birth name so only I could hear. "Please. This was the one thing Bex and I indulged in … our alone time together. Bring me to him. Let me have my time with him."

I reached out and took her hand. Pulling her close, I walked with her over to the railing beside the sail hold and we watched as the sun came up. It had been too long, even for me. Zola's fiery-red orb drew everyone's attention.

"Ow!" Matty reached sideways to swat at something by her ankle. Then her scream pierced the silence, echoed by shouts and cries from the crew change. I looked down as she stomped and shook her foot. A long, black eel fell from her ankle, lazily undulating its body across the moist deck. But as I crouched to inspect the bite mark on Matty's skin, it dawned on me that the deck should have been brown … instead hundreds, of black eels lay basking in the break of dawn.

Satie

Grasping at Straws

Scrambling back against the rail, Matty and I leaned back just far enough to raise our legs, balancing on our lower backs. I knew she wouldn't last long. The crews grabbed anything they could to push the wriggling black beasts back over the edge of the ship through the wash points, where swells and waves of water filtered back to the sea.

"NO! Catch them, you idiots!" Marxx's voice broke across the deck.

The man closest to us grabbed one with his hand, but it coiled around and bit him on the arm. He let go—it didn't. The man howled and ran at the hull, smacking the creature against the rail. It finally let go and lay there twitching. I signalled to Matty with a look that the deck below us was clear. First, I wrapped her ankle, then rushed over to the bleeding man. Pulling a clean rag from an apron pocket, I wrapped it around his arm double-time. But still, it wasn't fast enough.

The drops of blood at our feet called to the vicious fish.

"Matty! Back inside! In your hammock. Mister, move!" I pushed him along the rail toward mid-ship. *Are they poisonous?* I couldn't risk opening up the wrap to check his arm. *Gods, if they're poisonous and Matty is infected ...* "Are you feel—" The clang of multiple buckets crashing down made me jump. Marxx's crew contained as many of the eels as they could while Tony's crew cleared the remainder. Deep purple smears painted the deck as the crew killed as many as they saved. Marxx's men sat or pushed a foot down on the buckets to keep them from shifting. I turned back to the man before me and studied him: no sweats, clear eyes, no stumbling or shaking ...

"How are you feeling?" I asked.

"It hurts like bloody hell."

"More than usual?"

"What?"

"Is there any additional stinging, numbness, wooziness—"

"No. But it's deep."

I nodded, then tied the wrap tighter. He grunted and glared at me.

"Follow me back to Med-bay. You probably need stitches." We passed Marxx and Tony pacing the deck with more than a dozen crew stuck with down-turned buckets over trapped eels. I shook my head and wished them luck figuring that one out. I had a feeling I'd be getting more patients shortly.

Neeka, one of the kitchen staff, bumped against the door frame on her way in as the fourth bite victim headed back on deck for his shift. Neither apologized for getting in the other's way.

"Sister, I need your help."

She held her arm close to her chest. I pointed to the table and motioned for her to sit. "What happened?"

"I think I sprained it."

"Heavy pot?"

"Heavy man."

I looked her in the eyes.

"It's not that. He was thrown across one of the tables and landed on the serving counter just as I set out a couple more bowls."

I sighed. "Porridge again?"

She closed her eyes. "We don't know what else to make. We need Daria ..." But they couldn't have her, even if she wasn't locked in the hold.

"There must be someth—"

"There isn't. You've seen the hold. Over half our remaining supplies were lost during that storm, and the meat from the goats that went lame is still curing."

I felt her wrist for anything amiss before gently flexing her hand and rotating it. Neeka winced and gave a sharp intake of breath but nothing appeared broken. I worked on wrapping her wrist as another bite victim wandered in. They still hadn't figured out a way to put the eels into a barrel without causing more casualties. I nodded for the newcomer to pick a cot by the door.

As I fitted a sling around Neeka's shoulder and arm, she leaned in to my ear and whispered, "Please, Sister. Talk to her. Tony says the eels are poisonous and—"

"What do you mean, poisonous? None of the bites show—"

"To *eat*. If not prepared the right way."

"How does he know that?"

Neeka pursed her lips then spat, "The *Talian* told him."

"Doesn't he know how to cook them then?"

"No. But maybe Daria read that fishing guide ..." The same memory flashed to my mind: Daria's insistence on going fishing in the sharptooth waters. "Please. You're the only one she lets close to her."

"I'm the only one who doesn't blame her for poisoning the crew."

The surprise in Neeka's eyes showed her own fear and guilt. She looked away, then hopped down from the table and walked to the door. "Please ... It's only getting worse."

I finished chewing the last of my rubbery bread as I walked down into the hold carrying Daria's breakfast. Drax had been busy conferring with Marxx and Tony about navigational details, so I'd left his bowl on the deck. He had verified his concern about the eels though, based on comments Darius had made in his journal entries on the Purple Sea. So, we had a new source of food but no way to eat it. *Great. Just great.*

As I walked around the wall of crates trying to figure out what I could possibly say to a woman who was only alive because she promised me she wouldn't kill *herself*, I stopped short and gaped. There she sat, completely naked, on the same far crate she always did—that Drax always had. My gaze assessed the space in seconds, even as she ignored me: pants draped over the nearest crate, shirt over the next, underclothes and socks over the next two. I walked over and shifted her stockings to the crate with her under things—they were wet. Her wash bucket held some of the dirtiest water I'd ever seen. My heart spiked and my eyes widened for just a moment. *Don't say anything, Satie.* This was both potentially good *and* bad.

"Are you hungry, Daria?" I used her name because Eena had taught me that when dealing with people who were hurting, it helped create a connection however tenuous. I could only hope it worked for both kinds of hurt.

She didn't look at me or even move.

"I don't blame you. They're feeding this stuff to everyone."

Still no reaction. I set the bowl by her feet then crossed my ankle over the opposite knee and leaned my elbows on my leg.

"Neeka came in with a sprained wrist this morning. If the riot had gotten out of hand I might have needed to set her bones. I don't know how to do that, Daria."

Her eyes flicked to my face then back to the floor—No, to the chain keeping her from leaving this prison.

"We were attacked by eels today. The deck is stained purple from their blood. I had to stitch up six bite wounds—five of which Marxx caused by trying to save the things for food. But go figure, Darius' Journal says they're poisonous. They'll kill us if we prepare them wrong." I left that thought hanging in the air between us, careful not to mention that Drax supplied the information about the Journal.

I also knew I couldn't ask for her help the way Neeka wanted me to. That would only shut down all communication. Not that much happened between us anyway. Still, I knew the woman who'd risked her life to save me was in there somewhere. The dedicated wife. The loving mother.

"Hetly tried to cut one of the bludgeoned ones up on the prep counter."

She looked at me, gaze sharp, narrowed.

"No, the others wouldn't let him."

Her shoulders relaxed, and she let her focus wander to the high ceiling.

"Now, I know there's a certain type of fish the divers back home catch that only a few specialized chefs know how to prepare. I'm assuming it's the same situation with the eels."

Her lips flattened, and her eyes shifted back and forth as if reading something written on the beams above. I'd piqued her interest. A challenge?

"I'm going to ask around. See if anyone's eaten at one of those places." I moved to stand but Daria whipped her head around.

"Don't be daft. No one here could afford it."

"The Magistrate might have. He was asleep when the eels boarded. I'll ask him."

"Even if he did, he wouldn't have a clue how to prepare it."

I shrugged my shoulders and left to check on the still ... someone was still operating it. The catchment was empty again.

Satie

Three Trials

I scrambled through the dim lantern light over to Sister Meg. Her body spasmed and shook violently. Panicking, I threw myself across her. But she cracked her head against mine and kneed me in the gut. I let her go, crumpling to the floor beside her cot. A glance told me Ella lay quiet in her coma. A dark weight pulled at every part of me as I watched Meg writhe. I pressed a palm to my eye, trying to force back the tears. Drawing in shallow breaths, I fought against the insubstantial fog in my sleep-deprived brain ... searching for a prayer—something to end her suffering.

Somehow, forever crammed itself inside a minute until finally, Meg stilled. The sound of her gargled breath drove needles into my heart. I hurried to turn her head but it just lolled back again. Grabbing her hips instead, I worked my way up her body rotating her all the way up to her head. Drool slipped past a loose tongue, dripping long threads. I collapsed back onto the floor against the base of the table, my body jolting with silent sobs as I blinked back a crush of tears.

Through glassy eyes, I tried to focus on Ella instead: the rise and fall of her chest, her tousled hair, and smooth brow. I crawled over to check her vitals even though I knew nothing had changed. I needed the normalcy of the action, something logical and systematic to focus on. Then I checked Meg again before visiting the water closet, washing up, strapping my half-apron on, and grabbing the med-kit. It was almost sunrise, but not quite. I'd start my rounds with Drax again today.

As I walked across the quarterdeck to the long shadow behind the map table, the remaining starlight bathed the Talian lying on his back with his hands behind his head. I sat down by his feet and lifted his shackled ankle onto my lap.

"What's wrong?" he asked, still gazing up at the night's sky.

"Nothing. It's healing well, all things considered. I'll just change the—"

"No. What's wrong with you?"

"What makes you think something's wrong?" But even I could hear it in my voice. Still, he'd asked the question before I'd spoken.

"The sound of your walk, the line of your shoulders, and even"—he pushed up onto his elbows—"the feel of your touch."

My hand trembled until I gripped the gauze for a fresh bandage.

"So?" he drew out the word.

"So, what?"

He sat up and brushed my elbow with his fingertips before resting his hands in his lap. "What's going on? You haven't even whispered a prayer for me yet." He cocked his head to the side and narrowed his eyes. "It's the Sisters?"

I nodded. "Meg. She's not doing well. I—I keep second-guessing myself. I know there's no way Marxx will let them eat even if I manage to get them better. Every time I give either of them a drink of verrin I can't help but wonder who I'm potentially killing a month from now when we run out of our reserves …"

"Hey. We'll manage. By then we'll have landed and had time to look for more. Besides"—he cupped my chin with his fingers sending little waves of electricity through my body—"you have to focus on the here and now. Right now, they need you."

"There's so much I don't know. Eena only scratched the surface with what she imparted to us—me." I sighed, recalling the moment I knew Farrah wasn't sleeping anymore, and pulled away from his touch. He let his hand fall to his lap. I tucked away my supplies then stood up. As I passed the wheel, I nodded to the crewman monitoring it, surprised not to see Tony.

"I believe in you, Satie." Drax's words carried across the deck just as I reached the top of the stairs. I paused a moment before heading down to the main deck and across its expanse to the sail hold. A scream pierced the air seconds before several arms waved me into the small room.

"Has her water broke?" I asked, heading straight over to Matty.

"No. Not yet," a woman said, removing a cold compress from Matty's forehead before stepping away from her.

"How far apart are the contractions?"

"The last one was maybe half an hour ago, but before that it was a couple of hours."

"So, they're still erratic?"

Several *yeses* filled the cramped space.

"Can you give us some privacy? I'd like to see how far along she is."

The men and women who now resided in this small storage room left. Matty's breathing evened out as she inhaled deeper each time.

"Is it still the fake contractions?" she asked.

"I think so, but I want to be sure. Help me with your pants." Together, we managed to get them off, and I checked to see if she'd begun dilating. "No. Not yet. Someone just thinks you need the practice," I laughed, and helped her back into her clothes. Then I checked her belly. I caught sight of a small shrine Matty and her compatriots had put together in honour of the Sun Gods and felt both a jolt of pride and a stab of shame.

"Baby's turned now, so these practice ones could become real any time. Heartbeat's strong. I guess we should probably talk about the birthing plans you made with—"

"Sister. Sister!" Several voices crashed into the hold. I glanced at the door then back at Matty.

"Go," she said, waving me off. "We'll talk later."

I hurried outside. "What? What is it?" I asked. They parted before me to reveal the quarterdeck. An angry crowd gathered around the map table. My heart sunk. "No … NO!" Clutching the med-kit, I raced across the purple deck as red streaks of dawn pierced the early morning gloom.

The gang of bodies shifted and swayed as harsh laughter mingled with the hatred.

"—hands to yourself, White-y!"

Drax collapsed on his hands and knees.

"You've got no respect. Trying to taint our last Guardian?"

"A curse! You and the Kronik deserve to die!" A woman kicked him in the gut.

"A blight on this ship from the start!"

"You've angered the Sun Gods just being here, you—"

"STOP!" I shrieked, catapulting myself through the crowd as another punch caused Drax to spit blood before three different legs kicked at him for getting too close to the edge of the circle.

"Stop it, now!" Twisted faces filled with hate, sneered and spat at him like a carnival of horrors. "Back off! BACK! OFF!" I threw myself across Drax's crumpled form even as another hail of blows rained down on my back and side.

"It's the Sister!"

"The Sister! You hit the Sister!"

And just as they had twenty-six days ago, the enraged crew disappeared back to their jobs the instant someone laid a hand on me in anger. In their wake, a frowning Tony stalked across the deck. I rolled from Drax's back and landed on my hands and knees, winded.

"'Bout ... time ... you got ... here," I said. Drax just groaned.

"What the hell happened?" Tony demanded, dropping to his knees beside us. He looked around at the now dispersed crew.

I hugged my ribcage and tried to take shallow breaths. Drax was in no state to explain. That's when it smacked me in the face—I recoiled with the thought.

"Because of me ..."

"You?"

I looked down at Drax. "He touched my face when we were talking. One of the comments I heard—the man thought Drax crossed the line with me." I looked at Tony. "But he didn't. He was concerned about me." *That was more than just concern, Satie—or was I mistaken?*

"What were the other comments?" Tony ran a hand over his face before working to release the cuff from Drax's ankle.

"What?"

"You said *one of the comments* ... what were the others?"

"Oh, uh ... blaming him and the Kronik. Saying he's cursed the ship." I sighed. "He tried to save us by burning it down before the Kronik could trap us. You know he made the compass …"

"These people 've hated Talians fer a *very* long time. Most 've probably forgotten what you've *said* he's done, and t' others juss don' care. Come on." The old Shimug scooped the Talian up in his arms and brought him all the way down to the Med-bay for me.

"Will they be punished?" I asked as Tony made to leave.

"No."

"What? Why not?"

"Can ya say who hit 'im? Who hit you?"

I shook my head.

"I'll talk to 'em. I don' threaten like Marxx does, but I'll talk to 'em. Still, I'm not sure what good it'll do." And he left to get ready for the nearing shift change.

I blended some herbs Eena had shown me which helped with numbing pain; then added water to the mixture in a cup. Kneeling beside Drax's cot, I washed the blood from his face. He groaned when I touched the swelled areas around his eyes.

"Hey, sit up a bit, okay? I've got something to help with the pain." I brought the cup to his lips even as his silvery-white skin purpled. "I'll go down to the mess and get you cold water for a compress."

He coughed and set the mug on the floor. "Just don't bring me any of that slop they're serving. I don't think I could eat it anyway." He tried to laugh but inhaled sharply and held his ribs. *I'll have to bind them when I get back.*

I hurried along the corridor and down the stairs to the galley, only pausing long enough to grab a bowl of mush and some stale flatbread before flying down the stairs to the hold. Anger and frustration bubbled inside me, as echoes of complaints about the meal volleyed through the air. I inhaled sharply and wrapped an arm around my side—the pain fuelled the roil within.

Rounding the side of the prison wall, I slowed my steps. At least she wasn't naked today, though she still sat in Drax's spot. Not that she deserved to be here any more than he did. Her hands shook, body craving the liquor someone taught her to make. Too many thoughts fought for dominance in my head as I dropped the unappetizing meal on the crate beside her. She ignored it but looked at me.

"You're hurt."

"Another fight."

She glanced at the food. I wasn't about to dissuade her. Even with their prejudices, I didn't think those crew members would have beaten Drax if they hadn't already been on edge. We'd suffered a lot since setting sail, but until Daria gave up, at least having a home-cooked meal kept the feeling of family alive.

"Any words of advice I can give your protégés?"

"You mean, my usurpers."

"You were drinking on the job, Daria."

She narrowed her eyes at me, hearing the unspoken "it's your own fault". And then I broke my own rule …

"You're a great cook. We need you. The only thing holding this ship together was thought of a good meal. Now, we've got perfectly good fish that'll rot in the next day or two if we can't figure out how to prepare them—"

Daria launched to the end of her chain, snapping, "Don't you go chopping *my* head off, Sister. I'm not the reason the crew's rioting. You've been prancing around here from day one trying to help all the wrong people. It's *your* fault they're fighting, not mine."

I stared into her fevered eyes, livid, my mind fighting with itself:

Impossible! There's no way I'm the reason. I couldn't help everyone—my Observances …

Which you've clearly given up. Can you even call yourself a Sun Guardian?

I became a Guardian to help people and by working with Eena—

You could eat. You already had a job to do. Why didn't you do it?

But Meg and Ella …

Are dying. And you're just hiding behind the dead.

I did my job. I saved those souls—

You forgot about the living.

I turned and ran.

Satie

The Things that go Bump in the Night

I poked my head up, bringing my eyes level with the quarterdeck. Past the legs of the map table I caught sight of Drax lying on his back—eyes closed. I wasn't surprised since twilight was only half over. I was three hours early. Glancing up, I locked gazes with Tony. He stood at the wheel, actively on duty just as he'd been the last two nights since the incident. I wasn't necessarily checking up on him, more like making sure Drax was okay—maybe that was the same thing, but I didn't want to think too hard about it.

Slipping back down to the main deck, I walked toward the sail hold, my main reason for being awake at this hour. The scent of wet metal clung to the deck as I walked past the make-shift butcher block Hetly had set up for the eels. After cooling down from my confrontation with Daria, I spoke with the Magistrate about the situation. He mentioned there being a special technique the chefs of Darzeth used to make sure the meat of the fish didn't get contaminated, but that he'd never watched the process.

Then I remembered Daria yelling "don't you go chopping my head off" and realized that the poison likely came from the eel's central nervous system and the kitchen helpers just needed to experiment a little to determine where the largest chunks of meat were without hitting anything vital. They preserved the eels in a brine solution and experimented up here on deck. Last night we had eel stew. I could only hope they'd been working just as hard on "breakfast." But Daria had struck a chord—these people *were* being fed—I was the problem.

As I neared the small room under the forecastle, a deep, rich voice floated out beyond the open door.

"Yes, I do," the Magistrate answered a question I hadn't heard.

"But how can you be so certain?" A woman's voice asked.

"Because Captain Darius was. While it's true that neither he nor his crew ever set foot on the swell of land they saw in the distance, we know it exists. We know how to find it, and we're more than half-way there."

"But we were trapped in that storm for so long … there's no way we kept on track," a male voice persisted.

"Drax taught us how to make a compass."

"The Talian?"

"Yes. Between that key directional instrument and the star charts, we know for a fact that we're sailing in the right direction."

"That's good to hear," I said, walking in. Magistrate Delenon sat on a stool near the shrine, a perfect spot where he could see everyone and they could see him.

"Ah, I must be late for my shift." He stood and stretched, making the small room feel even smaller—but not in a bad way.

"No. I'm early tonight. Just checking in with Matty."

"Oh, good."

"Magistrate?"

"Yes, Quillis?" He turned to face the man who spoke.

"Will you be resuming your duties once we make landfall?"

"My … duties. Ah, yes. I see what you mean. Marxx makes an excellent Captain, and I'm grateful to him for stepping up to the challenge during my illness. He is, perhaps, more suited to making the hard calls out here. But life on land will require a somewhat different temperament, I think." He winked and turned to the door. "I'll leave you to it then and allow everyone some time to rest before dawn."

That temperament so suited to sailing was what had my Sisters hovering between life and death. I buried the thought and moved over to our mother-to-be. "How are you doing?" I pulled the stethoscope from my bag and searched for the baby's heartbeat.

"Haven't had a fake one for nearly a day now."

"Good. How's the swelling?" I checked her legs and ankles.

"The same. I'm trying to keep put, but I get restless around dawn and sneak out for a walk and some air."

I nodded. "Just don't overdo it." Her blood pressure was high, but not dangerously so; still, I felt it best to be cautious. "Are you eating?"

"Dinner was lovely, and the kitchen crew let me have extras." She smiled.

"But you're still avoiding breakfast?"

The smile disappeared. "Can't get that stuff past my lips. I'm drinking as much as they'll give me though—usually double rations."

"Good. Ask if they'll toast the bread. Might be easier to nibble on it throughout the morning."

As we talked, I tried to gauge her state of mind. She'd been less chatty of late and I wasn't the only one to notice. Likely she was missing her husband, her family, the closer it came time for the baby to be born. Eena warned about post-partum depression, but I had a feeling it was kicking in a little early. I gave Matty's belly a quick rub and then shifted over to check on Gina's sunburn. Now that the crew worked without the threat of rain, burns were becoming the norm again for the day shift.

"Here, take this salve and apply it when you're not working, as often as you can." I passed her a small, pocket-sized container. A sweet older man placed his hand on my arm and I turned to smile at him. It was a little early for our new ritual, but he was probably concerned I'd be busy later.

We knelt together and prayed to Mother Zola to care for all those souls so precious to him—those lost in the resistance and those not; even those on this ship who'd become his new family.

I left a short time later with a smile on my face and a spring in my step. At least, until I heard a bump and a thud across the deck. Using the dark to my advantage, I slipped over to the main mast and peered around its girth as a parade of men and women came down from the quarterdeck with chairs and mugs in their hands. When the last one disappeared down the stairs to the lower decks, I crept up to the quarterdeck, leaving my med-kit off to the side by the hull.

My gaze flicked over to Drax—still asleep. Delenon twisted around from his perch on the map table, the bright whites of his eyes expanding when he saw me. But it was the light spilling from the map room door under the poop deck that drew my attention. The Magistrate stood and walked toward it, even raised a hand … in warning? Caution maybe? But I ignored him and walked in unannounced.

The echo of faded laughter hovered over sparse circles of people, some standing, some kneeling. Dice rolled, hands slapped knees, and final bets slipped from sleep-weary tongues. Then a man at the narrow end of the room turned away from the only table and locked his gaze with mine. A cold feeling crept over my skin, needling up my bare arms. Slowly the others took note of the chill and slipped past me out the door until only Tony and I remained.

Neither of us walked toward the other; we just stood there staring at each other trying to read stray thoughts via contorting brow, mouth, and posture. That's when the smell hit me: the harsh, eye-watering fumes of that liquor Daria had secreted to me to help with the souls' transition. The same burning scent that clung to the mechanical room down in the hold where I'd found the ever-depleted still.

I gasped, "No ... Not you."

Confusion flashed across his face. He shifted, taking two steps forward, revealing a tin jug on the table behind him. My gaze flicked to it and then back to his face.

"Sister? We ain't doin' nothin' wrong here, now. 'S all carefully regulated and—"

"You taught her how to make it."

He cocked his head to the side then let his body swing around to look at the jug.

"We never stole good food, only what's rotted or tarnished by mould. Don't think we took—"

"You took her dignity."

"I took her pain away—for a few hours."

"Until a few became more, and more caused ..." I let the unspoken accusation hang in the air between us. And yet ... if he hadn't shown her how, my brain argued, I never would have found—but I refused to let it finish the thought. How could something ... someone ... be both a curse and a blessing?

"Now, that ain't fair. I didn't tip her hand. She did that herself. I didn't know she was skimmin' till I heard her singing at the top o' her lungs that day." He stepped closer, lifting his hands as if in supplication.

"And Drax. *This* is where you disappeared to when you were supposed to be on duty. You—"

I inhaled a shaky breath. I wanted to turn and report him to the Magistrate, but he already knew … and Marxx was probably in on it too, or at least suspected. This man whom I trusted in enough to organize a mutiny in favour of, who used words and reasoning with his crew instead of brute force and intimidation, had no one to be held accountable to. I'd been counting on him and Delenon, but now… now there was no hero to turn to. *Oh, Daria, you have no idea just how right you were.* I didn't have the right to lay blame at this, or any, man's feet. Had I done my job from the start, so much pain could have been avoided.

I dropped my eyes to the floor and whispered the Solemn Prayer as I turned and left.

Four hours later as Zola's warmth spread a radiance of crimson into the skies, the crews gathered on the main deck at the shift change after breakfast. Stationed on the forecastle, I raised my arms and sang the traditional *Welcoming* to Temple for the third morning in a row. My heart swelled as every man and woman on deck raised their voices to the heavens above.

I did not preach about my Sun God, Zerameteth. I did not recount the glories of our Sister Suns, Zola and Zita. And I most certainly did not condemn anyone for their misguided choices while on board this ship. We sang. We rejoiced. We focused on what we were thankful for, not what we'd lost. And each morning, my heart swelled with pride at subtle changes overtaking the crew.

On this particular morning, I threw my Luma into the Black Sea after our last prayer. Some people cheered, some clapped, some were down-right honest and said, "it's about time." I agreed. No longer could I be accused of not doing my job or "forgetting" about the living. This is what I was born to do.

Before I made my way down to the back of the rowing benches on the galley level, a meeting place for anyone who wanted to talk, a strange dark blip broke through the water off the port bow. I squinted, unsure if I actually saw what I thought I did. No, it wasn't land. But three more shadows rose up from the waters before crashing back into the black sea.

The Black Sea

Deeper Waters

Patches of what look, and feel, like black oil float in splotches across the surface of the water. We went out in the rowboat once but navigating through the oil slick was impossible, and the giant sea beast we speared capsized one of the boats. Dark footprints now mark beside long swaths of purple and black stains. Hauling the beast aboard was even a feat of team strength which left the side of the ship just as slick as the sea. Still, Cook was cautious and discovered that the creature's long arms were safe to eat.

Passing through five unique seas, I can't help but wonder what more might surprise us as we continue on our quest. After checking our stores in the hold, I've surmised we have about a week's worth of rations before we have to turn back. At least with the layer of black covering the water, those suffering from sea blindness after the storms have a few days' respite. I hope the waters of another sea might help wash away the black stain—not only of this sea, but of the losses we've suffered along the way.

Captain Darius

Satie

Spirit Flame

I dropped the moist cloth into the pail of water—freshwater. It was contradictory, seeing as how their bodies would be encompassed by the sea and not by fire; but this was tradition. I would not taint my Sisters' flesh with saltwater. They had devoted their lives as Sun Guardians and deserved every last attention to detail I could offer them—including their modesty.

Draping Sister Megrhen's bony arm across her breasts, I was careful not to bump the other arm—of whose hand lay strategically between her crossed thighs, just like Sister Ellanir's. Their long hair cascaded over their shoulders, offering a touch more modesty in these close quarters. Usually, only other Guardians ever saw committed bodies at close range. But this could not be a private ceremony. I had to include all those who'd survived into the Ceremony of Release. We'd set a new precedence with the storm and the poisoning victims, and to hide these two proud women away would mean admitting they were wrong, allowing dangerous thoughts to fully blossom.

"Sister Satie?"

I turned to the deep, masculine voice filtering in through the open doorway. The tip of his blue nose just in sight.

"Yes, we're ready now."

He and three other bearers walked in, heads down, eyes averted. I'd already warned them not to jostle the bodies too much. They'd listen.

As they collapsed the frame of each cot, securing the legs and lifting the stretcher-like form, I collected the necessary supplies into my apron, then paced my steps out into the hall and up the stairs. I couldn't be too far ahead, nor could I risk being a hindrance to their procession as they followed. Raising my arms high as I exited onto the main deck, my voice carried, singing first Zola's Prayer, for Meg and then Zita's for Ella.

A wide path wove amongst the survivors as they hummed, allowing my voice alone a chance to pay the respect owed these two great women. Passing the mainmast and curving toward the lower part of the hull's rail, I walked past the giant, black creature the fishing crew pulled from the waters only yesterday. Suspended by its bulbous head, a thick, ebony fluid dripped from somewhere in the middle of eight tentacle-like arms into several too-small buckets. My foot slid out from under me and I stumbled, landing harder than I expected. Of the nearly sixty people left on board, only a handful attempted to help me. Still, their "respectable distance" only meant I fell on my sensibilities that much faster. So much for a dignified service. Two of them set me back on my feet. I nodded and kept singing, wiping an oily substance on my apron from my hands.

My Sisters' bearers brought them to rest just before the lower rail, raising the stretchers on extended legs but not locking them in place. I gazed down not upon two forgotten and emaciated women, but two Guardians who had dedicated their lives to what they believed in, without compromise. Giving a blessing, I swept a circle over their hearts with the tips of my fingers before reaching for the Spirit Threads as the women of this vessel sang the Prayer for Death, and the men hummed—had they been male Guardians the opposite would have been true. I moistened the square of cloth with alcohol, first for Meg, then for Ella and then placed them over their hearts.

My hands shook. Tears streamed from my eyes. There was so much more I should have done—so much more I had yet to do to make them and our Divinity proud.

After a chorus of humming, the baritones in the group sang The Release as everyone else hummed. My heart both ached and soared as I struck the flint with my scissors and the Threads ignited in green and blue flame.

The bearers brought the stretchers to the rail and tilted them up.

I turned away—did not see them fall, nor hear them splash into the oil-spotted Black Sea. Instead, I raised my arms to speak with those assembled. A hush fell. I had difficulty seeing everyone. But the bearers noticed my concern and before I could say a word, they picked me up and stood me on the lower rail. I wobbled, arms still raised, but they held my legs fast. The realisation that only half of us remained since the Collection on the day of the Resistance needled my heart. I inhaled a shaky breath and lowered my arms to the shoulders of my bearers.

"If my Sisters have taught us anything, it's not to lose faith—not to lose hope. Here we stand, thirty days later, survivors. Their Observances were not their undoing, just as my breach of those same Observances will not be mine. We live … yes, LIVE! And we will only survive to find Darius' island if we remember to work together and honour our Gods by honouring ourselves.

"Don't let Guardian Megrhan and Guardian Ellanir's deaths be in vain. It was their sacred duty to connect us to our future, as well as our past, and remind us that no one person is more valuable than another. If we allow ourselves to believe that Prayer is only for the weak, then who will we turn to in our hour of need when there's no one left to offer a helping hand?"

I didn't want to get too preachy. It was bad enough several people kept sneaking looks at Marxx as he stood at the front of the quarterdeck beside Tony and Delenon.

"I invite you to join me now in one last song. Not for the dead, but for the living, for our future," and we sang the Solemn Prayer:

> *"May the Trinity's Light illuminate*
> *My soul and all its worth. Bring*
> *Guidance to the lost, strength*
> *To the weak, love to those forsaken.*
> *May the warmth of your rays*
> *Brighten the dark within and without,*
> *Uniting each soul with grace and wisdom."*

During the song's echo, as some voices dropped to hum and others continued to sing, I noticed several people in the crowd—specifically those on the forecastle—sniffing the air and glancing about. All I could smell was the inky oil draining from the sea creature and the residue on my hands from the liquor. Then a cry pierced the air and several people pointed out to sea. I swivelled on my perch to look behind me.

Dense black smoke rose from several oil patches on the water, near the ship ... and beneath the dark haze erupted a flash of orange as the *sea* caught fire!

"Marxx!" I yelled. He and Tony saw the danger and spurred both crews into action. Fire on the water was one thing, but a fire on board was another. We couldn't let that happen. But with double the number of people needed to perform jobs that had become second nature to the sailors, confusion quickly led to panic.

I jumped down and helped rally all unessential people down to the mess in case they were needed for rowing. But evening fell fast as Zita dipped beneath the horizon, leaving only little Zerameteth to light our way.

What happened? Why is the sea on fire? I just couldn't wrap my head around it.

After making a full circuit of the ship, as Marxx's crew flew above on the sails and Tony's went below to man the oars, I leaned back over the side of the low rail to watch the slow spread of the flames out across the water. Some morbid part of me looked for Meg and Ella's bodies, but even if they still floated on the surface, we'd long since travelled past their final resting place.

Then it struck me—the only way the oil patches on the Black Sea could have caught fire was because of *me*.

But the Spirit flames would have burned out before the bodies even touched the water. A flash, that's all, and release. Then I caught myself wiping my fingers on the side of my half-apron again. They still felt oily. And they were oily because I'd fallen. I glanced at the sea creature suspended over the deck by the forecastle and the over-full buckets which blessedly remained upright beneath.

The residue on my fingers must have transferred over to Meg and Ella... I gasped, holding my hands over my mouth, and not because I watched an oar extend and dip into the blazing waters below.

Satie

Enemy of my Enemy

Running past a myriad of crew hauling lines and adjusting sails, the scope and web of work being done brought me nothing but fear. The last time we were this frantic, the storms nearly devoured us. But how do you outrun the flame when it's you who's on fire?

I nearly fell headlong down the stairs but caught my balance on the Med-bay's door frame before pushing off along the corridor and down into the mess.

"Tony!" I screamed, rounding the passenger quarters to the back of the port oar-deck. "Tony, stop! The oar's on fire!" I fell into him as he turned toward me.

"What oar? I haven't given …" Steadying me, he then stalked the length of the oar-deck. "Whose is it?" he called.

"Ours, sir. It slipped. We tried—"

"It's on fire?" He leaned out the porthole to see for himself. "Meeka. It's crawling up the oar. Get some water on it!"

Two of his crew rushed forward with full buckets of sloshing seawater. I followed them down to the aft portion of the ship. They each took a porthole and chucked the water out. A fireball leapt up. Tony and the nearby crew backed away. When the flames died down he stuck his head back out, but not for long.

"No good! It's splashed the burning oil along the side! How do we put out the fire?"

"Drax!" I yelled, and scrambled back to mid-ship and then up, up, up to the quarterdeck. My lungs burned from overexertion. Flames licked up over the rail, threatening the sail lines. Several of the crew beat the fire with their shirts, which only became engulfed too. Nobody looked at the man waving his arm and holding his forehead in resignation. I ran over to him.

I pulled him toward me. His hands held the sides of my face—I couldn't read what his eyes were trying to tell me. "Do you know what to do? Did this happen to Darius?"

"Yes and no."

"What?"

"Darius knew about the black oily stuff floating on the sea. He never set it on fire though."

"I didn't know! I didn't know! Usually the flame burns out—" He pulled me into a brief, hard hug then held me at arm's length.

"They won't listen to me."

"You know what to do?"

"I have an idea. Don't know for sure."

I pulled away from him and stumbled over to Marxx who smacked the last of the flames from his sailor. My eyes skimmed over his skin—only first and second degree burns.

"Marxx. Marxx!"

He turned to me. "It better be damn important, Sister."

"Drax has an idea." I grabbed his wrist and yanked him to follow, stumbling at his resistance. He stood there staring with squinted eyes first at me, then over at Drax, then back to me again. I thought of the whirlpools in the turquoise sea, my mini-mutiny. I don't know if he read it in my eyes or on my face, but I knew it wasn't just Drax he didn't trust. What did I care? We needed answers. It was no use. I waved him away and ran back to Drax.

"What's your idea? I'll have to relay it to Tony."

"The black stuff is more like oil than anything else. If we can find something on board to neutralize it, we'll remove its capacity to burn."

"What in Xannia do we have on board that could do that?"

He ran his hands over his face and through his hair trying to force his brain to work harder. I knew he'd built this ship, studied Darius' travels, and likely oversaw the lists of supplies that a ship like this would need to carry—even if he hadn't been on board once the Kronik took over his museum.

"Salt," he said, dropping his hands. "The sodium crystals will act as an absorbent, effectively removing the oil from the equation. Helping snuff out the flames."

"Are you sure?"

"Yes, I'm sure. Now go!"

A loud clank shook the deck and resonated in the air between the shouts and cries of the crew. Drax and I spun around as Marxx slammed the heel of his boot against the mounting bracket of the shackles, knocking it free.

"Go on. I don't have the key to the cuff on me. If you can stop this, do it." Then he turned his back on us and returned to the crew.

Drax and I spared each other half a glance before I helped him collect the chain over one of his arms, and we sprinted down the stairs. A crash and a jolt, knocked me off my feet. I fell into him at the bottom of the risers. Heat radiated from his body—or was that me? Regaining our balance, we carried on.

Passing through the mess, I waved Tony away from the wildfire spreading along the oar-deck. Those brave enough were trying to bang it out using non-flammable stuff. I told him the plan. He sent six of his crew with us down to the hold.

"This way!" I yelled, and led everyone around behind the stairs to the sparse stores. "Check the casks across the front!" We split up and fanned out.

"Over here!" A woman called.

Only four barrels of coarse salt sat immediately below the back of the stair risers. With salting the eels recently, the cook team must have used a lot for their preservation.

"What do we do, Drax?" I held his free arm, feeling the flex and shift of his muscles. The crack and breaking of wood smashing made us all jump. We raced back around to the stables—it was a disaster. Smoke billowed from the maintenance room as ganoo tried to fly amongst broken fences and charging goats.

"Come on!" Drax yelled, running back to the salt. "You two take a cask to Tony. You four bring two up to Marxx. You need to get as much salt as possible on the source of the fire to trap the accelerant and choke off the flame. Sister … you're with me. Let's see how bad it is."

I nodded. We left the others to figure out how to move the heavy casks. I heard a set of rapid footfalls heading up the stairs—probably to get reinforcements.

I slipped on the straw as I tried to manoeuver around a charging goat and ducked to avoid panicked birds. I lost sight of Drax but knew he'd be close. Holding my shirt up over my nose and mouth, I crouched beneath the dark smoke and around the side of the crate wall. I staggered into the wall and fell to my knees, eyes wide and blinking. The constant drips from the leaks between the hull boards oozed black instead of clear water as flames engulfed the mechanism for the tiller.

A hulking form materialized on the other side of the long wall. In a break in the smoke, Drax's lean, shirtless body was not only covered in sweat and soot, but he'd wrapped the long chain still attached to his ankle up around his chest, under his arms, and around his neck in a wild pattern that held it in place and left his hands free as he breathed into the moist ball that was his shirt. He caught my eye and motioned his head. I slipped back to the other side of the wall, coughing. We met in the middle.

"What are we going to do?" I asked.

"Use the last barrel."

The last barrel. The kitchen staff would have none for the rest of the journey, but we'd be stuck at the bottom of the Black Sea if we didn't save the hull and the tiller.

"How did the fire get under the water?"

"Evasive manoeuvres. They must have crested a wave ..."

The jolt that knocked us from the quarterdeck stairs. I closed my eyes a moment, then nodded, and we raced back to the salt.

One partial barrel remained. Drax made sure it was sealed and then we tried to shove it over, shoulders to wood. It teetered and wobbled just as someone stormed down the stairs above us.

"Sister! Sister!"

I glanced at Drax before shouting, "Here! I'm over here!"

Delenon came whipping around the corner. "Thank the Gods!" He panted, holding his chest.

"Magistrate, we need your help with—"

"Can't. It's Matty."

Drax grabbed my elbow and kept me from collapsing.

"What about Matty?"

"The baby's coming. Hurry."

I looked at Drax and then past Delenon to the fire in the hull.

"Go. Go, Satie. I've got this." He backed away from the salt and moved across the hold.

"What? What are you talking about?" We had to save the ship. Fifty lives were more important than two ... But Meg and Ella's faces blurred my vision. Every life was important. I wiped my eyes with the back of my hand, pushing aside unwanted tears.

"I've. Got. This!" he yelled as he raced toward the prison. I followed him, but Delenon grabbed my arm.

"Sister, Matty needs—"

"We *have* to save the ship. Without it, we have nothing." I pulled away from him and he followed me. "One man can't move that barrel."

"What are you talking about?"

"*WE* have to help Drax!" The tears poured down my face—too many lives at stake. As we rounded the corner of the prison wall, Drax smashed a crowbar into a loosened shackle floor-plate. It crashed into the crate nearest Daria. She and Drax rose tall at the same moment, staring each other down. It felt like an eternity before she nodded, grabbed her chain and wound it around her torso.

The four of us raced back to the barrel, shoved it over, and lowered it carefully to the floor. Then Drax and Daria rolled it around to the stable-side of the stairs as Delenon and I cleared a path toward the black smoke.

At the nesting wall, Drax shouted, "Now GO, Satie. GO!" And I let Delenon pull me away from one disaster toward another.

As I breached the open air behind Delenon, the night's sky flared red and orange—not from a setting sun but *fire*. Stumbling along behind the Magistrate across the main deck, the crew worked within organized chaos trying to quench a sail fire on the mizzen mast.

"RELEASE IT!" Marxx waved his arms and the triangular sail fluttered away ablaze, igniting a nearby patch of oily Black Sea. The scent of burnt meat and a lump of dark shadows near the lower rail caught my attention: three people burned black lying crumpled like discarded garbage. I yanked my arm in Delenon's hold, turning to him with wide eyes.

"They're gone! Happened before I came to get you. Come on. Matty needs you."

I couldn't tear my eyes away from those charred remains, choking on the burnt scent and the black smoke—frightened at the growl in my stomach. A team of workers hauled the ropes for the rowboat through the pulleys raising two men and an empty salt barrel from over the side of the hull. My heart leapt when they gave a thumbs-up after releasing their burden just as Delenon steered me into the sail hold.

Cut off from the ensuing battle, I turned toward the laboured breathing and my patient.

"Status?" I surveyed the gore-laden hammock.

"Her water broke nearly twenty minutes ago. The bleeding started shortly after she tried to push with a contraction." Gina replied.

"When?"

"Maybe ten minutes ago?"

I nodded. *Meeka, not good.* I touched Matty's feverish forehead with my cool hand. Her eyes flickered up to my face even as she screamed with another contraction.

"I'm here now," I said as she gave a drawn-out whimper. "She needs cold water to bring her temperature down!" Someone left to find it, though I wasn't sure from where since any seawater would be contaminated.

"Release the foot of the hammock. Grab that stack of straw and form it under her like a chair. Make sure her feet are free."

Delenon and the remaining two residents worked as I checked Matty's belly. The baby was still head-down, but something was wrong. *What did Eena say, what did Eena say?* I grit my teeth and tried not to show my fear.

Matty's pulse raced faster than her breath as sweat ran down the sides of her face. I discarded her pants and Gina held a short length of sail cloth tented over Matty's legs for modesty. The light in here was dim and the tent didn't help matters. I knelt and checked Matty's cervix, wiping away what blood I could with her pant leg. The baby's head crowned but no more.

"Matty, on the next contraction I want you to push as hard as you can, okay?"

"Yeah," her voice wavered. I felt for her pulse again—it dropped!

"Here's some water from the kitchen. It's clean and cool." It was plunked down beside me. I motioned for Quillis and the other bystanders to leave. Delenon shifted to Matty's side and held her hand. Soaking the bottom of the pant leg, I carefully tried to clear as much blood as I could—but it just kept coming.

Matty tensed and screamed.

"PUSH!" I cried.

The baby didn't budge. Matty's scream turned into a shriek and she fell limp.

"What's going on, Sister?" Delenon asked when he saw my face. I shook my head. I didn't know. I just knew it wasn't supposed to be like this.

"Send someone for my med-kit."

He nodded and went outside. Gina shifted one hand over to Matty's, but her makeshift tent collapsed, blocking all light. I shoved it away, pulling it from her other hand. I heard a startled noise come from her but she wasn't my problem. I had to see what was happening.

"Matty? Matty can you hear me?"

"Mmm …" her weak voice confirmed my fear. I slapped her leg.

"Come on, Matty, stay with me. Get ready to push again."

"Mmm … AHH—" I looked up. She fainted!

"Matty! NO!"

More and more red seeped from around the baby's head. With all that blood it might be suffocating—I didn't know but it sounded logical. *What are you gonna do? What are you gonna do?* Delenon returned with my bag and placed it beside the pail of water.

"What happened? Is she okay?" He held her other hand, patting a damp kerchief over her forehead, then looked back at me.

"No. And neither is the baby." I shifted stuff around in the bag, then grunted and dumped the contents on the floor. *To meeka with sanitization!* I grabbed the scissors and held them out to Delenon.

"Cut open her shirt."

"But—"

"NOW!" I couldn't find it! I shook the bag and heard something shift in an inner pouch. Feeling around, I finally claimed it.

"Gina, wipe her belly clean." Again, we were far from sterile but I had no choice. With Matty's blood loss and her unconscious state, she couldn't push any more. I had to get this baby out!

I raised my scalpel. Gina gasped; Delenon tensed but nodded. I needed that. I'd seen birthing scars before, so I knew I had to aim low, but that's all I knew …

Placing the blade to her skin and puncturing her belly made my insides churn. The slim resistance and the give of her flesh made bile launch into the back of my throat. I couldn't swallow it, so I spit off to the side and kept going. Peeling back the layers of tissue I met another barrier. I had to go deeper. I inhaled three quick breaths then tried again, this time her stomach sagged.

"Here!" I handed the blade to Delenon then plunged my hands into Matty's womb and around her child … her very still child. Splinters of fear slashed my heart as I worked to bring the baby back out of the birthing canal. Gina and Delenon gasped as I pulled the small light-grey body out.

"Cut it off, Del. Do it now!"

I held the infant above Matty's stomach, unable to bring her closer. Delenon deftly grabbed the umbilical cord, severed it and unwound its length from the child's neck and chest. I pulled her close, cradling the limp body.

"Spread out the pants."

Gina froze, still holding Matty's hand, who was a mirror of her daughter's condition. Delenon sprang to action. I rested the baby on the cloth, cleared her mouth of blood and prayed, *Holy Trinity, guide me!*

PART III

Daria

Second Chances

The Gods-Forsaken goats wouldn't shut up, and there wasn't a bloody thing I could do about it. Not that I'd bother. The chain rattled as I shifted my leg to keep my foot from falling asleep. *Maybe this is it. Maybe this time the Nine Seas will kill us all. The Gods know I helped that along.* I let my head fall forward into my hands and crushed my knuckles into my eyes. *Hurry up and get it over with! Put me out of my misery...*

At the scrape of metal against wood, I raised my chin and opened my eyes—following the source of the sound. A moment later, Drax brushed around the corner of my prison, which had none to recently been his.

I scowled at the monster turned marionette.

"Ship's on fire. I need your help." Without waiting for an answer, he strode across the space in a blink and rammed a prybar under the metal shackle plate, gouging the wood. The acrid scent of smoke made me wrinkle my nose and spit the taste from my mouth.

With the nails mostly out of the board, standing tall on crooked, spindly legs, the Talian heaved the bar above his head and swung it down with a crash. The metal plate and nails smashed into the crate beside me.

I stood up, partly from the noise, partially because I wanted to kick his ass. But even as I stared into his eyes, I saw no malice, no anger like that first time ... or the time I rescued the Sister ... Every line of his body begged for help. I nodded. Just because I was ready to die, didn't mean the rest of the ship was.

Grabbing the length of chain still attached to my ankle, I wrapped it about my body like the Talian had. Even though I was mobile, the weight of the chain served to remind me—as I'm sure it did him—that I was still a prisoner. I caught sight of Sister Venra—I mean *Satie*. She looked different—scared but confident. A surge of mixed emotions battled within me: anger at her for trapping me down here; pride to see her come into her own; jealousy knowing that what she'd left behind weighed less on her than my losses on me; fatigue at the battle to come; and yet some glimpse at my old fortitude when it came to tackling a new challenge. We had a fire to put out and a ship to save. Perhaps I could redeem myself before the curse of the Nine Seas took me.

Sister Satie motioned to the barrel of salt. "We need to get it to the mechanical room. Help us get it on its side," she looked from me to Delenon and back. It took little time to get it down. The Talian and I pushed it across the warzone where the stables used to be as Satie and Delenon cleared debris and wayward animals.

At the ganoo nesting wall, the Talian shouted, "Now GO, Satie. GO!" And Delenon pulled her away. Perhaps to play nurse or to release the dead, I cared not. My world was now smoke and fire and... *salt?*

"Why do we have a barrel of salt and not a barrel of water?" I coughed and waved the black air billowing toward me.

"Oil-based fire. The salt will help soak up the oil and take away the accelerant for the flame. But you're right. The ship's made of wood …"

"Kitchen grease fires are managed by suffocating the flame—putting a pot or pan over it and cutting off the oxygen."

Our gazes locked.

"Why don't you—"

"Why don't I—" We spoke the same thought at the same time. Clearly, we needed both techniques to tackle this.

"Right. You shift those crates outta the way and I'll find some pots." I back-stepped then spun on my heels and ran for the stairs, dodging goats and frantic ganoo flapping around my head. Satie and Delenon were long gone. On the level above, the scene was no better. Spilled salt littered the planks as some crew tried to row and others tried to fight the smoke and flame. Tony turned and spotted me just as I whipped around the landing and passed the jumble of tables and chairs in the middle of the mess. Only two of the galley staff remained to protect the contents of the kitchen—food or otherwise. Neeka and Hetly linked arms and blocked the way, their eyes bright with alarm and glassy from the soot-filled air.

"Let me in!"

They didn't move.

I catapulted over the peninsula, chains rattling, limbs flailing.

"What are you doing?" Neeka shouted. Hetly cowered behind her. Tony strode up to the counter as I stood up.

"You should be using the larger iron pots. It's basically a grease fire," I chided, then squeezed her shoulders before moving her out of my way.

"What do you mean?" Tony asked, leaning over the counter.

I tossed him the two largest soup pots and pulled the biggest fryers down for myself. I quickly explained their purpose.

Neeka and Hetly unfroze, grabbed more pots and left for the upper decks. Tony tossed a "thanks" and a wink over his shoulder as he organized his chaos, and I raced back toward the enemy. Though, whether that was the fire or the man I couldn't have said.

Hurrying back into the mechanical room, my pan's clanged. The Talian looked up as he finished shifting the last crate out of the line of fire.

"No one else is with you?"

"Putting out their own fires or rowing the damn boat." I heaved over a deep-frying pan twice the size of his head and held up my matching one by the sturdy handle.

"Let's toss a bunch of salt on the hull first. It might help shrink the flames so that we can cover what's left with the pans."

I nodded. I'd been thinking pretty much the same thing. I filled my pan, squinted my eyes against the black smoke, and heat, then flung the salt at the fire. The Talian and I did it twice more. A pile of blackened salt collected under the tiller arm, but the flames got smaller!

Filling my pan again, I ran at the hull and slammed it over the lower portion of the flames—holding it in place to keep it from shifting and letting in more air. Drax mirrored me above and, between us, most of the flames were covered. A few determined tongues licked out from the sides and around the pan as the hull was rounded and the two married imperfectly.

The iron handle of the pan was an extension of the fryer's frame, allowing the heat to travel its length. Licks of orange flame wrapped around my exposed fists. I gritted my teeth to keep from crying out. Then I screamed, "Don't move it!" If we let the oxygen back in, it would only fuel the dying fire ... and it *was* dying—the flames were also frickin' hot.

As I felt the flesh on my hands pinch and then dissolve into a liquid flesh, I tossed my heat-seared face back and screeched at the top of my lungs. I thought I heard a man's scream too, but only the pain registered. *It's happening. I'm dying!* Tears sprang into my eyes, dissolving before they could fall as more and more black smoke and soot billowed out from beneath.

I don't know how long I stood there coughing and crying until only a strangled choking sound escaped my mouth and my legs finally gave out. I slid in slow-motion down the side of the blackened hull unable to let go of the handle, having seared its impression into my palms.

Some part of my brain registered a heavy clank, a salty drizzle of liquid from above hitting my upturned face and stinging my molten hands. The crack of wood splitting yanked me away from the cool darkness in my mind. I scrambled away from the hull just as Drax applied a sloppy layer of resin, straw, and sawdust to the weakened siding above.

The salty wet spray slowed, then stopped.

The handle slipped from my clawed hands.

I stumbled up onto shaky legs and rested my back against the crate wall. Drax moved deftly and surely, even with equally burned hands and arms. He knew how to care for this ship ... it was his after all, or so Satie claimed. The aching hollowness emptied my heart again. I wasn't needed anymore.

After staggering back across the mayhem of the stables and walking amongst a brood of ganoo pecking the floor, I dragged my feet back into the hall of my prison and laid down to die.

An eternity of pain later, several sets of footsteps smacked against the floorboards just beyond my mausoleum. The vibration of the floor against my cheek and ear made me cringe and pull into myself, chains rattling and pulling against me.

"Daria!" Satie cried. "Oh, Daria. What's happened?" A moment later, her small, strong hands touch my face and neck and arms. I sensed a warmth hovering over my damaged hands and opened my eyes when she whispered, "Daria," layered with such heartache and … hope?

I blinked as she helped me sit up, and the room came into focus. Delenon stood holding something by the entry, Drax looked at me over his shoulder. Then Satie's face hovered in front of mine, a look of concern marring her features.

"I'm going to touch your hands now, okay?"

I inhaled sharply and looked away. They were ruined, I knew it. I coughed and a tear squeezed out. The gods hadn't seen fit to grant me my wish.

Nowhere Satie touched felt incredibly painful, though she didn't linger in any one spot for long.

"Mostly second-degree burns, some first-degree. Based on Drax's story, I'd say the two of you fared much better than could've been expected." She sighed. "Daria. Daria, look at me."

I slowly turned back. Her eyes shone bright and the frown-lines had disappeared, though a trace of something like regret remained. She nodded toward my hands. I let my eyes track down.

My heart jumped a little. She was right. Some scabbing but mostly bright pink or red pinched skin. I turned my claw-frozen hands over to look at my palms. A wide, red line coloured each palm. No gore-laden, skin-blackened stumps, just a pair of long-abused hands.

A baby hiccupped and cried out. A spear of ache pierced my heart as I whipped my head toward the sound and stared at the bundle in Delenon's arms.

Satie stood and walked over to the man with the child. He slid the small bundle into her waiting arms, then she turned … and smiled at me. I sat up straight, never taking my gaze from the pale-grey infant. Satie knelt beside me and held the wailing child to my chest. My arms automatically cradled the babe who could have easily passed as my own, were she two shades darker.

"Her mother … you remember Matty?"

I nodded as I took in every perfect little feature and tiny ribbon of red colith.

"I couldn't save her, but I did revive her daughter."

I looked Satie in the eye, a million questions buzzing but none reaching my lips.

"She needs a mom. And she's hungry."

I shifted my gaze to Delenon, redemption written all over his face. Dare I believe it possible?

"She's mine?"

"She's yours."

The Red Sea

Distant Costal,
Cook is laid up in the Mad-bay after tasting the
red seaweed that grows in vast clumps just beneath
the waves. His assistant did not fare so well when
he tried the fish we caught. Unlike the eels from
the Purple Sea, even these flesh is poisonous. Food
has been simple this past week and will continue to
be so as long as Cook remains unwell.
We are not so brazen to assume that with poisonous
seaweed and marine life, that the water is not
contaminated somehow. Cook assures me that we
have enough fresh water reserves for another week,
but after that we'll need rain, or a new sea to break
our drought.
I've instructed the men to eat simply and not
overwork themselves. The less they sweat, the less
water and worrin' they'll need. Most days, little
attention is paid to the sails and we only row if
eight hours pass without a breeze.
Through the scope, the red-brown hue of the weeds
never breaks or falters. If we can't make it through
this stretch, we might not make it at all. This is
truly a sea of death. Perhaps I should rename it the
Dead Sea.
Captain Darius

Satie

Point of No Return

I slammed the Journal shut and stared where the leather spine lay against the weathered wood of the map table. What little remained of Darius' words answered nothing as the term "Dead Sea" repeated over and over in my mind.

Loose strands of hair grazed my jawline as the rest of the black mass remained poorly tied in a knot at the back of my head. It was at that awkward, in-between stage. I shoved it away from my face, behind my ears, and looked around. Drax, now chainless, helped a team of sewers edge the newly-cut mizzen sail as Tony oversaw the work. The steady tromp of the Quartermaster's boots on the deck echoed the endless ticking of a clock with no hour hand. My gaze latched onto the steady shift of Drax's shoulder blades under the pull of his borrowed t-shirt. I saw, in my mind's eye, each ridge of twisted flesh criss-crossing his back beneath.

I blinked, and the raised material flattened. My hands shook at the memory of washing his body all those weeks ago. Shaking my head, I turned as two more crew members brought up pieces of the still from the mechanical room to the poop deck. The chaos from the Black Sea fires saw the water distillation devices trampled and dismantled for parts—to snuff out smaller flames. The two workers both had bright burns on their arms and bandages over fingers or palms. No one was spared, especially not the dead.

I looked up into the clear blue sky and squinted to see each of our suns. My gut twisted with the half-formed thought, *I'm all that's left* ... These people needed spiritual guidance but the pedestal I now wobbled on refused to steady or diminish. I wanted to help people, not feed them false hope in exchange for blind reverence.

The clatter of toppled buckets broke the usual creaking of the ship and flutter of the sails. It hadn't rained since the White Sea, but Marxx insisted on placing empty buckets everywhere, just in case the thin clouds above turned dark. Darius wrote about the drought ... but he'd been prepared, mostly.

Marxx whistled. As Delenon climbed the quarterdeck's stairs, Drax set down his needle, and Marxx and the men joined Tony at the wheel. I opened the Journal to a random, ink-streaked and faded page. Drax's gaze held mine a second longer than was comfortable. I stared at the nearly blank parchment in my hands, and turned the page. Tony signalled to a female crew member who shimmied down the woven ropes and took his place at the helm.

I grabbed the Journal and sat on the poop deck stairs, the nearly empty book open on my raised knees. Drax and Delenon went inside the map room to retrieve several charts. I felt the burn of Drax's eyes on the top my head as he came back out. My cheeks flushed. He knew what I was doing—I wanted to hear their conversation.

The men spread the maps out over the table, fussing about which one to look at first. Drax relented and let the captain pull rank.

"You're sure?" Marxx asked Drax, picking up from some previous conversation.

"Yes. Darius was clear. It took about a week to cross the Red Sea."

"And we've been sailing it for two days." Tony stated the obvious.

"It's bad. Do we turn around and go back to the Navy Sea? Restock and then try again? The fires—" Delenon started, but Marxx cut him off.

"Then we'd have been out here for four days with nothing to show for it, and had we kept on course we'd be in clean water within another two days anyway."

"There's almost nothing left. We haven't had a drop of verrin in over a week and there isn't enough water to keep us alive for those two extra days." Drax pointed out.

"And if we go back, we'll have no food. No one will risk the Black Sea for another meal, and the choppy waters of the Navy Sea aren't ideal for the small rowboat. It was a fluke we caught the creature we did."

"But we can survive without food for a week."

The men argued back and forth. At one point, Delenon suggested altering course on the diagonal, but that was shot down unanimously since it was a complete unknown. They circled around the same points, no one gaining ground and no one willing to concede. I'd wasted enough time spying, so I returned Darius' Journal to the map room.

The lingering scent of alcohol and body odour made me gag. Still, I couldn't deny the fact that the nightly Gambler's Den helped stave off the stir-crazies. The Sun Gods didn't care what people did in their spare time—they welcomed every soul home again. Hell was an idea created by a storyteller, not a Guardian. No one was born "bad", they were shaped that way by who and what they were exposed to—their choices. I'd finally made peace with that in my heart, if not my head; he was a good man, even if he made poor decisions sometimes.

Walking back down the steps to the Med-bay I couldn't help but wonder how many times I'd gone up and down them over the past thirty-two days … how many more times I'd do exactly that before we found Darius' island.

"How is everyone?" I asked Reena, my new part-time assistant. She'd wrenched her shoulder adjusting the fullness of the sail on the mainmast a couple of days ago and refused to take it easy while it healed. The two crews were down to a skeleton team of men and women, so she was anxious to return to duty. Helping me, at least, kept her arm immobilized, but her mind engaged.

"I'm worried about Lind. He's stopped eating and refuses to take more than his regular share of water." She shimmied around the metal table and stood with her good hand on her hip. I pinched my lips together and frowned. He wasn't the only one who thought like that … and they both died yesterday.

"Did you explain about the dehydration, recovery—"

"Yeah. I even mentioned that with Ginnee and Red passing we had … well, a small surplus."

I nodded. She said it, but I knew she didn't believe it. She'd gone to get our share of the water supplies this morning and knew it was a lie. Still, one could hope it might rain and change all that.

"Keep trying. He might be losing track of time, and you could convince him to take extra between rounds. Just make sure it looks like you're making the rounds first. He's perceptive. I'll be back up in a little while. Send a runner if you need me."

She gave me a sad smile and then returned to monitoring our patients. Of the seven, five suffered from dehydration, and there was only so much water could do to help. We needed verrin. *We need this madness to end.*

Down in the mess, no one sat at the tables and few rested in the general quarters waiting for their next meal and the shift change. Daria stood with three of her helpers around the serving counter—the fourth lay upstairs in Med-bay recovering from severe burns. Baby Teena, named after Matty—Mateena—slept silently against Daria's breast, wrapped in a scrape of sail fabric bunting-style.

"It's simple, doesn't need yeast, and uses very little salt," she said.

They nodded, knowing they had only what salt didn't absorb the oil from the Black Sea fires. Half a barrel had been collected, so it had to last.

"We'll use the saved goat fat to replace the oil, and mix our grains in different combinations with an alternate spice each time to give the impression of something new to eat." During her absence, the kitchen staff had kept everyone fed, but the lack of variety made many of the crew unruly. Daria's knowledge of working with reduced supplies and interchanging ingredients calmed both hungry bellies and frustrated constitutions.

"Keep each portion of flatbread wrapped in cloth until you're ready to serve. Only put one source of protein in each wrap at each meal. Again, this will spread out our options ..."

I turned the corner to the oar-deck and nearly tripped over my own two feet. More than a dozen men and women sat in silence waiting for a Sitting. *Should I do a Temple service? No.* I knew what they were here for and would not be satisfied with generalities. They'd come for a Sitting, and that's what they'd get.

I pushed stray strands of hair from my face, squared my shoulders, and whispered a silent prayer to Zerameteth for guidance as I smiled and took my place at the back of the oardeck where it met the wall of the sleeping quarters.

As the last person slid onto the bench beside me, the clatter of pans and sizzle of food in the galley only served to remind me just how long this Sitting had taken. I smiled at the older woman who turned to face me, a keen gaze marking an even sharper mind.

"Welcome, sister," I said.

She nodded and closed her eyes as I held her calloused hands in mine and spoke the Prayer for Guidance, "... Let wisdom rule my heart, patience guide my soul, and truth breathe life into deed..."

We sat, eyes shut, for some time. The weight of the afternoon drawing my shoulders and the corners of my mouth down. She stirred, and we looked up. A glassy film shrouded her eyes. I had seen this look before in other eyes, and not just today.

"You miss them."

She gave a small smile.

"But they live and miss you too."

Her eyes cleared, as if asking how I knew this.

"They weren't part of the Resistance, right? You chose to fight alone, fight for their chance at a normal life."

"I felt it was my duty. My husband disappeared after protesting the purchase of our land. He was not hiding in the Underground—just gone. Our children started asking questions. Our grandchildren..."

"The Kronik does not punish those who follow, only those who break free."

She nodded, knowing the truth of my words, just needing to hear them spoken aloud. As long as they obeyed the rule of the land, they'd be fine.

"The captain isn't speaking to us. He looks more sullen and angry every day. What is happening, All Mother?" A spike of electricity coursed down my spine at the ancient name, spoken not for the first time that day. I was a mere "Sister" no more. I was simply the only one among us who knew all the prayers and had taken the vows—broken or not.

I could not lie to this woman, and yet I had to keep the captain's confidence. *How much can I say?* I asked myself multiple times with each Sitting. I'd mutinied against Marxx once before, but somehow, I knew if I did it again I'd be made an example of and risked causing a riot with the Followers of Light on the crew, those who believed and practiced the ancient ways.

"These waters are dangerous and we must be careful. The journey is long and so, the Cook has been forgiven in order to help us survive these trials. The Talian has redeemed his race by giving us a clear path to follow, and you and the other crew members work tirelessly to keep us sailing true. Do not forget the good. For it's when we lose hope that all is lost. As long as the suns rise, so too shall we."

It was a variation of what I'd said all day, but I wasn't so sure I believed it anymore. The more often we tell ourselves a thing, the more we question its authenticity. Some Followers asked if the Gods had spoken to me … thankfully, this woman did not—just squeezed my hands, said "peace" and left to join the line of hungry crew. I looked down at my folded hands, resting on the bench.

How do you tell someone, a Follower especially, that you've never heard the Gods speak—at least not directly? I'd been taught to read and interpret signs, become a student of life … to ask for guidance but never demand it. And through my own interpretations, I would know what I needed in order to help keep the old ways alive.

But no matter how hard I tried, I *didn't* know. No matter how many questions were asked, I gave no answers, not really.

Familiar strong hands massaged a radiating warmth into the tight muscles where my neck met my shoulders. Edged with a tingling sensation, the calm spreading through my limbs and into my mind threatened to erase reality. The mental strain to pull away nearly brought me to my knees. I wavered and leaned against the wall to catch my breath before turning to look at him.

I should have just left. My knees buckled. Drax leapt over the bench and gripped my elbow to keep me from falling. A sizzling jolt from his touch electrified my sensibilities—I suppressed a gasp and shook off his hand. I tried to explain everything in a look, because I didn't trust myself to speak, then hurried away.

Tears of confusion streaked my cheeks as I descended to the cargo hold. *I'm not supposed to feel this way! What's wrong with me?* Pushing the tears from my eyes, I blindly raced past the few remaining barrels and crates until I passed the dark, looming wall of the prison and collapsed in the straw by the half-ring of boxes. *Breathe. Just breathe, Satie.* My hands trembled as I released long, shaky breaths.

"Satie …"

I stiffened even as the sound of his voice melted hidden places inside me. He walked over and sat before me, his back against the nearest crate, just inches from my knees.

"I'm confused. Am I misreading you?"

I half-laughed, half-sighed. "I have no idea what you're reading because I'm just as confused. What I'm feeling ... I shouldn't be. My vows—"

"Are not relevant here."

I gave him a sharp look.

He sighed and leaned his wrists over raised knees. "You're recreating what it means to be a Guardian. Just because you agreed to something doesn't mean you can't change your mind ... or the rules for that matter."

I sat up straight and frowned. "Nonsense. I'm a Guardian. I'm the only Guardian now and my job has exploded. More than ever, I need to uphold *all* of my vows."

"Why?"

"What?"

"You heard me. Why? You've been making choices outside the known scope of Guardianship since the beginning. You told me so yourself—you became a Guardian to help others, to guide them and act as the voice of the gods. How is allowing yourself the capacity to love beyond your platonic vows stopping you from doing any of that?"

"You don't understand."

"No, I don't."

"Why do you care? You're a Talian for goodness sake."

"What's that supposed to mean?"

"I've read the old documents. I know I'll never be your Soul Mate. So why are you doing this?"

A sad smile tugged at his lips. "My wife died many years ago, and my son has likely taken over my practice now that I'm ... *gone.* Just because I've fulfilled that part of my destiny, doesn't mean I'm incapable, or will never love again. How could I not love you?"

A hot blush crept up the sides of my face and I looked down. He took hold of my chin and drew closer.

"You never once looked at me like the others did—like Talian scum. The colour of my skin, my culture, never once stopped you from being who you are or doing what you were meant to—*help people*. And if anyone needed help on this blasted barge, it was me. I'd given up."

He leaned in close, his fingers slipping along my jaw to cup the side of my head. I closed my eyes and leaned into the warmth, the strength.

His breath caressed my lips, "How can I not love the only person on this ship who sees me, for me?"

Soft lips cradled my own sending waves of hot electricity coursing through my body. *Gods! Could a person really feel this way?* But the conflicting ache of destroying my last link to the person I was before scrambling aboard this death trap, quakes my heart. I pushed him away and ran.

Daria

Lengths to Survive

He slammed his meaty fist down on the serving counter rattling the flatbread and eel skewers already set out. "Give me milk then!" The robust Jeridan demanded. Teena startled awake and cried. I rubbed her back as I watched him raise a flour-smeared black hand—remnants of dinner prep. Teena hiccupped, then curled her tiny face into my bosom and fell back asleep in her bunting wrap.

"What little we have is for baking. You want bread each day, yes?"

He scowled.

"Then take the water." I held the tin pitcher up.

"I'm not drinking that concentrated piss! You're insane!" He chucked his empty mug, and it clattered across the floor, landing by a bare foot beneath one of the tables. Those of the crew who weren't light-headed from dehydration, sat with one or more hands holding up their heads at the tables in the mess. Some chewed the poor excuse for dinner, others poked at it, nudging it around their plate. Few sat with a drink, and those who did eyed it warily.

The Jeridan man stormed off grumbling to himself. Hetly gave my shoulder a gentle bump with his and paired it with a sad smile. They'd figure it out eventually. I couldn't force them to stay alive. I breathed in Teena's new-born scent and let her presence calm my nerves before handing out the remaining plates of food.

I turned to Hetly and Neeka, "Can you and Kiian take care of clean up? I need to find Delenon." No one bothered to call him Magistrate anymore. We all hoped he'd reclaim the title one day, but as long as we remained at sea, there was only one man with the final say—and I needed to see him. Every day for the last four days I asked him the same question: will there be a course correction? And every day I got some version of a non-answer, and yet we seemed to keep sailing north across this blasted sea.

Satie called it the "Dead Sea." I supposed everyone did to themselves, but she actually said it aloud. I thought she would try to shield her followers from the severity of the situation, to pacify them—but no. She didn't pull her punches even though it was getting harder and harder to find something positive to say. Gods love her, she tried.

I couldn't help but shake my head at the gods. They'd seen fit to grant me both my wishes: to be with my child (close enough, all things considered), *and* to die. Fate had a cruel sense of humour. Wrapping my arms around Teena, I absorbed the shock of walking up two flights of stairs to the main deck. I had to know what lay ahead. I had to know just how much meeka I still had to wade through before I earned the right to raise this beautiful child.

Above, I caught sight of the backs of the top brass crowded around the port-side lower rail, and walked over. The faint humming of an all-too-familiar prayer lingered in the air. Of the forty-odd people still breathing on this ship, only seven stood in respect. The ten "fresh" crew members healthy enough to sail the ship were scattered among the rigging, teasing a few more knots from the paltry wind.

A splash brought my focus back as I joined Marxx, Tony, Delenon, Satie, Drax, Jip, Reena, and the newly deceased. My gaze drifted over to the make-shift memorial set into the corner near the bow, where the hull met the sail hold. Of all the hundreds of lives lost in the Resistance, only Matty's had pulled at the heartstrings of this dwindling community. Then Drax shifted, clearly uncomfortable. I followed his furtive glance over to Satie. Her eyes shifted back and forth and all around before settling on the body before her. Something was going on between those two.

I caught the distinct flash of blue flame and watched the strange, sooty handprint form on the dead guy's chest. They waited until the flame was completely out, then Jip and Reena lifted the stretcher—the fifth body in four days. Marxx grabbed the side of the frame.

"Wait."

Jip and Reena paused, the dead man's feet dangled over the lower rail. I never looked too close anymore—even if I didn't know names, every face from every person who was trapped on this Gods Forsaken barge remained locked in my memory. I didn't need a string of rope bracelets, kerchiefs folded to look like flowers, or etchings in wood to remind me—I fed these people.

"What?" Delenon asked even as Satie opened her mouth to speak.

"Look around. We've barely enough crew to keep the ship running." He turned his head toward me, his gaze piercing mine.

"Supplies are running low and more people are confined to their beds every day." He motioned with his head toward the deceased. "Why are we throwing away perfectly good meat?"

My heart leapt into my throat. I gagged. Satie and some of the others gasped. I looked away from him, from the man lying before me, but it didn't matter. Even out in the sea, I watched the blue skin of the woman already committed, float atop the Red Sea. Closer to the hull, swaths of poisonous weed and water sparkled in the late afternoon sunshine. I closed my eyes and tried to swallow.

"No," Satie whispered. No one else ever spoke outright against him. But then …

"No," Drax, Tony, and Delenon echoed stronger.

I opened my eyes. Marxx stood with his arms crossed, squinting at the group. I knew what had to be said, but I still couldn't swallow past the lump in my throat. When Marxx set his mind to something, he didn't back down.

"We're fine," I managed to push out. "Really. We don't need to desecrate the dead to survive."

"Is that so? Then why is this—" he waved his arms above the deceased—"a daily occurrence now?"

"We. Have. Enough. *Food.* What we don't have is clean water or verrin. That's why people are dying and feeling nauseous, unable to work. They're dehydrated, *not* starving. You need to decide if we turn around and go back to the Black Sea, where we can try to filter some clean water from the oil deposits, or keep going north and pray we get to the next sea sooner than later. It will have fresh water and more food."

"Not necessarily," Marxx countered.

"What do you mean?" Drax asked.

"I mean, the line between one sea and the next is not absolute. The contaminated water might mix farther than we'd anticipate into the clean stuff. We've got milk and that urine water, right? So we can stay hydrated. What we don't have is a guarantee that we'd be able to catch another giant oil fish in our weakened state or find something relatively uncontaminated moving forward. We risk dying out here if we keep going in circles. We're not going back. And since we can't be sure of what food is to come, it's only logical that we preserve our—"

"I said. We have. *Enough*. Marxx. We do. Drax, how long did it take Darius to cross the Red Sea?" I asked.

"About eight days, almost a week really. So, ten max."

"We have enough food for ten days. If we keep recycling our urine and filtering it through the distiller, we can survive up to another week just on water alone." I purposely left out the fact that verrin-shock could happen to anyone at any time, but eating a person wasn't going to solve that mess.

"We have no idea how long it'll take us to get anywhere, Daria." Not the answer I had come topside to learn. "If the wind dies down and we have to row, we'll have even more crew dropping like—"

The stretcher suddenly shifted and the body splashed into the sea. Jip and Reena's faces blanched as they dropped the stretcher. Everyone except Marxx jumped as it clattered on deck, and they rapidly professed not to have bumped the board. The rest of us looked just as surprised, or at least seemed to. Marxx waved us off and walked away.

I glanced at Satie. Her face remained blank, but her eyes sparkled more than usual.

The Rocky Sea

Shallow Waters

We're getting closer to somewhere. The sky still isn't reflecting any particular land mass on the horizon, but the size and the frequency of the large rocks and crags dotting this sea tell me water levels have dropped and land is near. We're still cautious about the water and aquatic life, since we've only just come into this sea and each destination has been gradual from one to the next, but any residual danger from the Red Sea should dissipate over the next day of sailing.

Morale is up and the crew are starting to talk and even laugh. Everyone is still cautious though, since running aground could happen at any time if the lookout doesn't have a keen eye or happens to be tired. We'll weigh anchor tonight so as not to risk ramming into any rocks, then in the morning we'll send the fishing crew out to see what we can find.

Medical issues remain the same: sunburns, dry and cracked skin, blisters, and the odd missing fingernail. Cook is back in the galley though and we'll all eat better for it.

Captain Darius

Satie

Science or Faith?

The last faint twinkle in the skies above washed away with the deep, red rays on the horizon turning indigo to purple. Just over a week had passed since the Black Sea fires, but my body refused to let me sleep in. Instead, I embraced Matty's morning ritual as I leaned against the rail overlooking the bow of the ship.

This morning I found myself thinking back to that first day when I'd hobbled along the rail to stretch out a cramped leg muscle. Who would have guessed about a pregnant woman getting caught up in the Resistance? I often wondered if she'd run a Junction Point or safe house like the Guardian's had at the Temple, was a getaway driver who got caught, or was simply in the wrong place at the wrong time when the Collection swept through the streets. I never did ask about her story, and she never told—she was too focused on living for the day to mourn the past for long.

She'd been so sure and happy. No one else shared a smile as genuine or inviting. I wish I'd spent less time worrying about what I couldn't change, what I was supposed to be doing, and just lived. *Then why don't you take your own advice?* I sighed and asked myself for the thousandth time, *what does it mean to be a Guardian?*

I closed my eyes and fell into the memory of that forbidden kiss … and yet, the very first vow I took as an initiate was to "wed none but the Gods above" and "love all equally." And I did, until… *But I can't. I'm the All Mother now.* I snapped my eyelids open and stared wide-eyed at the layered reds and blues blending with wispy clouds on the horizon. I couldn't justify potentially alienating the crew, Followers of the Light or not. They'd beaten him, for Gods' Sake, just for comforting me!

The wind tugged at the loose knot holding my hair back, flipping stray strands across my face, trying to bleed the anger and confusion from my soul. I squinted, but not because of my hair.

"A bird …" I whispered, seconds before the Lookout cried out.

"Rocks! Rocks off the starboard bow!"

Other voices echoed her call as the crew on deck climbed into the rigging to get a better look, and those just waking for the shift change stumbled up to the forecastle instead of down to the mess. Men and women jostled for the best positions on deck to avoid overloading the rigging. I swear, in under two minutes all forty-five Resistance survivors strained to catch sight of the Rocky Sea, gasping and crying at the simple sight of birds flying overhead and landing on the yardarms.

I moved away from the bowsprit into the crowd, placing my hand on a shoulder, the back of a neck, an arm, and even in another's hand with a firm squeeze—letting them know this was not a dream.

Thirty-six hours, just over a day later, as Zola's rays chased the last of the stars from the night's sky, Marxx's voice boomed "All Hands! All Hands on Deck!" down into the belly of the ship. I shut the cabinet doors and left off taking stock of the remaining medical supplies to join the night crew as they streamed up the stairs from the mess. The sight of tired but bright eyes joined happy smiles and fuelled the elation bouncing around in my heart.

Marxx and Tony shouted out instructions as we spilled out onto the main deck. Tony sent me to help wrangle the mainsail. Several crew members worked to unravel the ties from the posts at the base of the mainmast. A section of the large, smooth length of rope found its way into my hands and I helped adjust the fullness of the sail or the tilt—I really didn't know. I just did as I was told, working side-by-side with the men and woman of this crew, of my flock.

An enormous crag of brown rock split the pink and blue sky. Even as we skirted around it from a safe distance, my eyes feasted on the moss and lichen textures, the glistening damp layers below and the dry peaks above.

By the end of the second hour of manoeuvring through this rocky labyrinth, Daria disengaged from helping with the foremast and hurried across the deck to the stern and onto the poop deck. I tracked her progress out of the corner of my eye, holding firm when needed, pulling then releasing when directed. My hands ached from gripping the line for so long.

Daria hurried down the stairs to the lower decks with two full buckets of distilled urine-water straining each arm as baby Teena moved her head from side to side in her bunting wrap. Then, what felt like only a moment later, Daria raced back up again and poured *clear* water into the main chamber of the device. I looked over my shoulder and out past the lower rail to the sea beyond. No longer tinged red from poisonous algae, the light brown waters reflected the sand below and the rocks around us.

More and more people, Tony's crew actually, pulled away from their stations and rested or stumbled down to their quarters to sleep. Marxx's crew were into a groove now, and while the extra hands made light of the work, they showed no malice toward those who needed a break. Everything was under control now.

"This is it for me too," I said, nodding to the woman in front of me and the boy behind. They smiled and nodded back as I let go. My hands had stiffened into claws, and the air stung open wounds I hadn't realised were there. I leaned against the starboard rail and watched as Tony and Daria collected a few of his more resilient crew to haul the fishing nets from the rafters in the mess and lower the rowboats into the sea.

Marxx had his back to the whole operation, but I could tell from the set of his shoulders and stiff spine that he wasn't happy about the situation. Still, he didn't counter Tony's command, so he must have come to the same conclusion: time to restock.

With an ease away from this morning's urgency, and the lightness of spirit hope brings, several crew members broke into an old working song children often sang when jumping rope. In the span of time it took me to stop by the Med-bay to medicate and wrap my hands, when I returned topside, a portion of the crew worked together to heave a large net of fish on board as we passed close to yet another island crag.

But my smile slipped when I saw Drax scramble over the edge of the crow's nest and shimmy down the rigging. He signalled something to Tony who cupped his hands around his mouth and sounded the call for the other boat to return. When Drax reached Marxx, the Captain nodded and signalled to the crew. Sails were trimmed, and the ship gradually slowed from its steady pace toward salvation.

I climbed up onto the forecastle, where I'd stood only yesterday morning gazing out at a new sea, when minute by minute a wall of rock grew on the horizon. The closer it got, the more I found it grew in my stomach, as well as before my eyes, until we were close enough to see the breaks.

It wasn't a wall but a series of towering, oval-shaped rocks ringing our island. Marxx signalled the crew, who scrambled to roll up the sailcloth and tie it to the yardarms on each mast. Only the triangular mizzen remained to help if needed. All those of able body then hurried below, and the oars stabbed out from the belly of the ship.

We slunk ever closer to the mammoth ring of teeth-like stones set just wide enough for two ships to pass comfortably between each break. And then we hit a wall—but there was no wall!

I couldn't explain it. The ship kneeled and then bounced backward! I staggered and fell against the hull.

"Weigh anchor! Weigh anchor!" The crew took up Marxx's command, repeating it until the oars disappeared and a resounding splash signified the job was done.

Regaining my sea legs, I stood and stared between the two enormous boulders at ... *nothing*.

After tending to several bruised heads, knees, and shoulders with the only advice I could give: cold water to bring down the swelling and plenty of rest, which I knew no one would follow, I let my curiosity lead me back up to the quarterdeck.

Daria leaned against the wheel as she fed the baby, listening to the circle of arguing with a scowl lining her face. It wasn't my place to interrupt, so I stood beside her instead.

"There's no such thing as magic!" Marxx spat.

"He's right," Drax said. "There's a logical explanation for everything."

"Where is the logic in an invisible wall?" Reena countered.

"There wasn't anything in the Jour—" Delenon started.

"No. I told you. I memorised the damn book because I was the one who copied it out in the first place. He said they got as far as scoping the island from a distance, seeing the change in sea, and then turning around went home."

"Why would he turn the ship around if he needed supplies?" Jip asked.

"Who says he needed supplies?" Drax challenged.

"After a week on the Red Sea? Come on."

"They never lost their cargo in a storm. They never set their ship on fire. If any of those things happened, it was on the way back home, and there were no entries made after they left here. At least not in the Journal on display at the museum."

"I don't buy it. I think they got as far as we did and the Kronik just didn't clarify the whole story. Darius was the last man alive, for Gods' Sake!"

"Maybe he never lived long enough to translate his writings. It was all in code anyway."

That was news to me. Everyone else too, by the look of it— and that wasn't good.

"I think," Marxx intervened, "the Kronik never wanted us to know about what really happened, and I find it awfully coincidental that the only Talian on board this ship knows the contents of that Journal."

Drax's gaze shifted from face to face. I could see the realisation in the set of his features seconds before he held his hands up and shook his head. "Look, I don't want any trouble. All I'm saying is that we should take a closer look. There has to be a scientific reason why we can't pass between the rocks. Maybe when Darius told the Kronik what happened a century ago he was labelled as insane and the information was ignored. Maybe they thought the Gods were involved and didn't want to anger them. Goodness knows strange things have been happening with the planet's environment ever since. But that's beside the point." The faces staring back at him showed a growing awareness of just how significant his "off-hand" comment really was.

"Are you willing to lead the scouting party?" Tony asked.

"I am."

"Then I'll come with you. I know a couple of people who are just as interested in figuring this out. I'll see if they want to join us. That okay with you, Boss?" Tony asked.

Marxx waved him off before walking past us and leaning over the railing to the main deck, to glare at the monoliths guarding the island beyond. Drax glanced over at me, our gaze connecting for a micro-second, but it was enough. He was scared. We all were. It all came back to whether or not the people on this ship trusted a Talian, and it was no secret what side of the fence our Captain remained firmly planted on.

The cawing of sea birds drew our collective gazes skyward. Drax's lingered far longer than anyone else's as his head moved along with the soaring flow of the birds. His shoulder's stiffened just before he shook his hands out beside each leg. Then, with Marxx looking out over the main deck to the bow of the ship, Drax nabbed the corked needle from our water compass and pocketed it.

I turned and watched as he joined Tony by the port-side launch after the Night Quartermaster had collected four other crew members along the way. As Drax's body slowly disappeared down the side of the hull, my body twitched. At the splash-down, instinct propelled me from the quarterdeck, across the main, and launched me into the rigging. My palms burned as I climbed higher and higher, the width of the rope's weave becoming narrower and narrower.

My breath hitched in my throat. The wind buffeted me back and forth as I clung to the netting and waited for my heart to burst. Gritting my teeth, I kept looking up at that small basket and the woman who looked over the edge back at me.

Scrambling into the crow's nest, I clung first to the woman and then to the mast as even the smallest dip in the waves churned my stomach.

"Just take deep breaths, All Mother. Look straight ahead to the horizon and let your body find the rhythm. That's it."

Within a few minutes, I'd stabilised enough to lean against the side of the basket and search the sea for the small rowboat.

"There." The Lookout pointed and handed me the scope. She helped me dial in the magnifier as I watched Drax, Tony, and their crew try to breach the invisible wall. They crossed the entire span between the closest pair of rocks, getting as close as they could. Drax held a bucket at arm's length each time before rounding another set of towering boulders to try the opposite side. The nose of the small craft kept sweeping away from the rock several yards before they could touch it.

When the craft came back into view, I released a breath I hadn't realised I'd been holding. Drax worked fervently rubbing something small against the metal mooring bar on the side of the rowboat as Tony held his hands to collect the filings. Then Drax swapped with one of the other men and I caught sight of a large boat nail—they'd used the nail head to grind the metal down.

"What are you doing?" I asked aloud. Thankfully the Lookout ignored me.

Before I knew it, they were rowing back to the ship. I turned away from the drop, my stomach doing exactly that, and handed the spyglass back.

"How … how do I get down now?"

She smiled. "Don't look down."

I gave a breathy laugh. "Yeah, right. Easier said than done."

"Hold onto my arm, back up slowly—a little more. A little more." My heels touched the side of the basket. "Now, grab the edge. Look out at the birds flying, and swing a leg over." The way down was a lot harder than the way up had been. I noticed the sway of the rigging more and had difficulty finding the next foothold as they grew larger and larger the closer I got to the main deck. When my feet finally touched the upper rail of the hull, I thought I might wet myself. I didn't.

Two of the crew helped me to the deck and one walked with me a few steps until I found my equilibrium again. The rowboat dollies squealed and creaked as the crew hauled up the small craft with its six occupants. I paced myself, walking in time with Drax as he made his way over to the portside stairs. I climbed the starboard stairs and met him and Tony back on the quarterdeck.

Daria, Reena, Jip, Delenon, and even Marxx waited for the verdict. But it was Tony who spoke first.

"I wouldn't 've believed it if I hadn't seen it myself. I'm juss sayin', keep an open mind here." Then he nodded to Drax who replaced the corked needle back into the bucket of water on the map table before us. Marxx scowled.

"I needed it to test a theory."

"And that is?" Marxx leaned forward with both hands on the table and squinted at Drax.

"It's not magic. It's magnetism."

Daria and I looked at each other.

"How's that?" Jip asked.

"The rocks, they're special."

"Magic," Reena coughed into her hand.

"Science. The Kronik launched a satellite into outer space recently. Its sole job is to catalogue what it sees at different wavelengths. The first block of data came in about six months ago and gave us some dramatic results."

"What's this got to do with a bunch of rocks?" Jip asked.

"It had been studying Xannia. The planet as a whole. Apparently, *this* rather large rock works like a giant magnet. It confirmed Nadian's Theory of Geomagnetism, or at least partially."

"How could looking at invisible lines in space confirm that the planet has an iron core surrounded by hot liquid metal?" Jip must have seen the same documentary I had. I'd found it hard to believe, but then I didn't study science. Drax was an Engineer.

"Yes. It's the most plausible reason for the satellite to relay images from the infrared spectrum that show the planet has a north and south pole. Why else do compasses work? This one in particular, pointing us north in the storm when we couldn't see? The natural magnetism of the planet drew the needle that way."

"Then why is it pointing west?" Delenon waved a hand over the bucket.

"Exactly. There's another north that's pulling it away from true-north. Another, closer, magnetic field. Tell them Tony."

"That bit of equipment kept turning slightly the farther along the invisible wall we rowed. Then the iron shavings we made formed different patterns in my hand when I held it close to the wall."

"Iron shavings are susceptible to a magnetic force."

"Sounds like magic, not science," Marxx said.

"No. *Magnetism*. The iron, the compass, the birds—"

"What about the birds?" Daria asked.

"Look." Drax pointed to the sky above the rocks. "Magnetoreception. They can sense the presence of the magnetic field. They're flying in particular patterns, not just avoiding the push of the magnetism."

"You think what you're saying proves your point, but to us commoners who chose to believe in the gods, and not your fabricated notions of science, you've just confirmed our belief in the Divine. In magic. There's no way through. We're doomed," Reena said.

Drax looked at me. She'd said "Divine."

"Sister," Marxx made Jip and Reena cringe. I was *All Mother* now. "Is this an act of the gods? Is the island sacred or being guarded for some reason? What does your experience tell you? What do the gods say?" And the invisible knife that hovered over my chest for weeks now, plunged home.

The gods had never spoken to me and yet, somehow, I knew I couldn't tell the truth. Could I? Marxx was baiting me. If I said no, I'd challenge everything I worked so hard to restore. If I said yes, I'd be supporting his claim that Drax was wrong and should be ignored.

Daria held my hand, unseen by the table top. As she wove her fingers through mine, I was torn by her support, her faith … but I knew Daria didn't believe in the gods, not when they'd taken everything from her. She blamed the Kronik, the Talians, the faulty government structure for all of the heartache in this world—not the gods … because to her they didn't exist. Perhaps then, her faith simply lay in me?

"The gods work in mysterious ways, Captain. It's my job to interpret acts of the unknown, and yet it's science's job to dispel myth so that we may better understand the workings of our world—not so different. I am only a conduit. The gods have not spoken to me, but I do know that Zita is the Harbinger of

Destiny. Zola has cared for our dead and Zerameteth has found ways to guide our lost souls. The Kronik wants us dead and yet the gods saw fit to find ways to help us get here. They would not give us false hope." I looked at Drax.

"Then how do we break an invisible wall?" Marxx snarled.

"We ram it at full speed."

Daria

All or Nothing

"You want us to do what!" Marxx slammed his hands on the table and stood up straight. I looked at Satie, her eyes as wide as mine.

"We thread the needle. If we're travelling fast enough, we'll slip in between the two polar fields and push against them at the very centre of the span between the rocks. The ship is saturated with water, making it diamagnetic …" I locked eyes with the Talian and shook my head in short, fast bursts. *Don't talk over their heads!*

"Uh—making us push against the invisible forcefield and poking a hole in it. If we're going fast enough, we'll sail right through."

"And if we're not?" Tony placed a hand on Marxx's shoulder. The man seethed, ready to break Drax's neck.

"Same as before. We bump off, only harder."

"And risk capsizing the ship, cracking the masts, killing my crew. NO! I won't allow it. We'll just have to keep sailing until we find somewhere else."

"What if there is nowhere else?" Reena and Jip asked nearly simultaneously. A flawed plan was still a plan after all.

"Medical supplies are running low," Satie said.

"We've no more fruit. The scurvy might get us all before we make land," I added.

Marxx sliced his hand through the air for silence. "That Talian is the enemy, not me. I find it awfully convenient that the Kronik have new intel that the rest of the world doesn't know about yet. The Kronik is devious, manipulative. He planted you here to make sure we'd fail—finally get his revenge and wipe out the Resistance."

Tony gripped Marxx's shoulder and pulled him away from the table, up onto the poop deck for privacy. As if of one mind, Satie turned with me and walked Delenon backward toward the balcony overlooking the main deck.

"He's raving mad, Delenon. If Drax is some kind of suicide-spy he would've let us sail in circles in the White Sea until the storms destroyed the ship. Even if he was put on board to earn our trust for nefarious reasons, it's clear he doesn't want to die. Look at him. A man ready to go to his grave doesn't fight for a lost cause," I said.

"She's right, *Magistrate*. Drax has helped save the ship at every possible opportunity. He's not going to trap us now. He's an Engineer, science and logic are tools he works with every day. If he says those rocks are giant magnets or mini-plants, I say the gods made sure he was on board to keep us alive; because he's the only one among us who'd know that."

I stepped closer to Delenon, Teena just a hand's breadth away from his chest, and said, "He's dangerous. We won't survive disease if we don't eat balanced meals. I said I could get us this far on what we had, and I did. Now it's up to you."

"Me? What are you talking about?"

Satie placed her hand on his arm. "Sir, you said so yourself all those weeks ago—we need the right leader for the right job. I don't agree with Marxx's choices but I understand why he made them, and someone had to be able to."

"Land, Magistrate. Right there in front of us," I said. "Of all the commoners, you were the only one who ever cared enough about us to stand up to the Kronik. It's time to reclaim your mantle. You were right, you're not a Captain—you're our Magistrate and we need you now more than ever."

Satie and I took a half-step back as we watched the physical transformation of the man before us. His shoulders drew back, his spine straightened, his jaw angled up slightly, but most importantly, his eyes sparkled the same way they did every time he or Satie or Tony or I nudged one of our dead overboard before Marxx could claim it.

"How? The crew follows him."

"Most prefer Tony," I said.

"Just turn around, call out to the people, they're all topside waiting for us to reach land. No one has spoken to them in ages. Many don't know why we haven't breached the ring of rocks. They're hungry for information and hope—"

"And guidance. *Lead* them, Magistrate. Tell them what we need to do." I snagged Satie's elbow and stepped back. She followed as Delenon turned to the gathering crowd on the main deck below. He raised his arms, and a hush fell.

"My Fellow Xannian's, the journey has ended! We have arrived."

A deafening cheer rose up, and I could have sworn I saw Delenon's chest swell right along with it. As he spoke of everyone's courage, battling the hardships, and earning their rite of passage for a new life, I glanced over my shoulder at the poop deck. Tony stood facing a livid Marxx.

"That man won't be enough to stop him."

"What?" Satie followed my gaze. "He wouldn't try anything now, would he?"

"The Magistrate just took everything away from him." I gave the Sister's arm a brief squeeze then slipped down the stairs and around and around, all the way down to the kitchen. Sliding the lower cupboards by the spices open, I pulled the bottom-most drawer out and reached all the way to the back.

Satie

Fury turned Marxx's normally tanned face bright red as the hate radiated from him in waves. Daria was right. Tony could only hold him off for so long.

"What are we going to—" I turned to Daria but she was gone. I frowned and looked around. Reena, still standing with Jip and Drax by the map table, inclined her head toward the stairs. I nodded and moved to follow her when the Magistrate caught my hand and raised my arm high in the air.

"All Mother spoke of Zita's hand in our destiny even as the Kronik and the elements have fought against us. She spoke of Zola watching over us, making sure that should we not complete our trials in the mortal realm, she would greet our souls in the beyond. All this, as the Child of the Light helped guide us on our perilous journey. We were meant to live!" Then, amidst the cheering and applause, he whispered to me, "Give them your blessing. Tell them you support the plan."

Movement out the corner of my eye distracted me, but before I could turn my head to see what it was, the crew fell silent. *Say something Satie!*

"It is not up to the gods whether we live a sheltered life or one of challenge. But it is our faith in what's right and our hope for a better future that bring us strength in these trying times. And the knowledge that we are not alone in the universe, that not one but three gods wish nothing but the best for us, that convinces me the Talian was not placed among us to cause harm or act as a curse. He, too, rose to the challenge and has helped us reach this destiny. I believe that it is now our faith in his science that will allow us to finally reach land." Jip and Reena walked forward with Drax between them showing the solidarity of the Leaders.

"Hear him. Follow him. Believe in him as we do, and we may yet live to see the suns rise another day!"

A strange bristle up the back of my neck made me stiffen, just as a hot growl seeped along the nape as Delenon and I stepped back and let Drax explain the plan. The wall of Marxx's chest stopped me short.

"You're gonna regret this—" Deft fingers circled my neck. I gasped, then an arm slipped between Marxx's chest and my back.

"Uh-uh-ah. You wouldn't hurt a baby and the only person on this ship capable of feeding the rabble, now would you?"

I gulped, turned my head and caught a glint of sharp steel in Daria's hand seconds before she gave Tony a nod to say she had this under control. Slowly, filling the space between Marxx and me, she forced him backwards toward the map room. His hands loosened from around my neck and slipped to either side.

"Hands down," Daria said, pinning him against the wall. The ghost of his hands still gripped my neck, but I refused to rub it in front of him.

Tony stepped up beside Drax and, between the two of them, organized the crew to turn this ship around.

We found the longest possible straight then pointed the ship back toward the island. The Lookout relayed info to the scout, who passed it on to Tony, who decided how best to course-correct on our way to "threading the needle.. Reena stood at the top of the lower deck stairs, another scout at the top of the next run, with Jip at the bottom to instruct the few rowers on either side of the ship when to act. Delenon stood at the helm, with Daria still holding Marxx at knife-point by the map room door.

Excitement charged the air as a crew, trained by trials and experience on the open water, worked seamlessly as if this were their destiny all along—to breach the invisible magnetic field.

The wind blew hard as the men and women made sure each sail was trimmed exactly so. Drax stood beside Delenon, the image reminiscent of the stage at the Collection site and pyre— only this time, the Magistrate was not in handcuffs, and the Talian beside him wanted only the best for the people before him. I stayed by the starboard stairs, leaning over the rail of the quarterdeck with the wind whipping my hair from its knot, heart pounding in my chest and ears, as my entire body vibrated in anticipation.

The ring of rocks came faster and faster. Minor course corrections were called, until the cry rang out for "full speed ahead" and the rowers added momentum stroke for stroke as the vessel sped across the water. The invisible barrier was almost tangible as my eyes tricked my brain into sensing a visual barrier of reflected light.

Then a gasp.

Brace for impact!

...

I opened my eyes and shrieked, "We're flying!" I ran to the hull and leaned far over the rail toward the sea below as the ship slowly rose up out of the water and across no man's land. Cries of excitement and astonishment echoed throughout the ship, then laughter when we splashed down on the other side! I turned to look for Drax. He did it! We did it.

But as I stepped forward to hug him or jump into his arms or something else completely reckless and totally emotional, Marxx took advantage of Daria's distraction as she kissed the top of Teena's head. He smashed Daria's wrist with his fist, knocking the filet knife from her hand. Barrelling past her, the ex-Captain shoved woman and child aside. Daria shielded the baby from her fall against the map room door as time slowed. Marxx rammed into an unsuspecting Drax.

The two men staggered, grappling with each other, turning and turning and turning until they slammed into the portside rail.

"DRAX!" The scream tore from my throat. He was gone! As Tony and Delenon hauled Marxx away, I streaked past them. The ship ran aground, launching me at the rail. Winded, I gasped for air even as I watched Drax flail in the churning water below.

"NO!"

Tony grabbed hold of me.

"Save him! You have to save him!"

He called for the rowboats. A surge of people moved to help but got tangled up in the crowd they made.

"—don't know if we can in less than ten minutes. All Mother. All Mother! Satie! Do you hear me?"

Ten minutes? Ten minutes! He'll go into sodium shock and die!

"He doesn't *have* ten minutes!" Shoving Tony back with a strength I didn't know I had, I scrambled up onto the rail and jumped—

Images of soaking in the sacred underground verrin springs flashed through my mind as bird caws whipped past my ears and my body went from soaring to falling. I knew how to float, but would that be enough?

Reality crashed into me as my body cracked against the water and tore the air from my lungs. My head went under. I inhaled seawater, coughing as my head breached the surface, trying to empty my lungs.

"Drax!" I croaked, smacking my arms around trying to get my bearings.

A splash!

Kicking my feet and thrashing my arms brought me closer to the sound, but I couldn't get near his desperate flailing.

"Drax! Calm down. Just kick your legs under you! Kick your—" But it was no use. Fear marred his already pale face. I tried again and moved closer. His hand clamped down on my arm, forcing me under. Large bubbles fled past my eyes as I breathed out. Something soft and slimy wrapped around my foot.

I screamed inside my head. Prying his fingers from my forearm, I curled in on myself surrounded by crystal clear blue. I hugged my knees and ran my hands down my pant-soaked legs to my feet. Ripping the seaweed off, my lungs burned as I absorbed, in less than a milli-second, the vast acres of green weed, large brown rock, and massive hull of the ship before me.

Pushing myself through the water, I scrambled back to the surface gasping for air. I whipped my head from side to side, but mine was the only one above water.

"Drax!"

His shirt floated bunched up by his shoulders. *No!* I moved my arms and pulled myself over to his limp body. *No!* I grabbed him under his arms and pulled his shoulders onto my chest, his head flopping back beside mine.

"No!"

He gasped. My heart catapulted into my throat.

"Don't move," I said into his ear. He'd only exhausted himself fighting the water. *He's not dead.* "Don't move. Try to relax. I've got you." I slipped my arms all the way around him and hugged his chest. His shoulders sagged against me as he let out a shaky breath. Rotating our heads toward land, we floated on our backs, aiming for the shore.

I licked my lips, mentally wincing. But the briny blast never came. *What? Fresh water? Is that even possible?* I dipped my head back and looked up at the perfect blue sky as the water caressed my brow. Flying through the air in a giant ship wasn't supposed to be possible either, and yet ...

My heels scuffed sand and I scrambled to find my footing.

"Drax, put your feet down."

He struggled as if waking from a dream, staggering upright. We held onto each other as the clear blue water flowed around our hips. I dropped my forehead onto his chest, my body shaking, teeth chattering from shock.

"I can't believe you did that."

"What?" I looked up at him.

"Jumped." His gaze searched mine, confusion knitting lines in his forehead even as a faint spark of hope glimmered in the glassiness of his eyes.

I released a full-bellied laugh, reached up and pulled him closer.

"Yes. For you, I'd jump overboard any day." I kissed him, full on the mouth and fell headlong into my future. Applause erupted from the ship and nearby. The rowboat had finally reached where we nearly drowned. Tony waved to us from the bow.

I waved back, laughed again and splashed to shore hand in hand with the Talian prisoner who'd captivated me all those weeks ago, the man who pushed me to be more than the rules that threatened to define me.

Crystal Sea

Costal Island.
We arrived six days ago, breaching a
geomagnetic gate to these fresh, crystal
waters. Not only have the survivors of
the Massacre followed in the path of
the Great Captain Darius, one hundred
years after his fateful voyage, but we've
touched the land he never could.
Amazingly, after scouring this small
island we found one small well-spring
of verrin—Thank the Gods! Game is
small and sparse but the plant life is
wide and varied.
Magistrate Delenon has organized the
remaining forty-five souls into a new
community. Each day we work on
finding materials for shelter and
building according to our needs. We
share two temporary huts made of
branches and large leaves: one for the
men and one for the women. Race has
no sway here, only faith, science, and
friendship—tentative though they may
be.
Life will not be easy on an island
ill-equipped to nourish this many
mouths, but for a crew who defeated the
odds, we relish the challenge and hope
that someday we will make it back
home again.

All Mother

THE FOLLOWERS OF THE LIGHT
Xannia's Dominant Religious System

THE TRINITY

ZOLA
Goddess
Mother
(Red Giant Sun)
Giver & Taker of Life
Protector of Souls

ZITA
Goddess
Sister
(Orange Giant Sun)
Harbinger of Destiny
Diviner of Change

ZERAMETETH
Child God
Brother
(Yellow Dwarf Sun)
Protector of Children
Guide for the Lost

THE FOLLOWERS OF THE LIGHT
Citizens of the Planet Xannia who *believe.*

SUN GUARDIANS
Practicing Initiates, Faithful, and Devout.

INITIATES
Men and women who dedicate their lives to the faith, it's practice, and helping others.

THE FAITHFUL
Those Initiates who become skilled and knowledgeable in the ways of the Trinity and actively spread the word to followers (Assistants to the Devout who lead Temple Rites).

THE DEVOUT
Those of the Faithful who transcend and become a direct conduit for one of the three Gods. They follow a strict adherence to the faith and are the most highly respected of the Guardians. "All Mothers/Fathers" are formed when only one Devout watches a community.

TRANSCENDENCE
When a Follower of the Light dies, a Rite of Passage is performed via ritual and prayer that culminate in the cremation of the earthly husk to allow the spirit to travel on Zola's sunbeams into the afterlife.

THE GOVERNMENT OF XANNIA
Pre-Nine Seas Massacre

THE KRONIK
Of the Talian race, born *privileged*.

THE MAN
Of the Talian race, born privileged.

The Kronik is a dictator who has an advising council, also referred to as "The Kronik". Only a Talian who is born into a family with direct ties to the Council can ever rise to power. He must first rise through the familial ranks and take his place as a Councilman, serve the Council and the Kronik well, and then he can move into position to claim the title of Kronik (the man) based on seniority.

THE COUNCIL
Of the Talian race, born privileged.

As a member of the privileged or Elite Sect of the Talian Compound, families vie for 1 of 12 Council Positions. Usually a father passes his title to his first-born son. If there are no sons, the title then goes to the son of a close family member (brother first, then cousin) via age of seniority. As a council member, a man represents not only his county within the Compound, but his assigned county outside of the Compound; a place he's never seen before nor is ever expected to see.

THE MAGISTRATE
Of the Common races, elected from peers.

A single man elected by the Master Keepers for each of the 12 general citizenship counties. This average business-minded citizen becomes the key liaison between the Kronik (as council) and the rest of the populous. It is his job to placate and pacify as necessary. When asked, he may speak to the Kronik (as man) to clarify issues not fully understood by the Council.

THE MASTER KEEPERS
Of the Common races, elected by the populous.

One Master Keeper represents the people in 1 of 12 counties. He or she acts as a Senator and ensures the smooth running of their county. They deal with a representing body from each of the major sectors of society.

THE CONTRACTORS
Of the Common races, educated by Kronik-chosen instructors.

A microcosm of society, any graduated Contractor is considered the most Elite Commoner, bridging the gap between the Kronik and the Lower Government in status/respect. The CTF (Contractor Training Facility) educates exemplary commoners to be utilized in a variety of capacities throughout society according to law and position requirement—including advanced training as Military Personnel who receive orders directly from the Kronik as Council.

If you've enjoyed reading

Rebels Rein

please consider leaving a review at your favourite online resource.

Reviews are a wonderful way of helping an author shine.

Thank you.

Forgotten Fallacy
Book 4 in
The Chronicles of Xannia Series
Available 2018

Time's Tempest:
The Lost Chapters
ePrequel to Time's Tempest: The Chronicles of Xannia
Available for FREE mjmoores.com

Author M.J. Moores

Growing up in Ontario, Canada, M.J. was the only child of a single mom. M.J.'s passion for the arts ignited at a young age as she wrote adventure stories and read them aloud to close family and friends. The dramatic arts became a focus in high school as an aid to understanding character motivation in her writing. Majoring in Theatre Production at York University, with a minor in English, she went on to teach in both the elementary and high school divisions.

M.J. keeps busy these days with her emerging authors' website Infinite Pathways, freelance editing for two small publishing houses, volunteering with the Writers' Community of York Region, and writing, writing, and more writing.

Connect with M.J. online:

Author Website – mjmoores.com
Facebook – facebook.com/AuthorMJMoores
Twitter – twitter.com/AuthorMJMoores
Goodreads – goodreads.com/author/show/8104388.M_J_Moores